THE HOSTILE TRAIL

The first shot came from Ike's side of the ravine, the bullet kicking up some dirt two feet in front of the trench. Ike aimed at the spot where he thought he'd seen a muzzle flash and fired a return shot. Moments later, a barrage of shots rained down from both sides of the ravine, pinning Matt and Ike down in the trench. When there was a lull in the firing, they each returned a single shot. This was repeated several times, with the Sioux firing at random and the two white men responding with single shots spaced about thirty seconds apart. Thus far in the assault, there were no casualties and none likely since there were no clear targets on either side. There followed a lull in the firing from the Sioux, and Ike warned Matt to get ready. . . .

THE
HOSTILE TRAIL

Charles G. West

A SIGNET BOOK

SIGNET
Published by New American Library, a division of
Penguin Group (USA) Inc., 375 Hudson Street,
New York, New York 10014, USA
Penguin Group (Canada), 90 Eglinton Avenue East, Suite 700, Toronto,
Ontario M4P 2Y3, Canada (a division of Pearson Penguin Canada Inc.)
Penguin Books Ltd., 80 Strand, London WC2R 0RL, England
Penguin Ireland, 25 St. Stephen's Green, Dublin 2,
Ireland (a division of Penguin Books Ltd.)
Penguin Group (Australia), 250 Camberwell Road, Camberwell, Victoria 3124,
Australia (a division of Pearson Australia Group Pty. Ltd.)
Penguin Books India Pvt. Ltd., 11 Community Centre, Panchsheel Park,
New Delhi - 110 017, India
Penguin Group (NZ), cnr Airborne and Rosedale Roads, Albany,
Auckland 1310, New Zealand (a division of Pearson New Zealand Ltd.)
Penguin Books (South Africa) (Pty.) Ltd., 24 Sturdee Avenue,
Rosebank, Johannesburg 2196, South Africa

Penguin Books Ltd., Registered Offices:
80 Strand, London WC2R 0RL, England

First published by Signet, an imprint of New American Library,
a division of Penguin Group (USA) Inc.

First Printing, September 2006
10 9 8 7 6 5 4 3 2 1

For Ronda

Chapter 1

Ike Brister took a cautious step forward in the knee-deep snow, his gaze unwavering as he watched for the first indication that the confused bull elk was about to charge. His rifle was ready, but he hoped he wouldn't have to use it. The elk eyed him suspiciously, tossing his head back and forth and pawing the snow in warning. Moving very deliberately, Ike took one more step and stopped. He was as close to the huge animal as he dared. He glanced toward the clump of pines on the slope to his left. *Hurry up, dammit,* he thought. *This son of a bitch is fixing to jump into my lap.* The agitated bull elk had exhausted his patience, with the strange creature seeming to challenge him. He lowered his head and shook his huge antlers back and forth violently as he pawed the snow. Ike raised his rifle and aimed at the massive head, just in case the elk was preparing to charge. He waited, his finger on the trigger. A figure rose silently in the pines, and a second later the elk bolted sideways, an arrow embedded deep in his lung.

Enraged and confused, the bull tried to sidestep away
from the pain in his side, only to feel the lethal sting of
a second arrow a few inches from the first. Ike kept his
rifle sighted on the crazed animal in case it was still
thinking about charging him. A bull elk sometimes took
a little time dying, and this one might take a notion to
take Ike with him. If at all possible, Ike wanted to avoid
firing his rifle in this part of the mountains. The shot
would echo through the canyons for miles and might
bring a Sioux hunting party down on them. There had
been several Sioux hunting parties working this side of
the Bighorns within the past week.

Much to Ike's relief, the elk did not charge. Confused, it tried to retreat, bounding up the slope, still trying to sidestep away from the pain. But before it could
reach the top, its legs became wobbly, and it went down
on its knees in the snow. There it remained, waiting for
the two white men to finish the kill.

"What in hell was you waitin' for?" Ike asked when
he caught up to his younger friend. "I thought me and
that damn elk was fixin' to have us a dance."

Already preparing to skin his kill, Matt Slaughter
grinned up at his friend. "I'd have paid money to see
that," he teased. "Seein' as how you two are about the
same size, you'da made a handsome couple."

"Huh," the big man snorted. "Next time you can be
the bait, and I'll do the killin'." They both knew that
was just idle talk because Ike couldn't hit the side of a
barn with a bow. Ike would say that he had just never
had any use for a bow as long as he had his Spencer
rifle. Although he would never mention it, Matt knew

there were other reasons, reasons that Ike didn't care to acknowledge. Sometimes a man aged faster when forced to live by his wits. Lately, Matt could see signs of his partner's aging—a hand that was not as steady as before, an eye that was not as keen as when he was a young man. Still, the old man was not ready to return to the settlements just yet. And before he reached that stage, Matt promised himself that he would take care of him.

As far as the bow was concerned, Matt took to it like he was born with one in his hand. This particular bow was special. It held sentimental value for both men. It had belonged to a young Cherokee boy who had been killed only a few months before by a white bushwhacker. Crooked Foot had been held in high regard by Matt and Ike, and Matt had kept the boy's bow. He had spent a good deal of time practicing with the weapon, and it had proven to be time well spent. Making a winter camp in the Bighorn Mountains, the two partners found the bow essential. It was not only a silent weapon, it saved on the consumption of precious .44 cartridges.

The need for silence and secrecy was especially important now that there had been an increase in Indian activity between the Bighorns and South Pass. It was a dangerous time for two lone white men in the Powder River country, even in the dead of winter. The Sioux and Cheyenne had raided all summer along the Bozeman Trail, attacking any parties traveling that route to the Montana goldfields. It had not helped matters when the army built Fort Reno on the Powder River just that past August. The fort, originally called Camp Connor, had not been garrisoned as yet, but Chief High Backbone and Red Cloud knew there would be soldiers there soon. It was fairly obvious to the Sioux leaders that the purpose of the fort was to protect travelers on the Bozeman Trail.

At the beginning of winter, the partners had planned to wait out the cold weather at Fort Laramie. After a couple of idle weeks, however, they decided there was nothing for them to do for employment of any nature there. The army would not be hiring any more scouts until spring. And it was painfully obvious that what cash they had would soon disappear if they spent their days hanging around the post trader's store. At the beginning of their third week at Fort Laramie, Ike announced, "Hell, I'd rather head for the hills and live like an Injun than set around here till spring."

Matt wasn't sure the bushy-faced old trapper was serious, but the idea suited him just fine. He wasn't comfortable in crowded places, and Fort Laramie was beginning to close in on him. Ike's remark was all it took. They set out for the Powder River country the next day. Even a blizzard on the second day out failed to dull their determination as they made their way northwest, with the Laramie Mountains to the west of their trail.

After seemingly endless travel from one snowy camp to another, they found themselves in the Bighorn Mountains and decided to make their base camp there. In a narrow canyon, protected from the winter winds by steep, rocky walls, they built a shelter for the horses, using young pine trees. Game was not that plentiful where they made their camp, but they agreed that it was better to ride some distance from their base to hunt so as not to draw any curious Sioux. Firewood was also a problem. The canyon was convenient to abundant pine, but green wood burned with far too much smoke, so they had to travel considerable distances to find suitable fuel for the fire. If they had allowed themselves to consider the difficulty of their situation and the hardship it created, they might have headed back to the settlement.

"I'da heap druther you was a nice young cow," Ike commented to the elk as he worked to force his knife through the tough flesh. "This ol' boy was gettin' on in years. I'll bet he was as old as I am."

"I hope to hell he'll be better eatin' than you'd be," Matt teased as he packed snow into the chest cavity to soak up the blood. They had been so long without fresh meat that they did not have the luxury of being picky. Though old and tough, this elk was the first game they had found in almost a week. And to make matters worse, they had come across recent sign of Indian hunting parties close to their camp. Sioux or Cheyenne, they couldn't tell which, but as Ike had commented, two white men in their country were not welcomed by either tribe.

"I reckon the Great Spirit took pity on us, and sent this old bull wanderin' up here before we got so hungry we started eyeballin' each other," Ike said with a chuckle. "He musta got run off by some younger bull and lost his ladies." He sat back on his heels and threw off his bearskin robe to give himself more room to work. "Well, it was just a matter of time before he got took down by a pack of wolves. He'll serve a better purpose feedin' the likes of us." Ike rambled on as he worked steadily away at quartering the elk until he realized that Matt wasn't listening. He looked up to see his partner signaling him to be silent.

Matt listened for a few moments, his ear turned to the wind. He turned then to look at the horses. The buckskin's ears were twitching, and a moment later Ike's horse neighed softly. "Best get that meat loaded on the horses," he called back over his shoulder as he got to his feet and scrambled up to the top of the ridge.

Detecting a sense of urgency in his partner's tone, Ike dropped his skinning knife on the elk hide beside the half-butchered carcass, and hurried after Matt. "Damn," he exclaimed softly as he flattened himself beside Matt in the snow. Riding single file through a narrow gulch below the two white men, a hunting party of a dozen Sioux made their way at a leisurely pace toward the ridge. They were still more than half a mile away. "We ain't cut meat in a week, and when we finally find one ol' tough elk, along comes a huntin' party," Ike complained.

"I don't know if they've been trackin' the same elk," Matt said, "but if they have, he's gonna lead them right to us when they get to the snow line." A couple hundred yards more and the hunting party would reach a clear trail with not only the elk's tracks but also those of three horses, leading them right up the slope. "I expect we'd better get busy," Matt said, his voice devoid of any sign of excitement.

They withdrew from the crest of the ridge and wasted no time getting back to the business at hand. The safest action would have been to flee immediately, but neither Matt nor Ike had any intention of leaving the entire supply of fresh meat to the Indians. Working feverishly over the carcass, both men chopped at the bones and sliced the flesh into quarters. While Ike started hefting the meat onto the packhorse, Matt ran back up to the top of the ridge to check on the progress of the hunting party. There was no time to linger. The Indians were already closer than he had anticipated, and had just discovered the tracks in the snow. He could hear bits of excited words carried on the wind as the Lakota hunters talked among themselves. Matt didn't wait any longer.

"Tie down what you've got!" he sang out as he hurried down the hill. "We don't have time to take the rest." Ike did as he was told, and Matt grabbed one of the remaining sections of meat and tied it with the loose end of a strap while the big man ran for his horse. The pack secure, Matt stepped up in the saddle and held the buckskin back while he grabbed the packhorse's lead rope. Ike, his huge bulk plowing through the knee-deep snow like a buffalo bull, took a giant leap for the saddle, only to miss the stirrup with his foot. The resulting collision between man and horse caused the bay to sidestep and kick its hind legs in the air.

"Damn you!" Ike roared. "Hold still!" The bay, however, was leery of further contact with the big trapper, and continued to pull away until Matt drove the buckskin up to block it. "Damfool horse," Ike grumbled as he stuck his foot in the stirrup, embarrassed even in the face of imminent danger. It didn't help when he looked up and saw Matt's wide grin. "Let's get the hell outta here," he said, and gave the bay a sharp kick with his heels. Matt followed, and the two white men charged down the slope, driving their horses as hard as they dared through the snow.

Broken Bow paused at the crest of the ridge, and signaled the others. When the rest of the hunters rode up to him, he turned and pointed to the carcass in the snow some forty yards down the other side of the slope. Iron Claw, the leader of the party, nodded and pushed off down the hill toward the site of the butchering.

Arriving at the carcass, the hunters rode back and forth around the site of the killing, looking at the trampled snow and the signs of the activity they had just interrupted. *Wasicu*, Iron Claw thought as he stared at the remains of the elk. This had to be the work of the two white men who had camped in the mountains all winter. Iron Claw's nostrils flared in anger. None of his scouts had actually seen the two white men, but there had been occasional sign that told of their presence in the land of the Lakota. This day, the Great Spirit might be smiling upon them, for the *wasicu* could not be far ahead of them. Iron Claw jerked his head around to look at Broken Bow. "We may have caught the white coyotes this time. Leave the meat," he directed several of the hunters who were examining the carcass.

With Iron Claw in the lead, the Lakota hunters took up the obvious trail the white men had left in their haste to depart. Pushing their Indian ponies as hard as possible without tumbling in the snow, they followed the trail down the slope to the point where the line of snow stopped. There they paused only long enough to examine the tracks left in the loose shale to make sure they were still on the trail.

Broken Bow looked down the narrow gulch toward the valley beyond. The white men had made no effort to hide their trail. They had obviously been intent upon escaping as fast as possible. "We will catch these coyotes," he shouted, bringing a chorus of war cries from the others. Descending rapidly to the bottom of the slope, they raced down the gulch at a gallop.

Barely half a mile ahead of the Sioux party, Matt and Ike pushed their horses for all the speed they could muster. At first there was nothing but the sound of their hooves pounding upon the valley floor. But gradually the sounds of excited war whoops began to carry over the beat of the horses. It was not a good sign, for it meant their mounts were being outrun by the swift Indian ponies. To add to their disadvantage, the packhorse was slowing them down. Although not a match for speed with the Indian ponies, the buckskin was holding his own in endurance, but the other two horses were beginning to show signs of fatigue. The Sioux ponies were gradually closing the gap. With no other option available, Matt and Ike both started looking for a suitable place to make a stand.

As they thundered down the valley, Ike shouted something. Matt couldn't understand what he was yelling about, but the big man pointed toward a rocky defile near the end of the valley. Matt nodded and promptly guided the buckskin toward it. The big horse responded without breaking stride.

Into the mouth of a deep ravine they charged, dismounting as the horses slid to a stop. They led the horses back within the walls of the ravine where they would be safe, then hurried to take up positions on either side of the opening. "If we're lucky," Ike said, "they'll ride right on by."

With rifles ready and cartridge belts at hand, they prepared for an assault. While they waited, Matt couldn't resist taking a playful jab at his oversized partner. "Sometime when we ain't so busy, I'd like you to teach me that quick mount technique you demonstrated back there on the ridge."

The big man blushed behind his whiskers. "That damfool horse wouldn't hold still," he offered lamely. He grinned sheepishly. "I reckon I did come pretty close to bustin' my ass."

They didn't have to wait long. Within minutes, the Lakota hunters rode out of the valley, their ponies grunting with the effort. Deerskin fringes fluttering in the wind, the party drove toward the passage that led to the next valley. Suddenly the leader held up his hand and halted his warriors. He had seen something in the soft floor of the valley, a sharp hoofprint where the white men had swerved toward the ravine. "Well, I reckon we ain't lucky," Ike opined when he saw them stop.

"We have them trapped," Broken Bow exclaimed as he pulled his pony up beside Iron Claw. "There is no way out of that ravine but the way they went in."

"There are only two of them," one of the other hunters said. "Why don't we rush them?"

"We would risk losing lives if we charge them," Iron Claw said. "I think it would be wise to find out how well they are armed before we decide the best way to attack."

"Maybe they don't have guns," Broken Bow offered. "The elk was killed with arrows."

"I think they have guns," Iron Claw replied. "I think these are the two white men who have been camping in the mountains all winter, and some of our hunting parties said they have heard gunshots on several occasions." Iron Claw was especially interested in seeing the white men who had made their winter camp in Lakota hunting ground. There had been many times when evidence of their existence was found, even though no one had ever actually seen the white hunters. Some in his village were even beginning to speak of them as ghosts that were impossible to see. Iron Claw was not one to believe such stories, but he had come to be fascinated with the white men.

"I'll find out if they have guns," Gray Bull, the warrior who had suggested rushing them, volunteered. "Who will go with me?"

Two of the others quickly spoke up. Iron Claw cautioned them. "If you go charging into that ravine, you will be killed. A better plan would be to divide our party and climb the slopes on both sides. There is plenty of cover above them, and we will have them in a cross fire."

"Iron Claw is right," Broken Bow said. "Why risk our lives foolishly?" Without waiting for further discussion, he wheeled his pony and said, "Half of you come

with me. We'll circle around this side. The rest can go
with Iron Claw."

Matt and Ike watched the Sioux party as they decided
upon their plan of attack. "That one doin' most of the
talkin' must be the big dog," Ike remarked, referring to
Iron Claw. Even at that distance, the Sioux warrior was
an imposing figure.

"I reckon," Matt replied. Like Ike, he had focused
upon the warrior riding the paint pony. With deep-set
eyes glaring out from under a prominent brow, and a
pronounced hook nose, the warrior reminded Matt of a
hawk.

In the next moment, the Indians split up and rode off
in different directions. It didn't take a great deal of spec-
ulation to determine what was about to take place. Both
men looked around them at the steep sides of the ravine
and the rocky patches above. There was plenty of cover
for the Sioux on either side. "Next time it would be nice
to pick a ravine with a back door to it," Matt commented
as he repositioned himself to cover his side of the
ravine.

"Next time maybe we can ask the Injuns to give us a
little notice so's we can pick a better spot," Ike replied.

Using a trench for cover, both men knelt and watched
the rim of the ravine above them. "Most likely they're
gonna test us to see what kind of firepower we're
totin'," Ike said. "So when they show up, just shoot
once, then wait a little between shots. Make 'em think
we've just got single-shot rifles. My guess is they might
try to rush us if they think we have to take time to re-

load. That's when we'll have the best chance to cut down the odds, maybe make 'em think twice about jumpin' us again."

"All right," Matt said. The plan sounded good to him. He felt no need to comment that if it didn't work, they could be trapped there indefinitely.

The first shot came from Ike's side of the ravine, the bullet kicking up dirt some two feet in front of the trench. Ike aimed at the spot where he thought he'd seen a muzzle flash and fired a return shot. Moments later, a barrage of shots rained down from both sides of the ravine, pinning Matt and Ike down in the trench. When there was a lull in the firing, they each returned a single shot. This was repeated several times, with the Sioux firing at random and the two white men responding with single shots spaced about thirty seconds apart. Thus far in the assault, there were no casualties and none likely since there were no clear targets on either side. There followed a lull in the firing from the Sioux, and Ike warned Matt to get ready. "They're thinkin' it over now."

"We're wasting bullets," Three Horses complained. "They don't have the *spirit guns*. They are reloading after every shot. I say we should attack them after they shoot again. We can be upon them before they have a chance to reload."

Iron Claw considered Three Horses' words for a few moments. What his friend said was probably true, but what if the white men were trying to fool them? "What do you think, Gray Bull?" Iron Claw asked.

"I think Three Horses is right," the warrior replied. He, like most of the others, was getting impatient with the ineffective assault. "I think we should rush them after their next shots. We can kill them with our knives before they have a chance to reload." It was agreed then, and Iron Claw signaled to Broken Bow on the other side of the ravine.

Down in the trench, Matt watched the rim of the ravine carefully. "They've been talkin' a long time," he said. As soon as he had uttered the words, a fresh barrage of lead was thrown down upon them.

"Here they come!" Ike warned as they both answered with single shots. Moments later, the Sioux warriors poured over the sides of the ravine and charged down the slopes.

There was no time for either man to worry about his back. Each had to trust his partner to take care of business on his side of the fight. Matt raised up enough to clear his upper body so that he had freedom of motion to sweep the slope with rifle fire. Firing and cocking and firing again without pause, he proceeded to cut down three of the charging Sioux with deadly precision. He could hear Ike's Spencer barking behind him, but dared not take time to judge the results. The three remaining warriors on his side, realizing the killing machine they had triggered, tried to turn as fast as they could. But the steepness of the slope made retreat difficult. Two managed to escape over the rim of the ravine unharmed. The third, the hawk-faced warrior, was hit in the thigh but made it over the rim with the help of his friends. Only then could Matt turn to see what was taking place behind him.

"I got two," Ike said, reloading his rifle as quickly as he could. "I maybe hit another one. I ain't sure. But we sure as hell run 'em off for now."

Matt didn't wait to talk it over. He ran back down the ravine to get the horses. Leading them toward the mouth of the gulch, he yelled, "We need to get the hell outta here while we've got the chance. I don't fancy spending the night here."

Ike was in complete agreement. If the village the hunting party had come from was close by, the six or seven survivors of the fight would soon be back with reinforcements. He jumped up in the stirrup and followed Matt, who was already galloping out of the ravine, leading the packhorse with their supply of elk meat.

Back on the ridge, Iron Claw, furious over having been tricked by the white men, struggled to his feet with the help of his two comrades. Ignoring the blood that soaked his thigh, he stared angrily at the fleeing white men, burning the image of the young rifleman with the *spirit gun* into his memory.

Chapter 2

Libby Donovan Lyons paused to recall the day her first husband had bought the shawl of white lace she held in her hands. It had served as her bridal veil two months before when she married Franklin Lyons. She folded it carefully now to be put away once more in her trunk, where it would no doubt lie until some other special occasion called for it. What that occasion might be, she could not imagine. It would likely not be to celebrate the birth of a child. At her age, child birthing was a thing of the past. With a seventeen-year-old daughter, she couldn't imagine having a baby, anyway. Besides, Franklin had no desire to start a family, having already raised one.

Libby and Franklin's marriage had been one of convenience for both parties. Franklin's wife had succumbed to pneumonia more than two years before. He had a grown son with a family back in Omaha, but had lost touch with him after deciding to head west. He had intended to pass on through Nebraska City last winter, but decided the weather was too bad to push on. Like most folks who passed through Fort Kearny, he soon discovered Libby's Kitchen, the hotel dining room run by a widow woman with a daughter who could not speak.

Libby took note of the rather distinguished-looking middle-aged man who had begun to show up for every meal. He always took off his hat before seating himself at her table—obviously a man of manners and respect for a lady. And he always had a warm smile for her. Soon he began lingering a few minutes after eating to engage her in friendly conversation. He was a widower, he told her, and with no family to provide for, he had decided to follow the search for gold in the Montana hills. It was a daring thing to do for a man at his stage in life, she had told him. "What stage?" he had retorted. "I may be more'n half a century by yearly count, but I'm still a pup inside."

His remark had caused her to think about her own situation. She was pushing fifty herself, and she found that she was thinking a lot about Franklin Lyons. She must have exhibited signs of her interest in the polite widower with the graying temples, for he soon began to appear in her kitchen well before the advertised mealtimes. She was not quite sure when their relationship passed from casual to one of special interest, but when he proposed that she might consider a union between the two of them, she could not come up with a strong enough reason to refuse. It seemed that she had been unaware of how tired she had become of running a kitchen for the hotel until that moment. And she realized that she did not want to spend the rest of her life dishing out hash and beans until she dropped in the traces.

And what of Molly? Would Molly grow old slaving away in the kitchen if Libby declined? Molly had been her greatest concern when she was considering Franklin's proposal. How would the slender young girl react to the idea of her mother getting married again? As it turned out, her daughter was fine with the idea. She recognized the decency in Franklin Lyons and was happy for her mother. Franklin was more than happy to provide for mother and daughter.

Thinking of the seemingly melancholy young girl, Libby gazed again at the lace shawl she held in her hands. It was unlikely the lace would be worn in a wedding for her daughter. For whatever reason, God had not seen fit to provide Molly with the ability to speak. When she was a young child, Molly would attempt to speak, but the sounds that she made were cause for laughter and ridicule. So she stopped trying to talk, preferring to withdraw into a silent world. Libby often despaired over the shame of it. Molly was not a beautiful girl, but neither was she overly plain. If she had not been so shy and withdrawn, she might have had a chance at someday finding someone and starting a family. Libby shook her head sadly. Molly was destined to a life alone. The only thing romantic the poor girl could cling to was a little silver Saint Christopher's medal that she wore constantly, given to her by a young man dressed in buckskins. He intended it as a token of his appreciation after her quick thinking had prevented his being shot in an altercation at Libby's Kitchen. Though it was only a kind gesture, Molly treasured the medal as if it were a wedding ring. Of course, the handsome young scout had gone on his way, never to be seen around Fort Kearny again, just another one of the wild ones that rode the high plains. Libby was certain the young man had no clue of Molly's infatuation. She didn't even remember his name.

It was with little regret that she said good-bye to the hotel dining room that had known the name Libby's Kitchen for more than eight years. She had made only a few friends during that span of time—none that she couldn't bear to leave. John Bryant, who owned the hotel, was perhaps the saddest to see her go, for she would be hard to replace. She ignored the advice of those who thought it folly for a woman of her age to set off on a journey that would take the measure of someone younger. "How much do you really know about this man?" John Bryant had asked, referring to Franklin Lyons.

"All I need to know," Libby had replied, confident in the kindness she read in her new husband's eyes.

"What does he know about mining for gold?" Bryant had questioned.

"As much as any dreamer who's willing to risk a little hardship and disappointment," Libby said. She didn't add that it was better than withering away in Nebraska City.

It was early spring when Franklin Lyons, wife, and daughter had rolled into Fort Laramie. Already the trip had been difficult, the winter having been especially harsh that year. But they arrived at the busy outpost still in good spirits, their determination intact.

It had been Franklin's plan to join others who planned to follow the Bozeman Trail to the goldfields in Montana Territory. However, his eagerness to embark upon the journey brought his new family to Fort Laramie a bit too early in the season to rendezvous with other parties bent upon adventure. The decision left to him and Libby was whether to wait there at the fort until other gold seekers showed up or to strike out for Montana alone. They were strongly advised against the latter by Colonel Henry Maynadier, the post commander. There had already been some hostile Indian activity reported, and a wagon alone would be a risky endeavor.

"Are you familiar with the country between here and Montana?" Colonel Maynadier asked.

"Well, no," Franklin was forced to admit. "I expect we'll be looking for a guide if we decide to go on alone."

The decision had been a tough one to make. Franklin and Libby talked it over and reluctantly decided to take the advice given by the colonel. They camped there near the river and waited. A week passed with no appearance of additional prospectors. With their provisions steadily declining, it became more and more frustrating to sit and wait. To make their delay even more intolerable, the weather had turned pleasant, giving signs that spring may have arrived early. The incident that had reversed their decision to wait was the chance meeting of one Jack Black Dog at the post trader's store.

Jack Black Dog was well known around Fort

Laramie. The son of a white trapper and a Brule Sioux woman, Jack had dark, sullen eyes set deep within a narrow face, and he dressed in smoky buckskins. He worked off and on as a scout for the army, but was not trusted as a full-time scout, due to a tendency to disappear occasionally, only to show up a few weeks later looking for work again. None of the Crow scouts wanted to work with him, for it was widely known that he spent most of his life living with various bands of Sioux.

Jack Black Dog was prone to swap stories with anyone who was willing to buy him a drink, and he quickly befriended Franklin Lyons. Over a glass of beer, he had told Franklin of his many adventures in Indian territory and boasted about his intimate knowledge of every ridge and ravine between Fort Laramie and Virginia City. "Hell," he proclaimed, "I rode that country up the Powder, east of the Bighorns, long before John Bozeman even thought about markin' a trail."

The longer they talked, the more eager Franklin became to get started. Before the night was over, they had entered a contract together. Jack agreed to guide Franklin and his two women to Montana for wages of three dollars a day. Franklin did express concerns about the wisdom of passing through Sioux country, but Jack assured him that there was little danger as long as they were with him. "Hell, I go and come as I please, all the time," he boasted. "I live with the Lakota half the time. You ain't got nothin' to worry about when you're with me."

Libby was not confident that Franklin had made the

right decision, and she said as much to her husband. She was even more doubtful when the post trader, Seth Ward, advised against it. "Are you sure it wouldn't be a lot safer thing to wait till some other folks show up, so we could all go together?" Libby asked. "Most folks around here believe that half-breed you've hired would just as soon stick a knife in you as look at you."

Franklin was patient in answering, but he was convinced that it was not as risky as Seth claimed. "Jack says the soldiers always make it sound more dangerous than it really is," he said. "Don't you see? Seth Ward would like to have us hang around here all spring, so we'd buy more supplies. I think we'll be all right if we're careful. After all, the man travels through that country all the time," he insisted, referring to Jack Black Dog.

So here they were, four days after leaving Fort Laramie, gathered around the broken wheel of their wagon, the Bighorn Mountains watching silently from the west. "Reckon you can fix it?" Jack Black Dog asked. He seemed to be irritated at Franklin for the bad luck.

"I reckon," Franklin replied, "but it'll take some time."

"We can leave the wagon and take what we can carry on the mules," Jack suggested.

"No," Franklin replied with no uncertainty. "I need the wagon." He gave Libby an apologetic shake of the head, then set to work mending the wheel. Libby and Molly went about the business of making a fire and rustling up something to eat.

"I expect I'd best ride on up ahead a piece to make sure there ain't no hostile Injuns about," Jack announced. He paused for a moment to leer unabashedly at Molly, who accidentally exposed a milky white calf as she climbed down from the wagon. He grinned when she hurriedly pulled her skirt down. Then he stepped up in the saddle. "I'll be back directly. Maybe you'll have that there wheel fixed."

Libby stood, hands on hips, shaking her head, watching their scout ride off toward the north. "I reckon helping you fix wagon wheels ain't in his contract," she said in disgust.

Franklin was still working on the wheel when the sun went behind the Bighorns. Libby persuaded him to put it aside for the time being, saying the job might as well wait until morning. He reluctantly agreed, and sat down to a plate of side meat and beans just as Jack Black Dog returned. Without taking time to unsaddle his horse, he went immediately to the campfire to help himself to supper. With a lecherous wink for the silent young girl, he sat down beside her and proceeded to gobble his food noisily. Libby and Franklin exchanged frowns. It was obvious to them both that Jack might prove to be a problem before they reached Montana.

They had no way of knowing exactly how long the Sioux war party had been watching them. And they would not know of the Indians' presence until it was too late. As darkness settled in to surround the tiny campfire, Libby got up to collect the empty plates. She could not help but wonder at the foolish grin on Jack Black Dog's face as he handed her his plate. A muted sound in the darkness behind the guide caused her to look up in time to see a menacing-looking figure step into the firelight.

Followed immediately by several other warriors, Iron Claw strode up to the fire, glancing around him at the stunned family. His fearsome appearance rendered Libby as incapable of speech as her daughter at that moment. Desperately trying to gather his wits, Franklin made an attempt to offer hospitality. "We pretty much finished our supper," he stammered, "but my wife can cook up some more if you're hungry.

Iron Claw gazed at him for a long moment with eyes filled with contempt. Then he calmly raised the pistol in his hand and pulled the trigger. Libby screamed in horror as Franklin slid to the ground with a bullet hole in his forehead. Her scream had not died away before a second shot tore into her breast. Terrified, Molly ran to help her mother. Iron Claw raised his pistol again, but Jack Black Dog yelled, "No! She's mine!" And he grabbed Molly by the arms, holding her back.

Iron Claw hesitated. He fixed Jack with a cold stare while he deliberated. The Sioux war chief had little more than contempt for the treacherous half-breed, but he was useful on occasion. "I will take the girl," he decided. "Maybe I'll give her to you later."

"Please don't hurt my baby" were Libby's last words before a Sioux warrior silenced her for good with one quick slash across her throat.

The morning broke cold and rainy on the day Matt and Ike rode into Fort Laramie. It was sometime around the first or maybe the middle of March, by Ike's reckoning. There was no way he could be sure, since neither partner really cared to keep track of the days. At the beginning of winter, when they had left Fort Laramie before, they had not planned to return until late spring. The incident with Iron Claw's hunting party had caused them to change their plans, however. The Lakota war chief became obsessed with the capture of the two white hunters, and the weeks that followed the fight in the ravine became a deadly cat-and-mouse game. Sioux war parties combed the mountains east of the Bighorn River, searching for the two intruders who were trespassing on Lakota hunting grounds. Almost every scouting party they saw had the same leader. At first Matt recognized him by the paint pony he rode. On one occasion, when he and Ike were almost surprised by a small war party, there was no time to run. Figuring they were going to be forced to make a stand, they hid the horses in a ravine and took cover in some rocks along the top. The Sioux warriors appeared to be following their trail as they approached the ravine, but they made no motions directly toward the two white men hiding in the rocks. They appeared to be confused.

"Hold on a minute," Ike whispered. "I don't think they know we're here."

In fact, the warriors seemed to be arguing among themselves. Finally one of them, the rider of the paint pony, spoke, and the others immediately ceased their bantering. With the first real opportunity to see the man up fairly close, Matt looked long and hard at him, interested to see one who seemed so dead set upon finding him and Ike. He was certain he would recognize him again. He was even closer than he had been when Matt and Ike were trapped in the ravine. The pronounced hawklike quality of the warrior's face made him appear always to be angry.

After that close encounter, they decided it was too dangerous to remain in one camp for longer than a day or two before moving to another. Finally, after more close calls, they decided it was getting a little too hot altogether for them to stay in the territory. They had talked about moving on west toward the Wind River country, but the prospect of gainful employment with the army offered the opportunity to restock supplies and ammunition. The decision made, they returned to Fort Laramie, both men and horses lean and weary from a hard winter spent in the midst of hostile country.

On the day of their arrival, there was a full-dress formation on the parade ground. The two hunters skirted the formation, heading for the post trader's store. "What in tarnation is that all about?" Ike exclaimed. "Nobody but soldiers would dress up in their Sunday suits and march around in the rain for no reason at all." Matt didn't reply. He had served in the army, although it was not the Union Army, and he knew that all armies were prone to parade for no reason at all.

Seth Ward glanced up through bushy black eyebrows to squint at the two men dressed head to foot in deerskins. "Well, Ike, I thought you were gone till spring," the post trader said. "What's the matter? Too cold up there in the mountains?"

"Too damn many Injuns," was Ike's gruff reply. "How you doin', Seth?"

"Tolerable," Seth replied. "I swear, I'm surprised to see you back so soon, though. Thought maybe you'd go Injun for good, maybe join up with ol' Cooter Martin." He chuckled when Ike grunted in response.

"Hell," Ike opined, "I ain't gone loco yet." He turned to explain to Matt. "Cooter Martin's some old man that's supposed to been livin' with the Sioux and Cheyenne for so long he's gone Injun hisself—or maybe crazy—or both. Lot of people talk about him, but ain't many seen him. I never saw him. I don't know if he's even real or not, might be just another tale some folks made up."

"Oh, he's real all right," Seth insisted. "He's been in here a time or two tradin' pelts for ammunition and coffee." He grinned at Matt. "I expect ol' Ike here will end up like Cooter." With his attention on Matt, he went on. "How you doin', young feller? I'm sorry I don't recollect your name right off."

"Slaughter," Matt replied, not surprised the post trader hadn't remembered his name. He had met the man only once, and that was several months past.

"Right. Slaughter," Seth echoed. He looked back at Ike and grinned before adding, "Well, Slaughter, I've gotta hand it to ya. You've gotta have plenty of starch to put up with Ike for one whole winter."

Ike grunted briskly, giving back as good as he got. "That's mighty generous praise from a man that's made a fortune off'n poor folks like me and Matt here."

"Now you know I deal fair and square with ever'-

body, even Injuns. To show you my heart's in the right place, I'll buy your first drink for ya. Come on over to the bar."

"Now you're makin' sense," Ike said. "Say, what's all the hoopla on the parade ground? Is this a holiday or somethin'?"

"Nah, it's a welcomin' formation for the new post commander, Major Evans," Seth answered as he led them to the other side of the store.

Ike looked surprised. "Hell, I thought Colonel Maynadier was the commanding officer when we left here."

"He was," Seth replied, shrugging his shoulders. "There's been a couple since you've been gone. You know the army. They just turn 'em over like flapjacks. I took over the store here in 1857, and I could count on one hand the number of post commanders to hold the job long enough to take a comfortable squat in the outhouse."

"How 'bout chief of scouts? Is Captain Boyd still the man?"

"He is," Seth replied. "Why? You and your partner thinkin' about joinin' up?"

"Maybe," Ike answered.

"Well, he might have a job for you, since you've been livin' in the Powder River country all winter. I expect he might be interested in what the Injuns has been up to." He shifted his gaze toward Ike's tall young friend then. "Your partner don't say a helluva lot, does he?"

Ike smiled. "He takes spells. Sometimes he might say three or four words at once."

Leaning against the counter, Matt laughed. "Ike does enough talkin' for the two of us," he said.

"I expect that's a fact, all right," Seth said with a chuckle. "I'd be glad to put in a word to Captain Boyd for you."

Captain Parker Boyd of the Eleventh Ohio Volunteer Cavalry, chief of scouts, had been appointed to his position by Major Evans' predecessor, Colonel Henry Maynadier. His qualifications for the job of commanding the scout detachment at Fort Laramie could be summed up in the fact that he was Colonel Maynadier's nephew. While he had as yet never taken the field in this position, he was nevertheless determined to be successful as commander of the scouts, if only to prove the validity of his uncle Henry's judgment. In the only private meeting he had with the new post commander, he came away with the distinct feeling that he had not impressed Major Evans. When Evans had pressed him for information on the activities of the Sioux during the past months, Boyd had been forced to admit that he had very little knowledge of even the location of the larger hostile villages. For this reason, he eagerly received the two hunters who came to his office seeking employment.

"Seth Ward tells me you men have been camped in the Powder River country all winter," Captain Boyd said in greeting Matt and Ike.

"Yes, sir, that's a fact," Ike replied. Matt stood silently by, content to let Ike do the talking, since his partner took to the job so naturally.

Boyd paused a few seconds while he looked the two

over. Dressed from head to foot in deerskins, the pair looked little different from a great many rudderless drifters who wandered through army posts all over the western frontier. The big one was obviously older than his friend, and Boyd could not recall ever having seen a man of larger size. When he pulled his fox-skin cap from his head, he revealed a bald dome where not a single hair found purchase. In contrast, his face, from his ears down, was hidden beneath a great bush of gray whiskers from which his deep voice resonated when he spoke.

"What can you tell me about Sioux activity in that area during the winter?" Boyd asked. "Do you know where Spotted Tail's band is located? Or Red Cloud?"

Ike looked puzzled for a moment, thinking that everybody should know what activities any Indian village would be involved in during a cold, hard winter. "Well," he answered after a long pause, "I s'pect they was doin' about the same thing we was—tryin' to keep warm and find somethin' to eat." Seeing the disappointment in the captain's face, he glanced over at Matt before embellishing a bit on his report. "I don't know whose camp it was, but there was a big village on the Powder, maybe two hundred tipis. We come across huntin' parties ever'where. That's why we finally had to get out. There was too damned many Injuns."

"Where on the Powder?" Boyd asked. He opened a drawer and pulled out a crude map. "Show me."

Ike immediately glanced back at Matt, looking for support. He really had no idea of the location of the Sioux camp. He and Matt had never actually seen a village. They had made it a point to confine their hunting to the western side of the mountains and the Bighorn River valley. They had just assumed there had to be a big village somewhere along the Powder River. Matt rolled his eyes, doing his best to suppress a grin. Seeing that Matt was going to let him worm his way out of it without help, Ike leaned over the desk, squinting his eyes at the map. For a long moment, he said nothing, appearing to study the map. Finally, Boyd placed a finger on the map and said, "Here's the Powder where it branches off from the Yellowstone."

"Yes, sir," Ike replied at once, thankful that Boyd had pointed it out, for Ike couldn't read. "That's the Powder all right." He poked the map with his finger, about halfway down the river. "About there, that's where they was." He turned to Matt again. "Wouldn't you say so, partner?"

Without bothering to look at the map, Matt replied, "I reckon."

Boyd turned to study the heretofore silent partner then. Up to that point, his attention had been captured by the formidable figure that was Ike Brister. Upon a closer look, he realized that Matt was a big man as well, although not as thick of trunk as Brister. Rather, he was tall and lean, giving a sense of animal grace even while standing patiently by. His eyes were alert and clear, like the eyes of an eagle. *Maybe,* he thought, *this is the man who should be doing the talking.* Before he could voice it, Ike continued.

"'Course I doubt if they're there now," he said. "They've probably moved that village by now. I expect me and my partner could find 'em again, though." He glanced over at Matt and winked.

Boyd continued staring at the map for a few moments while he decided whether or not to put the two on the payroll. In numbers, he already had a full complement of scouts, both Indian and white. In quality, however, he was lacking. He had no qualms about the Crows and the Rees. But there were only a couple of the white scouts who had impressed him as men of integrity. Most of the others were little more than whiskey-soaked vagabonds, too lazy to do anything else.

There was something about the two standing before him now that gave him a sense of assurance, however, especially the young one. Slaughter looked like a man who was born to ride the high country. He seemed to have said more with his eyes than what his huge friend had blurted out for the last twenty minutes. The decision made, Boyd concluded the interview. "All right, I'm going to take a chance on you. The corporal will show you where to sign up." He called his clerk in to escort his new recruits out.

"Well, I reckon we're gainfully employed," Ike announced with a chuckle as they left Boyd's office and led their horses across the parade ground. "Don't seem like too hard a job, does it? Lay around the post here while the army buys our supplies and feeds our horses." So far, their only orders were to stay close and to report in with the other scouts every morning. The idle time lasted for only two days, however, for they were posted on their first assignment as scouts on the third day after signing up.

A settler named Robert Hostetler, his wife, and two teenage sons had built a cabin near the south fork of the Cheyenne River during the past summer. They had been advised that the Sioux considered that area their own and did not welcome white settlers. But Hostetler was firm in his conviction that when the Indians saw that he was a peaceful man with no intentions of spoiling their hunting grounds, he would not be harassed. Maybe, he thought, his family might even become friends with the Sioux.

His son, Albert, in later conversation with army scouts, said it appeared that his father was right. They had seen occasional Sioux and Cheyenne riders stopping on the bluffs above the cabin. The Indians would simply watch the activities of the white family for a while, and then disappear again. There were no threats of any kind. The Sioux merely seemed to be curious. The Hostetlers were left in peace until two days after Matt and Ike arrived at Fort Laramie.

There was no warning. Suddenly, in the middle of the afternoon, a line of thirty or forty Indians appeared upon the bluffs across the river. Albert's brother, Joseph, was the first of the family to spot the war party. He ran to alert his father. Upon seeing the line of hostiles, still silently watching from the bluffs, Hostetler was undecided what to do. Maybe, he thought, like the small groups of two or three that had wandered by before, they were simply curious, and might fade into the prairie as the others had. Still, they might have their eyes on the livestock. So as a precaution, he sent Albert to bring the horse and mules back to the corral.

As Albert later related, by the time he had rounded up the two mules and his father's horse and was headed back to the cabin, the line of warriors had forded the river and ridden right up to the cabin. From the hill south of the homestead, Albert saw his father standing in the yard awaiting the visitors. The boy paused when he saw his mother come from the cabin to stand beside her husband. She was holding up a cake of corn bread that she had baked just that afternoon. Before Albert's horrified eyes, one of the Indians raised his bow and drove an arrow deep into his father's chest. Stunned, Hostetler sank to his knees, only to receive a second arrow just below the first one. His wife, stricken with terrified disbelief, dropped the corn bread and tried to scream. The arrow that slashed through her throat cut her cry short, and she collapsed to the ground beside her husband. Joseph tried to escape to the river, but was ridden down before reaching the bank. It had all taken place within the span of a handful of seconds, during which time Albert was rendered helpless, paralyzed by the horror he had witnessed. Too far away to have come to his family's aid, he realized at that moment that he had not yet been discovered by the Sioux warriors. With no other choice, he dropped the mules' reins, jumped on the horse's back, and sped away down the other side of the hill.

Hearing the departing horse, the Sioux gave chase, but Albert's lead was enough that they gave up the pursuit after a couple of miles, more interested in looting the cabin. Albert pushed the laboring animal through the night, reaching Fort Laramie just before sunup. The exhausted horse foundered on the parade ground.

Lieutenant Frederick LeVan had been charged with the responsibility of seeking out the hostile Sioux party, with orders to bring them back in chains if possible. With a column of eighty troopers, eight Crow scouts, a seasoned white scout named Zeb Benson and the two recently hired white scouts, LeVan set out for the Cheyenne River.

Following the Bozeman Trail, the first day's march found the column some forty miles northwest of Fort Laramie, where they made camp in the shadow of the Laramie Mountains. Even though there was very little daylight left, Lieutenant LeVan sent the scouts out to look for any evidence of recent hostile activity. Zeb Benson had ridden scout for LeVan before, and he told Matt and Ike that the lieutenant was strictly by the book when it came to patrols. Most of the other officers were somewhat relaxed when in the field, but LeVan ran his command with strict adherence to prescribed military conduct. It did not make him popular with the rank and file. But most of the men would grudgingly admit that in a fight, you could count on him to lead the action while still remaining dedicated to a responsibility for the safety of his command. "He ain't gonna set down and chew the fat with you at suppertime," Zeb summed up, "but you know he ain't gonna run off from a fight without his dead and wounded."

Matt glanced over to take another look at the lieutenant, seated apart from the men, his only companion

Lieutenant James Leland O'Connor, his second in command. As respected as LeVan was, O'Connor was equally disliked by most who had served under him, according to Zeb. Matt had known officers like LeVan in the Confederate Army, all spit and polish, no button unbuttoned. Some were good officers, some were not. You never knew for sure until you were caught in the middle of a hot fight. Zeb seemed to think LeVan could be counted upon. Zeb was probably right, Matt decided. LeVan had that look about him. Slim and fit, he appeared capable of command, a soldier's soldier, born to the service.

The column was in the saddle again shortly after sunup, following the general trail Matt and Ike had taken when they had first set out for the Bighorns. It was the middle of the day when they arrived at the Hostetler homestead. Nothing remained of the cabin except a jumble of burned timbers, still smoking, with scattered flickers of flame here and there. The little corral was still standing, and the bodies of Hostetler, his wife, and his young son were hung on the rails, spread-eagled. It was a grisly sight. The bodies were mutilated and scalped, staring in sightless horror.

"Get them down from there," LeVan ordered, his voice crisp with anger. "Sergeant, detail some men to dig graves for these poor souls." When the sergeant moved sharply to obey his orders, LeVan turned to Zeb. "Get the scouts out and find me a trail. I want the bastards that did this."

It wasn't hard to find the Sioux war party's trail. There had been no effort to disguise it. Back the way they had come, the trail led toward the Powder River. It appeared that the raid had not been a random strike. The war party had specifically come to murder Hostetler and his family. With scouts out on the flanks, as well as about a half mile in advance, the column set out at a brisk pace, confident that there would be a Sioux village at the end of the trail.

Midafternoon found them at the lower end of the Powder. For the rest of that day the column pushed deeper into Sioux country with no sign of a village or any hint of Indian activity. Ahead and to the west, the Bighorn Mountains stood silent and forbidding, their upper slopes white with snow. Matt, along with Zeb Benson and three Crow scouts, crossed over to the western bank of the river, while Ike and the other Crows continued to follow the trail along the eastern side.

"I expect the lieutenant's gonna find more Injuns than he knows what to do with if we keep goin' much farther up this river," Zeb said. "I ain't sure but what we ought'n to turn back before we get in over our heads."

Matt didn't reply, but it was a thought he had already had. He and Ike had seen enough hunting parties in the area from the Powder, across the ridges to the Bighorn, to know that there had to be a sizable Sioux village farther upriver. They had just never felt the need to find it.

A little before sundown, LeVan called a halt to make camp for the night. The scouts were called in to report. No one had seen any hostiles or signs that any had been in the area recently. The only evidence that Sioux had been in the valley was the obvious trail left by the war party. "What do you think, Brister?" LeVan suddenly asked. "You think we're anywhere near that Sioux village?" According to what Captain Boyd had told him, Ike knew where the village was located.

This time, Ike was honest in his answer. "I swear, I don't know, Lieutenant. Like I told Captain Boyd, I expect that village has wore out the grass and moved on to somewhere else by now."

LeVan studied the huge scout for a long moment, considering his answer. Then he turned to Zeb Benson. "Can your Crows tell anything about the trail we've been following? Is it any fresher?"

Zeb knew what he meant. "You mean, does it look like we're gainin' on 'em?" Zeb said. "No, it don't look that way. That trail don't look no fresher than the day we started." He paused, watching LeVan while he digested the words. "And we're gettin' pretty deep into hostile territory," he added for emphasis.

"You don't think we'll catch the war party," LeVan said. It was not a question.

"Not a chance in hell," Ike suddenly interjected, not about to be left out of the discussion. "Them Injuns are most likely already home, and I got a feelin' their village is bigger than this patrol can handle."

LeVan studied the bear of a man for a moment, as if trying to decide whether or not to take him seriously. Then he spoke. "My orders are to find the guilty war party if possible, and to punish them." He turned then to Lieutenant O'Connor. "We'll follow this trail for one more day. If we don't turn up some hostile contact by tomorrow night, we'll return to Laramie."

"Damn good idea," Zeb mumbled low after the officers had walked away. "Be a better idea if we was to head back in the mornin'. We'd need a regiment if we *was* to happen onto that Sioux village."

Two Kills dismounted and walked over to the edge of the bluff to join Yellow Hand. "It would be an easy thing to steal some of their horses. They left them all together with only two sentries to watch them. It is a dark night. We could be away with half of them before the soldiers knew they were missing."

Yellow Hand smiled at his friend. It was an interesting thought, but stealing the army mounts would let the soldiers know they were being watched. And Iron Claw would not be pleased if his plan was compromised by losing the element of surprise. "It is for us to count the soldiers, and nothing more," he said.

"I know," Two Kills replied, "but it *would* be easy."

The two Lakota scouts remained on the bluff, counting the individual campfires, watching the soldiers settle in for the night with apparently no concern that their presence might be discovered. Most of the fires were dying out when they led their ponies down the far side of the ridge where they mounted and silently melted into the darkness to inform Iron Claw of the approach of the soldiers.

Chapter 3

The morning broke clear and cold. During the night a thin cover of clouds had drifted over the Powder River basin, dusting the mountains with a light snow and spreading a white mantle across the floor of the valley. The tracks now effectively covered, there was no longer a trail to follow. Lieutenant LeVan was determined to stay the course in spite of this, so the column continued, following the general path of the Bozeman Trail.

By sunup, the clouds had disappeared and the snow-covered peaks glistened silver in the bright sun, causing Matt to squint when he looked toward the mountains. As he rode, moving comfortably in rhythm with the buckskin's gentle gait, he couldn't help but wonder what the army had hoped this patrol would accomplish. The trail was too old, even before the snow covered it. The war party that killed the Hostetlers was long gone. He had to agree with Zeb on that. There wasn't one chance in a hundred that they could run the raiders down. *What the hell,* he thought. *I'm getting paid by the day, and I've got nothing better planned.* He glanced over at Ike then, and guessed that his partner was probably thinking the same thing.

It was close to midday when the first hostiles were spotted. Ahead of the column by about half a mile, Matt and Ike pulled up beside one of the Crow scouts who had stopped to await them. "There," Spotted Horse said, pointing toward a low rise about a quarter of a mile ahead. Following the line indicated, Matt saw them, two Sioux warriors calmly sitting their ponies, watching the column's progress.

"Better go back and tell the lieutenant," Ike said. He signaled Zeb, who was out on the flanks with the other Crows. Then he galloped off to meet Lieutenant LeVan and the column. Matt waited with Spotted Horse.

"Where?" LeVan wanted to know as soon as he rode up to them. Spotted Horse again pointed toward the rise. The lieutenant stared at the two hostiles, still calmly sitting and watching. After a few moments, he turned to Ike. "What do you think, Brister?"

Ike, never one to complicate an issue, replied, "I think it's two Injuns settin' on their ponies." It was obvious to him that the two were there to keep an eye on the soldiers, and he didn't see the need for LeVan's question.

Irritated by the big man's flippant reply, the lieutenant directed his next question toward Matt. "You think they're scouts or just a couple of hunters?"

"I'm pretty sure they're scouts," Matt answered. "My guess is they knew about us since yesterday, and I expect there's a helluva lot more of 'em waitin' somewhere up ahead." He had been studying the land that lay ahead of them, and he directed LeVan's attention toward the gently rolling hills that gradually transitioned into the base of the mountains. "There's a lot of good places to set up an ambush in those hills."

While Zeb and the other Crow scouts rode over to join them, LeVan took a few moments to consider Matt's remarks. With a column of eighty troopers, armed with Sharps carbines, he felt confident that he could rout any band of hostiles looking for a fight. "All right," he said when Zeb pulled up before them, "we'll continue on the present line of march."

"I'd keep a sharp eye on them ridges," Ike warned.

"That would be your job, Brister," LeVan replied shortly. He turned to summon the column forward. "Scouts out!" He commanded.

The soldiers continued along a trail that led them closer and closer to the mountains that divided the Powder River valley and the Tongue River. The two Sioux scouts disappeared when the column was within a quarter of a mile, only to reappear a few hundred yards farther on. This time, when the soldiers drew near, the two were suddenly joined by six or seven more warriors. No longer content to merely watch, one of the warriors fired a rifle at the approaching troopers. Well out of range, the shot fell harmlessly short.

"Hold your fire," LeVan ordered, lest some of his anxious command should waste ammunition at that range. A few more shots were fired by the small band of Sioux, all considerably short. Gradually, the shots became closer. Still LeVan held his men in check, until they were within a couple hundred yards. Then he dispatched Lieutenant O'Connor with a detail of fifteen troopers to rout the warriors. Ike and four of the Crow scouts were assigned to accompany them. "Just drive them off, Jim," LeVan told O'Connor. "Don't give chase, and keep the column in sight. I want to be able to see you."

O'Connor charged up the ridge after the Sioux. Before they had reached the top, another small band of Sioux appeared on the ridges on the opposite side of the valley. Like the first group, they fired at the column of soldiers. "Sergeant Barnes!" LeVan ordered. "Take ten men and dispatch those hostiles."

Matt pulled up even with the lieutenant. "Looks to me like they're tryin' to split us up," he cautioned. "There's no tellin' how many Indians are hiding on the other side of these ridges."

LeVan paused to consider Matt's warning. He looked at Zeb Benson, and the scout nodded his agreement. "You may be right," LeVan conceded. He was not one to ignore his scouts' advice, but he was still of the opinion that he could repel any assault by a sizable band of hostiles. "Barnes," he ordered, "chase them off that ridge, but keep the column in sight. Take Slaughter and a couple of the Crows with you. Benson, you stay with me. And Barnes, don't pursue them beyond the ridge. I want to be able to see you at all times."

"Yes, sir," the sergeant replied and was off.

With his column reduced by thirty-five, LeVan continued his advance toward the end of the valley, confident that whatever the hostiles had in mind, he could call all his men back into one fighting unit as long as they were in eye contact. Although careful to hide it in his expression, he was aware of a certain sense of excitement at the prospect of finding the Sioux village. He knew he was getting close because of the efforts of the hostiles to draw him off in other directions. He remained cognizant of Matt's warning that the valley narrowed into an ideal setting for an ambush, however. No matter how much he had heard about the fighting skills of the Sioux warriors, he felt certain of his superiority in a skirmish. What he feared most was the possibility that the hostiles would scatter and escape.

Ascending the slope on the column's right flank, Sergeant Barnes led his troopers up toward the waiting Sioux warriors. One of the warriors raised his rifle and fired at the approaching soldiers. Barnes ordered return fire, and the resulting volley served to rout the hostile party. After only a few more random shots, the hostiles turned and ran. The soldiers gained the top of the ridge and, following Lieutenant LeVan's orders, continued their pursuit along the crest of the ridge, keeping the column in sight. "Looks like they're tryin' to cut back to cross over again!" Barnes shouted to Matt. "I think we can cut 'em off before they make that ravine."

Matt looked at the ravine that the hostiles seemed intent upon reaching. It ran down to what appeared to be a narrow gorge, and he had a strong feeling that there might be considerably more Sioux waiting there than this small detachment of troopers could handle. "I think that's just what they're hopin' you'll do," Matt replied.

Barnes was about to lead his men down from the

ridgetop after the fleeing Indians, but he hesitated. Slaughter might be right, but Barnes had the feeling the scout was primarily concerned with avoiding risk to his own neck. Barnes had been in the army too long to ignore a command, however, and the lieutenant had ordered him to chase the Sioux off the ridge and keep the column in sight. He held up his hand to halt his men. "Let 'em go," he ordered. "We done what we was told. Let's get back to the column." He led them off in a diagonal direction to intercept the column near the end of the valley.

On the opposite ridge, Lieutenant O'Connor heard the shots exchanged between Sergeant Barnes' men and the Sioux. When he looked across the valley and saw the Indians taking flight after Barnes' troopers opened fire, it served to make him eager to confront the half dozen or so warriors still watching his advance. He gave his horse his heels. "Come on, men. Let's get after them before they get away!"

Like their brothers on the opposite ridge, the Sioux began shooting as soon as the soldiers climbed within range. Then they too turned and fled down the back side of the slope. Ike pushed his horse hard as it labored up the steep incline just below the ridgetop. Once he reached the top, he prodded the bay to lope along the crest until he pulled up even with O'Connor. "Don't let 'em lead you off down over that hill," Ike warned.

"After them, boys!" O'Connor shouted, ignoring the big scout's advice, and led the way. With only a few shots fired at the charging soldiers, the warriors turned and fled down the slope. "Don't let 'em get away," O'-Connor yelled as he raced along the crest.

In the valley below him, a small group of Indians rose up from the rocks and began firing at the main column. In response, Lieutenant LeVan ordered a charge. Sweeping down the narrow canyon with carbines blazing, the cavalry troop thundered toward the ambush. Seeing what appeared to be an all-out rout, O'Connor caught the fever and plunged over the top of the ridge after the handful of Sioux now fleeing through a stand of stunted pines near the base of the slope. LeVan's order to maintain visual contact with the column was discarded as unnecessary caution. His soldiers were rapidly gaining on the hostiles, and O'Connor was determined to overtake them.

The only member of the detachment not overcome with the scent of blood was Ike. He alone saw the folly of blindly galloping after the departing Sioux, and he tried to catch up to O'Connor before the foolhardy lieutenant charged into the trees. He was too late to head him off, but the troopers emerged from the pines without harm. They found the Indians waiting for them in a small clearing, no longer running. Behind them, in the trees they had just passed through, several dozen warriors rose up from the brush. Too late, O'Connor realized that he had been drawn into a trap. He was caught in a cross fire and was heavily outnumbered.

As one, then another trooper was cut down by the hostile fire, O'Connor tried to rally his small detail into a skirmish line. Seeing the futility of such a defense, Ike wheeled his horse around to block the lieutenant's. With lead flying all around his head, he shouted, "Up the slope! It's the only chance you've got!" He pointed toward the side of the ridge they had descended just moments before. "You try to make a stand here and we're all dead."

O'Connor, his eyes wide in shock, his brain befuddled, eagerly conceded to a calmer voice. "Follow me, men!" he shouted then, and immediately fled up the slope, not waiting to see if anyone had heard him.

Seeing the lieutenant's total lack of concern for his men's safety, Ike held his horse back to direct the withdrawal. He waited to make sure all of the detail retreated toward the slope where O'Connor had fled, and he remained there until all had started up the hill. He turned the bay to follow, but suddenly his horse screamed in pain, dropped to its knees and tumbled, dumping Ike in the process. The big man rolled over a couple of times before coming up to one knee. The last of the soldiers were struggling up the steep side of the hill, oblivious to his situation. He looked around him for his rifle. Seeing it a few feet away, he reached for it just as everything went black in his brain.

Down on the valley floor, Lieutenant LeVan had succeeded in pushing the Sioux back from their position in the rocks, and was now in pursuit of the fleeing Indians. He could no longer see Lieutenant O'Connor, the headstrong young officer having evidently ignored his orders to remain in view. On his right, LeVan saw Sergeant Barnes angling across the slope to catch up with the column. He didn't wait for them, figuring they could trail along behind him. In the excitement of the moment, when his cavalry was clearly the superior force, he threw caution to the winds and recklessly led his men through the narrow gorge at the end of the valley, following the confining passage as it wound between steep cliffs. There was no sound except the thunderous pounding of the horses' hooves upon the hard, rocky soil. Rounding a sharp curve, the lieutenant suddenly found himself facing the hostiles he had pursued. No longer running, they now turned to fight the charging soldiers.

The Crow scouts were the first to realize they had been tricked. They tried to call out to LeVan to stop, but it was too late. The door had been closed. In the next instant, the walls of the gorge erupted with rifle fire and arrows in flight. Caught in a virtual shooting gallery, LeVan found his command outnumbered and fired upon from every direction. He immediately began taking casualties as his troopers broke ranks and tried to find cover from the blistering gunfire. Still taking casualties, he was finally able to fall back toward the entrance to the canyon and form a defensive circle, using the horses as a revetment. Even then, he knew it was only a matter of time before they exhausted their ammunition and were overrun. His only hope was help from Barnes and O'Connor.

Sergeant Barnes was intent upon following his commanding officer into the gorge, but Matt persuaded him to halt before committing his men to the narrow passage. He could already hear rifle fire emanating from the canyon, and moments later a continuous roar of gunfire broke out. "Damn!" Barnes exclaimed. "The lieutenant must be givin' 'em hell."

Matt wasn't so sure. He figured it more likely the lieutenant had ridden into a beehive of angry Sioux, maybe more than he could handle. "You couldn't pick a better place for an ambush," he said. "'Course, you're gonna do what you think is best. But my advice is not to go ridin' into that canyon. I figure it'd be a better idea to split up and climb up on both sides of this gulch, work our way down to the fight and see what's what. If the lieutenant is in trouble, we might be of better use from up above."

Seeing the wisdom in Matt's suggestion, Barnes immediately agreed. They split the detail into two groups. Barnes took five of the men and started climbing the ridge on the left. The remaining five soldiers and Spotted Horse followed Matt up the ridge on the right.

It was a rugged climb up the steep slope, but the buckskin proved to be up to the task, keeping up with Spotted Horse's nimble pony. The army mounts labored along some distance behind them. Matt and Spotted Horse rode along the top of the gulch until they got to a point that they figured to be parallel to the fighting below. They waited until the soldiers caught up to them. Then they dismounted and, leaving one man to watch the horses, worked their way down to the rim of the gulch.

The scene was pretty much the way Matt had expected. Below them on the canyon floor, boxed into a tight defensive circle, LeVan and his men were fighting for their lives against hostiles on all sides. Between him and the lieutenant were countless hostiles hidden in the many gullies in the sides of the gulch, keeping the soldiers pinned down. Matt looked over toward the far side of the gulch, but he could not see any sign of Barnes and his men. Although he could not see them, they were working their way down through the gullies, just as he had. And unknown to him, they had been joined by the remnants of O'Connor's men from the other side of the ridge.

Matt directed the soldiers to spread out along the rim of the gorge. When everyone was set, he aimed at a pocket about fifty feet below him where four hostiles were positioned. His shots served as a signal for the rest of the men to open up, pouring deadly fire down upon the unsuspecting Sioux. A few seconds later, rifle fire broke out from the opposite side of the gulch, and Matt knew Barnes had made it to the party.

With little cover from the soldiers above them, the hostiles, at first confused by the lethal rain of lead, soon found their position a little too hot. After a blistering barrage from the carbines on both sides of the gulch above them, they were soon forced to retreat. In a matter of minutes, the Sioux were in full flight. Below, on the canyon floor, LeVan pressed his troopers to pursue the retreating Indians until the last warrior rode clear of the canyon mouth. Then, fully realizing that he was badly outnumbered after suffering a considerable number of casualties, he ordered the column to turn back and depart the gorge. The Sioux were bound to regroup and return to renew the battle. LeVan was no longer interested in endangering his men again to a force he reckoned to be well over a hundred strong and armed as well, if not better, than he. He picked up his dead and wounded and left the bloody gulch behind him.

The column moved at a smart pace back up the valley toward home. About a quarter mile past the mouth of the canyon, they found the rest of the soldiers awaiting them. LeVan galloped up to a stop beside Lieutenant O'Connor. "By God, Jim, you saved our bacon back there, and no doubt about it."

O'Connor, his campaign hat missing, his blouse stained with sweat and dirt, shook his head in response. "I'm not the one to take credit for that. We ran into an ambush down below that ridge. We lost some men back there, and the rest of us were damn lucky to get out of that trap alive. We ran into Sergeant Barnes on the ridgetop."

Surprised, LeVan looked at Barnes for an explanation. The sergeant turned to glance at the buckskin-clad scout just now approaching them. LeVan followed his gaze. "Slaughter?" he questioned.

Barnes nodded and replied. "Yes, sir, we was about to ride into that trap right behind you, but Slaughter come up with the idea of climbing the ridges."

LeVan was about to commend Matt for organizing their rescue when Matt spoke first. "Where's Ike?" he asked, looking around for his partner. The big man was nowhere to be seen, and no one could answer him. "Where the hell's Ike?" he demanded, turning a concerned gaze on Lieutenant O'Connor.

O'Connor shrugged uncomfortably. "I don't know.

He was behind us when we climbed out of that ravine. I thought he was with us."

"You thought he was with you?" Matt echoed, more than a little concerned now. Then, becoming fully angry, he demanded, "Dammit, do you *see* him with you?"

His feathers ruffled sufficiently by the disrespectful dressing-down he was suffering at the hands of a scout, O'Connor tried to defend his actions. "Dammit, man, we were under a great deal of fire in that ravine. I gave the order to withdraw. I was too damn busy to hold anybody's hand."

"Too damn busy savin' your own hide to worry about anybody else is more likely," Matt shot back. "You didn't even wait to see who you left behind."

"You'd best hold your tongue, mister!" O'Connor sputtered, aware that their argument was being watched with keen interest by the men around him.

LeVan decided he'd better step in before something already ugly developed into something unmanageable. He had just discovered that he had a helluva scout in Matt Slaughter. He didn't want a spat between the civilian and an officer to escalate to the point where he would have to back O'Connor. "A lot of us made mistakes back there," he said. "I take the responsibility for riding into that trap. There were just too many hostiles for this column to handle. We suffered a helluva lot more casualties than we should have." He turned to O'Connor. "How many did you lose?"

"Four, I think," O'Connor answered, still ruffled.

"Four, you think?" LeVan demanded. "Don't you know how many men you left behind?"

"Four," O'Connor replied meekly.

"Beggin' your pardon, Lieutenant O'Connor," a corporal who had ridden with the ill-fated detachment spoke up then. "But there was five left behind, not countin' that big scout." Seeing the angry scowl building on LeVan's face, the corporal quickly added, "I don't think you saw Baskin take an arrow in the throat when we was scramblin' up the side of that ridge."

LeVan didn't say anything for a few moments while he stared accusingly at O'Connor. When he spoke again, it was in quiet, even tones. "We'll go back and recover your dead while the Indians are withdrawn." With that order issued, he led the column after Matt, who was already headed down the slope.

As the corporal had stated, there were five bodies left in the clearing. There was, however, no sign of the huge civilian scout. The bodies were all mutilated, some to a more barbaric degree than others. The one shocking mutilation, common to all five, was the absence of ears. All had been sliced off. It was a sickening sight, and an initial introduction for most of LeVan's green troopers to the cruelty of the enemy they fought.

"Let's get 'em up," LeVan ordered sharply, trying to keep the emotion from his voice. "I don't know how much time we've got before they regroup. Let's get 'em under way, Sergeant." He then turned to O'Connor. "Jim, head the column out." Turning back to Matt, he said, "Slaughter, I'm sorry about your friend, but I guess it couldn't be helped. You and Zeb can take the point."

"Zeb can take the point," Matt replied. "I'm goin' back for Ike."

LeVan didn't respond at once. It was obvious that the broad-shouldered man in buckskins did not make idle statements. He thought to try to persuade Matt that he could not go back alone, but decided it was a useless endeavor. "Suit yourself, man." He wheeled his horse to join the column already under way. Then he turned back once again. "Good luck," he said.

Zeb Benson looked at Matt and just shook his head, figuring that this might be the last time he would see the young fellow. *It's a shame, too,* he thought, for there was something he saw in Slaughter that told him he was a man you could count on. Turning then, he galloped off to take the point. One remained beside Matt for a few moments longer. Spotted Horse looked deep into Matt's eyes for a long moment, reading the courage there. He solemnly nodded his head in respect. Then he joined the others.

Chapter 4

"It is the same man," Iron Claw said upon first seeing the captive. "There couldn't be many men of such great size." He continued to stand over Ike, staring at the huge man held helpless by the rawhide thongs tying his hands and feet. "I cannot be sure, but I think the other one was on the ridge above us. There was one with a rifle that spoke like the *spirit gun*, but I could not see him clearly." Iron Claw's mind was on the incident in the ravine weeks before, when he and his warriors were tricked into a deadly ambush by the two white hunters. As he re-created the scene in his mind, the lead slug embedded deep in his thigh began to ache. He would carry the *spirit gun*'s bullet for the rest of his life. The bullet was lodged too far into the muscle to be removed. The wound was almost healed, but he now walked with a slight limp and probably always would.

Broken Bow studied his friend's face for a moment. Like Iron Claw, he too still carried a hunger for revenge after the fight with the two white men. But he carried no physical scars from the battle, only the shame he had felt for being so blatantly tricked. Lakota warriors had been killed on that day, most of them by the hand of the white man with the *spirit gun*. Behind him in the village, the sound of the dancing carried triumphantly on the evening breeze. There was cause to celebrate. It had been a great victory over the soldiers on this day, even though his warriors had been forced to withdraw from the valley. They had killed many soldiers, and the dancing would continue for most of the night. It would have been complete if the big white hunter's partner had also been captured.

Gazing down at the battered body, soaked in blood from head to toe, Broken Bow could not help but marvel that the white brute was still alive. His ankles bound, he had been dragged all the way back to the Lakota village, an ordeal that would have killed most men. It had been Broken Bow's bullet that killed the big man's horse. A bullet from one of the other warriors had been the blow that grazed the white man's head, leaving him unconscious on the ground. The bullet had laid open a long, ugly gash along the side of his smooth bald head and streaked his heavy gray beard red with blood. While the two men talked, an almost continuous parade of spectators, mostly women and children, gathered around the captive, curious to see a white man of such proportions. They prodded the huge body with sticks, or threw stones, seeking some response. There was none. The body, battered and broken, appeared to be oblivious to additional pain.

"This crazy buffalo is too dumb to die," Iron Claw

commented, his thoughts running along the same trail as his friend's. "It pleases me, for he will be a long time dying." Broken Bow nodded. There was a long moment of silence while both warriors thought of their desire for revenge, and the partner of the huge captive, the man with the *spirit gun*. "He will come," Iron Claw finally pronounced softly. "We have not seen the last of that *wasicu*."

Broken Bow nodded, knowing of whom his friend spoke. "Maybe so," he allowed, "but he would be foolish to do so. I think maybe many soldiers will come, a lot more than came today. The soldiers will be seeking revenge for their defeat. I think it would be wise to move our village before they come. Some of the elders have already been talking about moving soon, anyway."

Iron Claw shrugged indifferently. "Yes, it's time to move. We have killed off most of the game, and the ponies need new grass. The talk has been mostly in favor of moving to the valley of the Greasy Grass. We have not camped there for many moons."

"Is the white giant still alive?" Wounded Bear wondered aloud as he walked up to join Iron Claw and Broken Bow.

"I don't know," Iron Claw answered, his attention focused upon a grisly necklace he was stringing. "He hasn't moved or made a sound for a long time now, even when the women kicked him. Maybe he is dead." Not really concerned at the moment, he held the necklace up for Broken Bow to see. Broken Bow grunted when shown the macabre ornament of human ears, sliced from the bodies of the soldiers.

Wounded Bear decided to see for himself if Ike still lived. He aimed a kick that connected solidly with the big man's chest. It was powerful enough to rock the huge body, but there was no response from Ike. Wounded Bear grunted, not satisfied. "I'll see if he's dead or not." He drew his knife, and dropping to one knee beside Ike, pressed the blade against his cheek until it drew blood. "Ha!" Wounded Bear grunted when he detected a slight recoil from the big man. Wounded Bear laughed. Pointing to Ike's smooth pate, he said, "He has no scalp to take." He then decided to take the next best thing. In one brutal motion, he sliced Ike's cheek down to his chin and ripped almost half of his beard from his face. Ike finally cried out in pain. Wounded Bear issued a loud war whoop and held the bloody trophy up over his head. With fatal resolve, Ike struck. With his hands tied together, he suddenly reached up and caught Wounded Bear by the throat, choking off the triumphant war whoop in a death grip. Wounded Bear struggled frantically, but to no avail. The powerful hands locked down on his throat, crushing his windpipe. In desperation, the trapped victim tried to free himself by jabbing his knife again and again into Ike's arms and shoulders. Broken Bow was not slow in reacting, but by the time he could come to his friend's aid, Wounded Bear's eyes were bulging wide. Seconds later, his body went limp. Still the huge hands tightened around Wounded Bear's neck, until they heard it snap. Broken Bow could not break the big white man's grip until, finally, Iron Claw stepped up behind them, placed his pistol against Ike's head, and ended his torment.

Broken Bow was beside himself with grief and anger. Wounded Bear had been his friend. In a fit of rage, he picked up a heavy rock and slammed it against Ike's head again and again, until his arms were weary.

The shot that finally ended Ike's life went unnoticed due to the shooting and dancing going on around the fire in the village's center. The dancers were not aware of the death of one of their brothers until one of the young boys ran to tell the elders. Enraged, they dragged Ike's body to the edge of the river and tied it spread-eagled between two stout willows. When they had vented their wrath upon his mutilated corpse, they left it suspended between the two trees as a grisly warning to other white men who might think to enter their country. Before leaving to take care of Wounded Bear's body, Iron Claw went back to Ike's corpse and hung his grisly necklace of human ears around the bloodied neck. He backed away to stare at it for a moment. Then, satisfied that it conveyed the message he desired, he joined the others.

As the column filed out of the narrow valley, heading for home, Matt immediately expanded his search around the clearing, looking for some sign that might help him find his friend. Entering the stand of pines near the bottom, he proceeded cautiously lest, like himself, some of the hostiles might be lingering after the battle.

In a small clearing beyond the pines, he found the carcass of Ike's bay, but no sign of his friend. Dismounting, he looked around the area for sign. The tracks he saw told him what had happened there. The detachment had been drawn into an ambush. Indications

of a fight before they escaped up the eastern slope of the
ridge confirmed O'Connor's testimony. The trail left in
the slope revealed signs of the fleeing soldiers' panic.
As he walked slowly around the clearing, something
else caught his eye. The gravel and dirt bore evidence
that a heavy object had been dragged away behind the
Indian ponies. Matt knew at once what that object had
to be.

He was struck with a cold, clammy feeling as if the
blood in his veins had suddenly chilled. The blatant trail
could only mean that the big scout was dead. He wondered if he was already dead when they dragged his
body away, or if he was cruelly battered to death behind
an Indian pony. Without his realizing it, his fists were
clenched so tightly in anger that his fingernails were
drawing blood. He had known that Ike was probably
dead when he did not return with O'Connor, but there
had been the remote possibility that he was still alive—
held captive or maybe hiding out somewhere, wounded
and waiting for Matt to find him. Now there was little
doubt that Ike was gone. Still, Matt was compelled to
search for him, hoping for a miracle and knowing that
had the roles been reversed Ike would be looking for
him.

Back in the saddle, he started out, following the trail
left by Ike's body as it was dragged through brush and
rocky soil. Down the length of the ravine and out onto
the rolling prairie, where the tracks were joined by those
of other ponies, the trail led northward. The combined
tracks converged yet again with tracks from another
party, and Matt could see then the full strength of the

war party that had lured the military column into ambush.

It was close to sundown when the trail led him to the river, then turned to follow it upstream. No more than a mile farther, darkness began to fall upon the river valley. He was going to have to make camp and continue by morning light. It would be a safe guess that the Sioux had a village farther upriver somewhere, but there was still the chance that the trail might cross over to the Tongue and he might miss it in the darkness. With a great deal of reluctance, he looked along the riverbank for a suitable place to make his camp. Only then did he realize that it had been some time since he had last eaten. He had nothing but some jerked venison and a little sack of green coffee beans. It would have to do. More important, there was plenty of grass along the riverbank for his horse. He could supplement the buckskin's diet with some bark peeled from a few cottonwood branches.

Worrisome thoughts crowded his mind as he went about making a small fire to boil his coffee water. He could not avoid thinking that it might have made a difference had he been with Ike. He could do a great deal of damage with his Henry rifle. Maybe it would have been just enough to drive the hostiles off. *Things happen the way they're supposed to,* he told himself, but the troublesome thoughts remained.

Daylight brought a cloudy, chilly morning with a dusting of spring snow that left a thin blanket over the ground and covered the bearskin Matt slept under. He awakened to the sound of the buckskin gelding gently nuzzling the light covering of snow to get to the grass beneath. He arose at once. Anxious to return to the trail, he did not waste time rekindling his fire or making coffee. Another piece of deer jerky would suffice for breakfast. He saddled the buckskin, checked his rifle, and was soon on his way once more.

Although light, the snow was enough to cloak the trail he had followed the day before. It perturbed him to realize that he had no choice but to follow his hunch and continue along the river, even though he had stopped the night before for fear he would lose the trail. Now he couldn't see the tracks anyway. He pushed on, following the general direction of the gently winding river, half expecting to find a village around each turn.

A large portion of his day was wasted when he decided to search the opposite bank for tracks that might indicate the Sioux warriors had crossed over, still following the river. However, there were none. His hunch had been wrong, and he was forced to turn around and retrace his route.

He was within a mile of the previous night's camp when he encountered the broad path of a large band of riders where they had come out of the river. Looking at the shallow crossing, he could not help but picture the battered body of his friend as the hostiles dragged it across the river. The image brought a stabbing pain to his chest. He looked toward the west, following the general line of the tracks. They led toward a broad ravine that appeared to be a passage through the hills and the mountains to the river beyond. *The village is on the Tongue, and not the Powder,* he thought.

Before the sun climbed directly overhead, he began to see other trails crossing the one he was following, and he knew he must be approaching a village. He warned himself to sharpen his eye and tune in to his senses. He could not afford to be spotted by a Sioux scouting party as he crossed the open meadows, so he stopped often to search the valleys and hills before him, always keeping a route of escape in mind. As he crossed over a tree-covered knoll, the river suddenly appeared below him. He had found the village, but he was too late. The people were gone. His ear immediately picked up the sound of snarling animals below him, seeming to come from the edge of the river. Descending into the valley, he didn't immediately see the reason for the sounds, but as he rode slowly into the abandoned campsite, a macabre apparition suddenly seized his attention.

Bound by the wrists and ankles between two willows and suspended several feet off the ground, the body of Ike Brister hung spread-eagled, like a bear hide strung out to dry. The sounds he had heard had emanated from a pack of snarling coyotes. The surly animals were fighting for dominance of the body, trying to leap high enough to tear at the flesh. Matt jerked hard on the buckskin's reins, pulling the big horse to an abrupt stop. Although he had thought he had prepared himself for the worst, the shock of seeing his friend displayed in such a horrific manner was enough to freeze the blood in his veins. For a long moment he could do nothing but stare at the ghastly scene. It was not until the buckskin pawed the ground nervously and backed away a few feet that Matt brought his senses back in focus. With no concern for the sound, he cocked his rifle and fired as rapidly as he could, trying to kill as many of the offending scavengers as possible. The sudden burst of rifle fire served to scatter the survivors of the pack and left four of their number lying dead at Ike's feet.

He wheeled the big horse around then and rode the length of the deserted Sioux encampment, chasing the last of the coyotes, yelping and snarling, into the cottonwoods. When he was certain that he was alone in the village, he returned to take care of Ike.

"Damn, partner," he muttered softly, "look at what they did to you." The buckskin was reluctant to move up close beside the corpse, and fidgeted nervously while Matt drew his knife and cut the thongs holding the body. As soon as he cut those on one hand and ankle, the trees separated and straightened, throwing Ike's body against the trunk he was still bound to. The buckskin almost bolted, and would have backed away had Matt not held it firmly.

"Damn," he muttered again, apologizing for the rough treatment, but there was no gentle way to free the huge body. He pulled his horse around the other tree so he could cut the two thongs still holding Ike. Seated on the horse, he found himself face-to-face with his former friend and partner. The sightless eyes stared at him from beneath blood-crusted brows, seeming to demand vengeance. A ghastly string of human ears hung from a rawhide cord around Ike's neck. The shock was unnerving, causing Matt to gasp involuntarily as he saw the results of Broken Bow's anger upon Ike's head. He had obviously been bludgeoned repeatedly with a heavy object. Matt quickly cut the two remaining thongs, and Ike's body dropped to the ground. Matt knelt beside his old partner, pulled the macabre necklace from his neck and flung it to the ground.

With a mixture of sorrow and anger boiling in his veins, Matt was determined to give Ike a decent burial. He looked around him, then up and down the river. It struck him as a strangely peaceful place in spite of the violent people who had camped there. Then he looked across the river to the mountains beyond. That was where Ike should be laid to rest. He had loved the mountains, and often said he wanted to ride out the last of his years on a high mountain where he could look down on the world. Matt looked back at the bulk of Ike's body. It would be a job, but it was the least he could do for his old friend.

Matt was a strong man, but the task of lifting Ike's massive bulk up onto his horse was almost beyond his capability. He struggled to get the body to a standing position in an effort to load it on his shoulder. But the body, already stiff, with arms and legs spread wide, proved to be too awkward to load on a skittish horse. After one unsuccessful attempt, he lowered the corpse back to the ground and tried to bend the arms and legs in closer to the body. "I swear, Ike, you're just as damn stubborn dead as you were alive," he couldn't help remarking as he struggled with the limbs frozen in death.

After considerable effort, Matt succeeded in laying Ike's body across the saddle. Taking a look at the massive load awkwardly balanced on his horse, he decided it best to walk instead of trying to step up behind Ike. He started out slowly, leading the buckskin away from the camp and toward the ridge that protected the valley. It was not an easy climb, but he was determined to get Ike to the top of the slope. Even though it was not a high mountain, like the ones he could see beyond, it would give a commanding view of the river below, and he thought the big scout would like that.

He had almost reached the top of the hill when the huge body began to teeter and suddenly slid off, landing heavily upon the ground. Matt stood gazing at the grotesque corpse for a moment, perplexed. It had been hard enough to lift Ike up onto the horse when he was on level ground. On the slope it might prove to be near impossible. After a few moments more, he said, "Well, I reckon you've decided this is the place you wanna be buried." He started digging right where he was.

Transporting Ike's body to the top of the ridge proved not to be the real task at hand. Digging a grave adequate to accept the huge remains took Matt into the late afternoon, and by the time he filled in the hole and smoothed the dirt, shadows were long in the valley. He gathered a few rocks to place in random fashion upon the grave, hoping they would disguise it. His grim task finally finished, he stood at the spot for a few minutes more. He felt he should say something, but he was not given to eloquent speech. "I know you ain't even here," he finally muttered. "You're most likely laughin' at me for totin' your big ass all the way up this hill. But you were as fine a friend as a man could have." He paused to think a moment. "And the worst cardplayer I've ever seen." He smiled at the thought of Ike getting fleeced in every poker game he played. Then his mind flashed an image of the battered face lying in the grave, and his thoughts became stone-cold sober. "I promise you this, partner. That band of Sioux will pay for this. I swear it." As he sat there, his blood boiling with anger, he suddenly thought about the ornament that had been hung around Ike's neck. There were ten ears strung on the rawhide, five pairs, sliced from the bodies of the five troopers. "Ten, Ike," he said solemnly. "I swear I'll kill one Sioux warrior for each one of those ears they hung on you."

He sat by the grave long after the sun had disappeared beyond the mountains to the west and the valley below him became cloaked in darkness. He might have sat there longer had not his horse nudged him impatiently. Bringing his mind back to the present, he got to his feet, realizing then that he had not eaten since chewing on that stick of jerky early that morning. He took one last look at Ike's grave, wishing there was something he could do in his friend's memory. The only thing he could think to do was to see that the big man's name didn't die. He hoped Ike wouldn't be insulted. He had never named the buckskin horse he rode, so he decided it was time he did so. "Come on, Ike," he said to the horse as he stepped up in the saddle and headed down toward the river to pick a place to camp for the night.

Chapter 5

With Ike laid to rest on the hill overlooking the river, Matt was at last able to think about basic needs for survival. The only staple left in his saddlebags was the sack of green coffee beans, and it was half empty. He had consumed the last of his jerked venison the day before, and his stomach was telling him that it was time to hunt for solid food. "There sure as hell ain't nothin' to hunt around here," he remarked to the buckskin, "unless a man wants to eat coyote." He looked back toward the scattered carcasses and curled his lip in disgust. "And I ain't that desperate yet."

The Sioux village had depleted all the game in the small valley. "I reckon we'll have to ride downriver, Ike," he said, addressing the buckskin by his new name. He left the abandoned Sioux village and followed the river north as it made its way toward the Yellowstone. He decided to stay with the river in his hunt for food, then come back to pick up the broad trail left by the Sioux village. He was now entering an area that was new to him. During the past winter, he had roamed much of the Powder River country and the Bighorn Mountains, but he and Ike had avoided the areas to the north because of the Sioux villages they knew to be there. Late on this day in early April it appeared to be a hostile country that surrounded him, empty of all game.

It was beginning to look as if he would go to bed hungry that night, for there was no sign of game of any kind as he followed the winding river through occasional gorges and across open meadows. "Complainin' ain't gonna help," he told his growling stomach as he gave up on the hunt and dismounted at a sharp bend in the river. "At least there's some supper for you," he said to the buckskin, for there were plenty of young shoots along the water's edge, as well as new spring grass on the banks.

He pulled the saddle off his horse and watched for a few moments while the big buckskin ambled down to the water to drink before grazing among the tender shoots. *It sure would be a lot easier if I'd learn to eat grass,* he thought before turning to gather some dry sticks for a fire. At least he could boil some coffee. He almost missed his one chance for solid food, and would have if he had not suddenly caught a flicker of movement out of the corner of his eye. He glanced up to find a lone pronghorn antelope on the opposite bank. A doe. She stood watching him. He froze, afraid any sudden movement might send her flying, but the pronghorn remained motionless. He turned his head slowly to see where his rifle might be and saw it lying across his saddle, some three or four yards behind him. He wondered if he could get to the rifle, cock it and fire before the doe bolted into the willows behind her. He wasn't sure if he could move that fast, but he was hungry, and there was meat staring him right in the face. Hoping to give himself a little head start, he moved one foot very slowly back toward his saddle. She tossed her head, sniffing the air. Ever so carefully, he drew the other foot back. That was all the doe would tolerate. She immediately sprang sideways, toward the cover of the willows. Almost as quick as the pronghorn, Matt dived for the rifle, grabbing and cocking it as he rolled over and came up on one knee. His first shot was fired too quickly, missing the bounding antelope as she swerved to avoid a bank of berry bushes. The second shot caught her behind the shoulder, knocking her off balance. She attempted to run again, only to stumble and fall, and he knew she was supper.

He was after her immediately, leaping from rock to rock over a series of small boulders that took him halfway across the river. He then plunged into the chilly water and waded the remaining distance to the other bank. When he reached the dying antelope, she struggled to move her legs briefly before lying still in shock. He drew his knife and ended her misery.

She was older than he had first thought, with gray around her ears and eyes. *What were you doing out here all by yourself?* he wondered as he examined his kill. *Did you get chased out of the harem by the younger gals?* He took hold of her front legs and pulled her up, testing the weight, wondering if he should go back to get his horse to carry her. He decided he could ford the shallow river without help from the buckskin.

Kneeling on one knee, he got his shoulders up under the antelope's belly and hefted her up. With a small amount of effort, he stood and shifted the carcass across his shoulders to balance it. He heard Ike snort and blow as he walked into the water. Looking up toward the other side, he was startled to discover two Indians seated upon their ponies, silently watching the white man's efforts. What happened next took only seconds, but it seemed to Matt that white man and Indians were frozen in time before one of the Sioux hunters suddenly loosed an arrow that barely missed Matt's head and buried itself in the pronghorn's carcass. It was enough to set off the lightning reaction that had served to save his life before. The carcass dropped from his shoulders as he brought the Henry up, firing and cocking again before it was shoulder high. The Sioux who shot the arrow slid over backward and fell from his pony. His friend immediately turned and ran, lying low across his pony's neck. There was no opportunity for a second shot as the hunter disappeared in the trees.

Before wading across with a cautious eye on the body sprawled upon the riverbank, Matt glanced quickly downstream to see his supper drifting with the current. Climbing carefully up the bank, his rifle trained upon the body, he paused to take inventory of the Indian's weapons. He saw no sign of a rifle or pistol, only the bow. He figured neither man had a rifle, and that was the reason this one's partner had made a run for it, rather than dueling with a Henry rifle. He turned the body over. A quick check confirmed that the man was dead, shot through the chest, probably in the heart. He gazed at the dead man's face for a few seconds, wondering if the warrior had had a hand in Ike's death. *This changes things,* he thought. *Now they'll know I'm coming.*

He had no idea if he was close to the Sioux village or not, but it was getting darker by the minute. Even if the village was close, they would hardly come looking for him before daylight. *But that buck might lead them back to this spot to get his friend,* he thought. With that in mind, he threw his saddle on Ike and left to find another campsite. Since his supper was drifting downstream, that was the direction he chose to ride. He found the antelope carcass a short distance downriver, lodged against a rock. "Come on, sweetheart," he said as he pulled the doe ashore. "Sioux or no Sioux, you and I have plans for supper."

Walking Ike slowly along the riverbank, the pronghorn carcass riding before the saddle, and an almost full moon lighting the way, he continued until he came to a tiny waterfall created by a rock shelf in the middle of the river. He judged it to be a safe distance from his first camp and a good place to butcher the pronghorn.

Supper was late, but it was worth waiting for after such a long time between meals. The doe was old and tough, but she had flavor befitting a lady, and Matt was inclined to compliment her after he had filled his belly. Washed down with black coffee, it was a repast fit for a lord. The only thing missing was the bulk of the big man who had been his partner. Ike's passing left a considerable void in the world—not just the size of the great man but the size of the life in him. Loud, swaggering, at times downright exasperating, but he was a friend who would lay down his life for you. "Dammit, Ike, what the hell did you have to go and get yourself killed for?"

The butchering done, he wrapped what he could use in the hide and packed it away for later. Disposing of the remains in the brush, he made his bed beneath a cottonwood where he could keep an eye on the riverbank in case he was wrong about the dead Indian's friends. *That's one of them, Ike,* was his last conscious thought before drifting off to sleep.

Morning brought a clear day to the valley of the Tongue. Matt awoke with a start, sensing that he had slept later than usual, for the first rays of the sun were already reaching the tops of the cottonwoods on the far side of the river. *A late sleeper might be a dead sleeper in Injun country.* The phrase passed through his thoughts. It was one he had heard Ike use on several occasions. He attributed his tardiness to the full stomach with which he had gone to bed.

He sat up and reached for his rifle when he heard the buckskin whinny. Quickly scanning the area around him, he could see no reason for alarm. From his bed under the cottonwood, he had an unrestricted view of the riverbank, both upstream and downstream. A gentle mist rose above the waterfall, causing the willows on the opposite bank to appear dreamlike. He rose to one knee, the Henry ready, and peered through the mist in an effort to see everything more clearly. Ike whinnied again, and when Matt turned to look at the horse, he detected a slight movement in the bushes that fringed the river below him. His reaction was instantaneous. Flattening himself upon the ground, he cocked his rifle and aimed at the spot that had caught his eye. At the same time, he couldn't figure out how they could have found him so quickly.

He waited, wondering if he should shower the bushes with a barrage of .44 slugs. Then, a few feet over, he saw the berry bushes move again, this time closer to the edge of the thicket, and he got ready to pull the trigger. After what seemed an eternity, the branches parted to reveal a horse's head. Matt lowered his rifle. It was the dead Indian's pony. The horse had followed them from the first campsite.

"Damn," Matt mumbled and lowered the rifle. "That's all I need, an Indian pony following me around, leading 'em right to me." He got up then and took a cautious walk around the area to make sure the pony had not already led a war party to his camp. Then he walked down to the thicket to see if he could shoo the pony away. "Git!" he shouted, waving his arms over his head. The horse, a mare, backed a few feet away, then stopped to marvel at the man's antics. "Git, dammit!" Matt insisted. He picked up a pebble from the water's edge and threw it at the pony. The horse was moved to depart, but only to a distance of forty yards or so. "Am I gonna have to shoot you, dammit?" he pleaded, knowing he didn't have the heart. He gave up on trying to scare the horse away and returned to his small campfire to cook breakfast. By the time a few strips of meat were sizzling over the fire, the Indian pony had sauntered back toward him. When he glanced over his shoulder to look at Ike, he discovered the pony standing next to the buckskin, the two horses whinnying softly.

"Damn," he uttered in disgust. "It looks like I've got me a horse, whether I want one or not."

After he had eaten, he walked over to saddle Ike. The Indian pony backed away a couple of steps, but then stood there, head and tail drooping submissively. Matt paused to scrutinize his uninvited guest. A dun like the buckskin, the horse was a darker shade, what he would call a mousy dun, with a black tail and mane and a faint white blaze on her face. Moving slowly and deliberately, he walked up to her, expecting her to bolt. Instead, she raised her head and submitted her muzzle to be stroked.

"Hell," he said, "you ain't nothin' but a pet." Her former owner had obviously spoiled her. No doubt she was the Sioux warrior's favorite pony, probably tied by his tipi instead of running free with the rest of the horses. He thought about the Indian he had killed then. A young man. Matt wondered if he was one of the bunch that killed Ike. In death he didn't look as brutal and savage as the image Matt was beginning to form of Sioux in general. *Maybe he was just a hunter like myself,* he thought, *just trying to get by.* Then a picture came to his mind of Ike's mutilated body, hanging in the willows, a necklace of human ears around his neck. "Hell, no," he blurted, lest he forget the graveside promise he had made to his former partner.

He rubbed the mare's face lightly as he examined her more closely, surprised that his smell did not seem strange to her, enough to make her cautious, anyway. There was no saddle on her, only a bridle fashioned from a single length of rope with two half hitches in the middle, looped around the horse's lower jaw. He had to admit that the mare was a fine-looking animal. With a deep chest and legs a little shorter than the buckskin's, she looked to be a strong runner.

He returned to finish saddling Ike. Giving the girth strap a final tug, he dropped the stirrup and said, "Looks like we've got a new addition to the family. Is that all right with you?" The big buckskin made no response beyond a disinterested snort. "You're an indifferent son of a bitch, aren't you?" He stepped up in the saddle then, and turned the buckskin toward the river. Looking back at the mare, he said, "Well, come on, then. We'd best get movin' before some of your relatives show up." He didn't bother to tie a lead rope on his new horse, thinking there was still a possibility that she might change her mind about following him. She loped along behind him, however, as he followed the riverbank, looking for a shallow ford.

"Little bird with no song."

Startled, she did not hear him when he walked up behind her. But she recognized the voice she had come to despise—the sneering tone of Jack Black Dog. Helpless to flee his presence, she tried to pull away from him, straining at the rawhide rope that held her captive. Her efforts served to amuse him as he walked slowly around her, leering openly. He laughed when she looked frantically toward the river, where Iron Claw's wife, Rising Moon, had gone to bathe.

"Looks like little bird's been left all alone," Jack said. "So me and you can have us a little visit." He would not have been so bold, but he knew that Iron Claw had left the camp with three others to search for Black Shirt's killer. He reached out to take her chin in his hand, laughing when she pulled away, her eyes flashing with the hatred and contempt she felt for him. He reached again, this time trapping her chin firmly. She spat at him. Reacting furiously, he slapped her hard, knocking her back against the tree. She glared at him defiantly, determined not to shrink before him. He drew back his hand to hit her again, but a thin trickle of blood at the corner of her mouth made him hesitate. It might not be healthy for him to leave evidence that he had approached Iron Claw's captive.

"I will have you, little bitch," he threatened, his black eyes blazing with undisguised lust. "Rising Moon will soon tire of you." He grabbed her thigh, leering wickedly when she was unable to escape his grasp. "Even if she doesn't, I will come for you, and take you anyway." Then, glancing toward the river, he saw Iron Claw's wife returning. Releasing Molly's thigh, he gave her one last smirk and repeated his promise. "I will have you, little bird with no song." With that, he turned to slink away behind the tipi before Rising Moon saw him.

Molly released a sigh of relief. For once, she was glad to see her cruel mistress approaching. This was the first time the despicable half-breed had been bold enough to physically accost her, such was his fear of Iron Claw. The Sioux war chief barely tolerated the devious half-breed, yet Jack continued to show up in the village from time to time, like the cur dogs that followed the camp. The fact that he was hanging around even more of late was solely because of the presence of the young white captive.

"Huh," Rising Moon grunted listlessly as she stopped to stand over her slave. The blood that traced a thin line down one side of Molly's chin had caught her attention. Curious, she took the girl's chin in her hand and turned her face up so she could examine it more closely. *Jack Black Dog*, she thought, and quickly looked right and left on the chance she might see him hurrying away. Everyone else had lost interest in the skinny white girl who couldn't talk. Only Jack Black Dog continued to skulk around, watching her. Maybe Iron Claw should give in to the craven half-breed, and then she would be free of the nuisance of having to keep an eye on her. "Huh!" Rising Moon grunted again at the thought, knowing she would rather work Molly to death than let the lecherous Jack Black Dog have her. "Wood!" She suddenly screamed at Molly, and began to whip the helpless girl repeatedly with a willow switch, ignoring the fact that Molly was still tied to the tree and could not respond.

Unable to protect herself from the blows, Molly did her best to stand up under the unwarranted attack, uttering not a whimper, until Rising Moon tired of the beating and untied her so she could fetch some wood for the fire. As she stumbled painfully before the cruel Sioux woman, she wondered how much longer she would be able to survive the harsh treatment before she became too weak to work. She feared that when that time came, they would kill her, or worse, give her to Jack Black Dog.

Iron Claw rose to his feet and stood gazing out across the river, sniffing the morning air as if searching for a scent. The body of Black Shirt lay at his feet, shot through the chest. Black Shirt was his wife's brother, and would be mourned by the village. Iron Claw's emotions ran more toward anger than sorrow, however. He truly hated the white man—and this particular white man more than all the others. The lead slug lodged in his thigh caused it to ache in the cool morning air, and he subconsciously rubbed at the dull pain. The white man and the giant he had ridden with had spent the winter in Lakota country, hunting their game, defiling Lakota country. Iron Claw could not rest until the white man was dead.

There were some in the village who said these two white men had shown no signs of disrespect to the land, killing only the game they needed for food. But Iron Claw had no patience for such talk. The white man clearly intended to drive the Lakota out of their sacred country, and he intended to kill every white man he found in Lakota country. Red Cloud and some of the others were discussing the possibility of attending peace talks with the soldiers at Fort Laramie in the summer. Such talk sickened Iron Claw, and he had vowed that he would never attend any peace talks. There could be no peace with the *wasicu*. It would soon be *peji to wi*, the Moon of Tender Grass, and the white men would again be following their fools' trail through the Powder River country on their way to look for the yellow dirt. If the white man really wanted peace, he would go away and leave the land as the Great Spirit had made it.

"Here!" Lame Deer cried out. "He follows the river."

Iron Claw walked over to see for himself. He stared at the hoofprints for a long moment, hating even the tracks left by the white man. It galled him to see that the white man was riding deeper into Lakota territory. Anxious to get after the intruder, he turned to Lame Deer. "Take Black Shirt back to the village. I will find this white dog and gut him."

Lame Deer protested. "There will be only three of you. Maybe I should go with you, and we can come back for Black Shirt. If this white man is really no man at all, but a ghost, as some say, he may be hard to kill."

"No," Iron Claw replied. "Three warriors are more than enough. I will go after him alone if you all think this puny white man is a ghost, and all three of you can take the body back to the village."

His comment was met with immediate protest, Broken Bow foremost. "I go with you," he said. "I don't believe he is anything more than a man. He has been lucky so far, that's all."

"I go with you," Yellow Hand echoed.

Iron Claw nodded. The four Lakota warriors then wrapped Black Shirt's body in a blanket and lifted it onto Lame Deer's pony. Lame Deer started toward the mountains to the west and the village beyond them on the Little Bighorn. The others set out on the trail along the Tongue, tracking the white man.

As the afternoon wore on, Matt became discouraged with his search along the river. The only sign he discovered was an occasional hoofprint that had been left long before. There was no evidence of recent Indian activity in the valley of the Tongue. Maybe, he thought, the band of Sioux he sought had crossed over the mountains dividing the rivers and were camped somewhere on the Bighorn or the Little Bighorn. *Hell, I could keep on this way until I hit the Yellowstone*, he thought. His gut feeling, however, told him that the village he sought was not that far away. He decided to cross over to the Little Bighorn. Although he was now farther north along the Tongue than he had ever been before, he had the pattern of the rivers in his mind, so he was fairly confident that he could strike the Little Bighorn if he crossed over the mountains, keeping to the west and maybe bearing a little to the south.

Following an old game trail, he made his way up into the hills. The dun mare followed along behind him like a pet dog. He had thought about putting a lead rope on the Indian pony, but it appeared the mare had no intention of letting him and Ike out of her sight. It had also occurred to him that the persistent pony might help him locate her former master's village. *Maybe*, he thought, *if I get close enough, the damfool horse will strike out for home.*

Near the top of the second ridge, he came to a small meadow where a tiny stream, fed by the recent snowmelt, carved its way through the rocks. Thinking it a good place to rest the horses, he decided to take advantage of the grass and water, and maybe roast a little more of the meat from the pronghorn. Ike gave him a questioning look when he retrieved the meat from his saddle pack, and Matt explained. "We ain't gonna camp here, boy, so I'm leavin' your saddle on."

After making a small fire, he unwrapped the chunk of pronghorn haunch and examined it. The air was still cool enough to have kept the meat from spoiling, but he decided it wouldn't keep much longer after that day. He should have taken time to dry the meat when he first killed the animal, but his urgent desire to extract payment for Ike's death had not permitted him to linger.

He thought about his promise to his late partner and the five soldiers whose ears had been hacked off to make the grisly necklace around Ike's neck. The thought served to stir the anger in his blood, but the passion with which he had made the vow had faded somewhat. Reflecting now, he questioned the practicality of his intent. He had promised ten dead Sioux, one for each ear on the rawhide string. *Then what? Just go on killing every Indian I see?* His thoughts flashed back to the recent war between the North and the South, and the part he had reluctantly played—a sniper, a job he had likened to that of an assassin. He recalled how much he had always hated the assignment. Now he was once again an assassin, seeking targets of opportunity, regardless of the time or situation, just as long as the victim was a Sioux. The mental image left a bitter taste in his mouth, and he knew that he really wanted only to extract vengeance from the individuals who had slain Ike—primarily the hawk-faced war chief that rode the paint pony. *I promised*, he thought, reminding himself, and put it out of his mind.

Chapter 6

Stripped of the blanket of snow that had covered their slopes during the past winter, the Bighorns seemed almost benign. With snow covering only the higher peaks, the lower elevations offered a varied display of terrain, from pleasant meadows to thick stands of pine forest and rocky cliffs. There could be little wonder why the Indians loved this land. Game of all kind abounded. Already there were signs of deer and occasional elk along the streams and lower meadows. Matt could not deny a feeling of reverence for the work of the Great Spirit. On this bright new morning, it was difficult to retain his purpose of vengeance. His feeling of peace would not last long, however.

They spotted each other at almost the same instant. Several hundred yards lay between the white scout and the three Sioux warriors, Matt higher up the slope, Iron Claw and the other two warriors in the valley below him. He realized then that he was the one who was being tracked, and not the other way around. "Fine," he said softly. "Come on then."

Both parties stood motionless for a few seconds, gazing at their adversary, contemplating the battle that was to follow. After a moment, Iron Claw raised his rifle high over his head in a gesture of defiance, a promise of what was to come. Matt did not respond to the challenge. Instead, he unhurriedly looked around him, selecting a place from which to await the attack. "That looks as good as any," he murmured, spotting a rocky apron below a steep cliff some thirty or forty yards farther up the slope. Still with no sign of haste, he turned the buckskin toward the cliff. As if on signal, the three Sioux warriors broke into a gallop, charging up the slope after him.

"He's going to stand and fight," Broken Bow yelled to the others as their ponies labored up the steep incline.

Seeing this to be the case, Iron Claw motioned for them to let up on the ponies. "Save the ponies," he directed. "The white man is taking cover in the rocks. There is no need to hurry." Looking the situation over, he said, "He has chosen a good place. It will be hard to rush at him across that open meadow. One of us should climb up on the cliff above him."

"I'll go," Broken Bow volunteered and immediately veered off to his right to work his way around the slope.

Iron Claw frowned, gazing after the white man, who by this time had reached the safety of the rocky apron. The menacing face that had struck Matt as hawklike before was now even more pronounced with the intense hatred of the man who had caused him to walk with a limp. He lifted his rifle, the Spencer he had taken from the body of the giant white man, and held it high over his head as if challenging the spirits themselves. So intent were his thoughts upon his vengeance that Yellow Hand was moved to question him, thinking that the war chief had lapsed into a vision.

"Are we not going to kill this white man? Broken Bow will soon be at the top of the cliff."

Iron Claw shifted his gaze to fix upon his companion. A slow smile formed at the corners of the cruel face. "Yes," he said, speaking softly, "we are going to kill him." With that, he sank his heels into his pony's ribs, and the paint sprang into a gallop, leaving Yellow Hand to follow.

Like a natural fortress, the boulders that formed a half circle at the base of the cliff were tall enough to provide protection for Matt and his horses. Moving quickly, but without undue haste, he led the buckskin back to the wall that was formed by the steep cliff and looped the reins around a scrub pine bough. He paused briefly to look at the Indian pony before deciding there was no need to tie her. The persistent mare had adopted the buckskin whether Matt approved or not.

His horses protected, he moved back to position himself for the assault to come. Settling in behind a boulder, he laid his cartridge belt out beside him for quick access, cranked a cartridge into the chamber, and waited. In less than a minute, he saw them approach. *The hawk-faced warrior on the paint pony!* Their paths had crossed again. Matt began to believe that one of them must have been destined to kill the other.

Skirting a clump of pines below him, they stayed short of the clearing that led up to the cliff, using the trees for cover. Matt followed their progress carefully until they disappeared from his view. *They'll be moving up to the edge of the pines on foot,* he thought while scanning the line of trees for likely places for the hostiles to fire from. After several minutes, he saw them again, inching up to the trees on the edge of the clearing. He could see only two of them, and he automatically looked up behind him at the ledge some fifty feet above his head for signs of the missing member of the party. As a precaution, he moved back a little to position himself farther under the overhanging ledge. Confident that it would be difficult for anyone to get a clear shot at him from above, he returned his attention to the pines.

The distance separating him from the two hostiles below was no more than a hundred yards, a range where any weapon other than a bow or a pistol would be accurate. He wondered what firepower the Indians could bring to bear on his position. In the next few seconds, his question was answered when the stillness of the quiet afternoon was suddenly shattered by the initial barrage of shots. He recognized the sharp snap of a Spencer rifle at once. He had heard Ike's weapon enough to be familiar with the distinct sound it made. The thought reminded him that the rifle Ike had carried was now in the hands of the hostiles who had killed him. Matt felt a sudden numbness, knowing that the weapon was now being used to try to kill him. The other weapon sounded like a single-shot rifle, like the Springfields most of the soldiers had been issued during the war. The shots from both rifles ricocheted harmlessly off the boulders protecting him. At this short range, the outcome was going to be determined by which one of them was careless enough to expose himself to take a shot.

He continued to wait, knowing the hostiles had not pinpointed his location and were just wasting bullets, hoping to draw his return fire. He counted on their impatience, and pretty soon his strategy bore fruit. From the base of a small pine, one of the Sioux suddenly jumped up and sprinted toward an outcropping of rock farther up the slope. Quick as the strike of a rattlesnake, Matt stood up and pumped two shots into the running warrior, causing him to tumble, turning a double somersault before landing in the grassy meadow, dead. Not waiting to judge the results of his shots, Matt turned at once to spray the pines with three more shots, effectively keeping Iron Claw from getting a clear shot. At the same instant when he pulled the trigger on the last shot, he felt a spattering of loose dirt on his head and shoulders. Without having to think about it, he turned the Henry up and emptied the magazine. He heard a grunt of pain, and a few seconds later, the body of the third Sioux came crashing down almost at his feet. It had all happened within moments, and now Matt thought about the one remaining as he methodically reloaded the magazine of the Henry rifle. It was a duel now between the hawk-faced Sioux and himself, at a distance of one hundred yards.

In the cover of the pine trees, Iron Claw was almost staggered by the suddenness with which the odds had been changed. He stepped back, mentally recoiling from the loss of his two closest friends within seconds of each other. His brain was pounding with the rage that filled his entire body as once again he had suffered at the hand of the white demon with the *spirit gun*. A thought flashed through his mind then. Was this truly a ghost he was trying to kill—as some had feared? Though it gave him pause, it was for only a moment. He vowed to kill this white evil spirit, be he man or demon. Clutching the Spencer rifle, he moved to take cover behind a tree closer to the edge of the meadow.

After making sure the warrior at his feet was dead, Matt moved to the other side of the apron of rocks and settled himself between two small boulders. With a flicker of movement of pine boughs, a shot rang out, the bullet glancing off the rock Matt had just vacated. Matt returned fire, clipping the pine bough in two. His shot was answered by Iron Claw, this time the bullet ricocheting off the rock by his head.

This exchange of shots went on for half an hour, neither man willing to risk stepping into the open, where sudden death was sure to come. An extended pause followed while both men considered their options and their chances for survival. Though almost consumed by anger, Iron Claw was not willing to rush foolishly at the white scout with the *spirit gun*. He wanted more than anything else to tie this white man's scalp to his lance, but he recognized the fact that they were at a standoff for the time being. He decided to change tactics, thinking to circle around the scout and surprise him. First, he must convince his enemy that he was quitting the fight.

Suddenly the silence was shattered once more, this

time not by a barrage of rifle shots but by the loud wailing of the Sioux warrior in the pine trees. The ranting went on for several minutes, leaving Matt to speculate on the message, since he understood no more than a few words of the Lakota language. Minutes later, he heard the sound of hooves, and he ran to the edge of the rocks in time to catch a glimpse of the paint pony as it topped a rise in the prairie beyond the pine forest.

Gone. Somehow he had not expected the hawk-faced warrior to retreat from the duel. Maybe it was as Ike had sometimes said: "An Injun will stay after a thing till he decides he's spent enough time on it. Then to hell with it, he'll go do somethin' else." Matt walked out into the meadow, staring at the rise where he had last seen the belligerent hostile. The sun was sinking ever closer to the craggy mountains to the west. Soon it would disappear behind the hills. Perhaps the warrior had decided that he had fought enough for one day. Maybe Ike was right, and the Indian just decided he had dueled long enough. There was a distinct feeling of regret that the issue had not been settled, for Matt somehow felt that his promise to Ike might be forgiven if he had killed this one particular Sioux. He was convinced that this hawk-face was the man responsible for Ike's death.

He walked halfway down the meadow to the body of Yellow Hand to see if there might be any .44 cartridges on the corpse. There were none, only some .58-caliber shells for the Springfield lying a few yards away. He picked up the rifle and began to climb back up the hill. Almost back to the rocks, he was startled by the sudden appearance of the paint charging up from a ravine that ran from the other side of the cliff. Iron Claw rode low on his horse's neck, his rifle aimed for the kill. Caught in the open, barely thirty yards from the charging warrior, Matt knew in that instant that the Indian couldn't miss. Iron Claw squeezed the trigger, but nothing happened. The cartridge had jammed in the chamber.

Matt dived to the ground, expecting a bullet that never came as the paint thundered past him. Hardly able to believe he had escaped being hit, he rolled over on his belly to try to get off a shot of his own, only to look directly into the setting sun. Blinded for the moment, he nevertheless fired at the retreating savage, hoping for a lucky shot.

Iron Claw heard the snap of the bullet as it passed over his head. He flattened his body as low on his pony's neck as he could and whipped the paint mercilessly for more speed. The Spencer had misfired, costing him the chance for an easy kill. He wasn't sure if it was because the white man's medicine was strong or because his own medicine was weak. The white man had also missed. Maybe both men's medicine was strong. Iron Claw was uncertain if the spirits were taking a hand in the confrontation between the two men, but he felt strongly that he was being given a message to wait another day to kill the white scout.

"I think we've seen the last of that son of a bitch for this day," Matt said aloud. He wasn't sure why; it was just a feeling. He had had enough killing for the day— he was sure of that. As he made his way back up to the rocky fortress, he thought again of the close call he had just survived. He had been caught dead in the Indian's

sights—at point-blank range. He had never been one to
entertain thoughts of the spirit world, but he couldn't
help but wonder if Ike's rifle had just refused to kill him.
It was a sobering thought, but one he preferred not to
explore further.

"We'd better get on outta here and find us a place to
camp with some water while there's still some light,"
he advised the buckskin. Leading his horse out between the boulders, he paused when he started to walk
around the body of the Sioux who had been on the cliff
above him. He put the toe of his moccasin under Broken Bow's shoulder and rolled the corpse over on its
back. When he did, the setting sun caught a glimmer of
metal on the dead warrior's neck. Matt knelt down to
see what had caused the reflection. It took a few seconds to register in his mind, but then the reality of
what he saw caused his heart to skip a beat. There were
thousands of Saint Christopher's medals, and a Sioux
warrior could come by one in any number of ways. But
this medal was on a silver chain like only one other he
had ever seen. It was the medal given to him by his
mother, and the very one that he, in turn, had given to
a young girl at Fort Kearny.

"Molly," he recalled softly as her image formed in his
mind. Molly, the shy girl who could not speak, who had
been a mute since birth. She was the daughter of the
woman who ran the dining room in the hotel in the town
close by the fort. Libby was her mother's name. He
couldn't recall the last name. He might not ever have
known it. Feeling the silver medal between his fingers
brought back the memory of the night he had given it to

Molly. He would most likely be dead now if Molly had not acted when she did. Unarmed, he had found himself staring into the muzzle of a Spencer rifle, held on him by an outlaw named Tyler. There had been no doubt concerning Tyler's intentions: He had come to kill him. Matt had not thought about that night for a long time. How, he wondered, had the medal come to be in the possession of a Sioux warrior? So far from Fort Kearny? Somehow it didn't seem probable to him that Molly would have given it away. Stolen? Maybe. There were other possibilities, none of which he cared to consider. The thought of Molly being taken by savage Indians almost sickened him. If that were the case, even if she was still alive, she would be living a virtual hell as a captive of the Sioux. He feared that he was letting his emotions run away with him, but there was no decision to be made. He had to know the answer.

Red Hawk flinched with the pain when the Lakota woman administered a stinging lash across his bare shoulders with a cottonwood limb, but he refused to cry out. He was not walking fast enough to suit the old woman, but then, she would not have been satisfied if he ran. The burden of wood that he labored to carry was hard enough to manage at a normal pace. She could whip away at his shoulders and back until he dropped. He still would not be capable of moving any faster.

It had been almost a moon since the Lakota war party had ambushed Red Hawk's hunting party. Red Hawk and his friends were Crow, and they were all aware that they were hunting deep in Lakota territory and the danger involved in that. The hated Sioux had watched them kill three deer, and waited until they had removed the hides and butchered the meat. Then, when the meat was packed on their horses and they started back home, they were suddenly swarmed by a large war party.

All of the Crow hunters had been killed except Red Hawk, who had suffered a shoulder wound and had been knocked unconscious by a Sioux war club. When he came to, it was to find the Sioux warriors standing over him, arguing over the way he should be killed. One among them was more fierce than his friends, and seemed to be the leader of the warriors. Red Hawk was to learn later that the man was called Iron Claw. Iron Claw stated that it was his bullet that had wounded the Crow and he would decide how the hated enemy of the Lakota would die.

"Give me my knife, and I will fight you. Then we will see who shall live and who shall die." Red Hawk had suddenly blurted the challenge, startling the Sioux warriors.

Broken Bow had reacted by aiming his rifle at Red Hawk's face. "Crow dog! I'll send you to the spirit world right now."

Iron Claw had laughed, amused by the Crow's insolence. "Wait," he said, placing his hand on Broken Bow's rifle barrel. "I think this coyote wants a quick death." He reached down and grabbed Red Hawk by his hair and jerked his head back, looking directly into his eyes. "I think my mother could use a slave to do women's work for her. We'll see how good a woman you are. Then I'll kill you when I'm ready."

The weeks that followed seemed like months. Iron Claw's mother proved to be as ruthless and cruel as her son, forcing Red Hawk to suffer humiliation as her slave. His shoulders and back were crisscrossed with a pattern of stripes from her cottonwood whips. At night, he was tied hand and foot and left to sleep outside the lodge with Iron Claw's favorite pony. What food he was given was barely enough to keep him alive, and his shoulder wound was left to heal on its own. The one constant thought that sustained him was the promise he had made to himself that he would escape as soon as his shoulder was strong enough, and return to exact vengeance upon the hated Sioux.

He was not the only captive in the Sioux camp. A week after he had been captured, Iron Claw returned to the village with a young white woman. The war chief made a present of the woman to his wife. Red Hawk never talked to her, for she was allowed to sleep inside the lodge, while he remained tethered outside like a horse.

"Hurry!" the old woman screamed, punctuating her command with another stinging swipe of the cottonwood switch. She followed along behind him, holding the rawhide rope that was tied around his neck. When they reached the tipi, she suddenly jerked on the rope, causing him to stumble under the huge load and dump the firewood before the entry flap. "Clumsy dog!" she screamed. "Pick it all up! You will get no food tonight because of your carelessness."

On his hands and knees, he gathered up the scattered

wood, aware of the constant surveillance he was under. He could easily overpower the old woman, but there were always others close by, and there were always many eyes watching him. He sensed that most of them were hoping he would try to escape. It would provide great sport for them to punish him for his efforts. Once again, he felt the sting of the cottonwood branch. He braced himself for the next blow, but it did not follow. She had been distracted by a welcoming cry on the other side of the village. Soon other cries were heard. Iron Claw had returned.

The fearsome war chief had been gone for several days, and in their excitement to welcome him, most of the people rushed toward the edge of the camp to watch him approach, only to suddenly lapse into silence. Red Hawk gazed toward the river and watched as Iron Claw rode through the pony herd on the opposite shore and crossed over. He was alone. The two warriors who had remained with him after Lame Deer returned with Black Shirt's body were not with him. A soft murmuring of concerned voices soon escalated into a general dirge of mourning, for the people knew that the white ghost had killed them as well.

It occurred to Red Hawk then that he was being allowed to pause and stare for quite some time without a threat or a blow from the old woman. Then he realized that only he and the old woman were left on this side of the circle of tipis. There was no one else within thirty yards or so. Distressed to see her son returning without Broken Bow and Yellow Hand, she looked around her frantically, trying to decide what to do with her slave.

"Come!" she commanded and jerked on the rope, pulling him toward the tree where he was bound at night.

He got to his feet as if to obey, one large piece of firewood still in his hand. It happened so quickly that the old woman had no time to react before the makeshift club thudded against her skull. She dropped the rope and staggered backward but did not fall down. Stunned, she did not cry out for help. Moving swiftly to finish the job, Red Hawk set upon her immediately, clubbing her again and again until she crumpled to the ground. He turned then, expecting a mob of angry Sioux charging upon him, but no one had noticed the isolated bit of drama near the edge of the lodges.

He pulled the rope from his neck and threw it upon the fallen woman. Alive or dead, he could not tell, and he didn't take the time to find out. There was no time to waste. Iron Claw would most likely come directly to his lodge. Red Hawk ran from the village, keeping Iron Claw's tipi between him and the throng of people for as long as possible before cutting back toward the river below the camp. Luck seemed to be with him, for he heard no outcry by the time he entered the water and began to make his way downstream. He was a long way from home with no horse and no weapon. Though he was free, his situation was precarious at best. He would be hunted like a rabbit.

Chapter 7

Matt paused to listen. The buckskin whinnied inquisitively a couple of times, and Matt sensed that something or someone had caused the horse to inquire. He had long since learned never to ignore the big horse's warnings, so he got up from his campfire and took a quick look around. Nothing seemed out of the ordinary along the bank of the creek where he had made his camp. He took another look at the buckskin he had christened Ike. The horse did not seem to be agitated or alarmed. *Probably a muskrat*, he decided and returned to the chore of fashioning a spit to roast some of the deer meat.

He had followed the trail left by the hawk-faced warrior for most of the previous day before losing it where the Sioux had entered the creek. The Sioux village had to be close now, however. The Little Bighorn River should be just beyond the line of hills that stood to the west of his camp, so he was naturally cautious about any strange sounds. Deciding he was probably just a little jumpy, he propped his rifle beside him and turned his attention back to his supper. The buckskin cocked his ears and snorted. Matt paused to listen again. After a long interval when no strange sounds reached his ears, he admonished the horse, "You're gettin' more jumpy than I am. You're just hearin' a muskrat or somethin'."

"You should listen to your horse."

Matt snatched up his rifle and dived for the cover of a cottonwood log. The voice had come from directly behind him, and in a fraction of an instant his rifle was cocked and leveled at a clump of berry bushes, ready to fire.

"Wait!" the voice cried out. "Don't shoot. I am Crow."

Angry at himself for being so careless, Matt spat out, "Yeah? Well, come on out here where I can see you."

With hands held high over his head, Red Hawk stepped out of the bushes that had concealed him. "I have no weapon," he said, pleading for mercy. "I am Red Hawk. I rode scout for the soldiers at Fort Laramie. My brother, Spotted Horse, rides with the soldiers. I was a captive of the Sioux." He paused to judge the effect of his words. When Matt relaxed his hold on the rifle, allowing it to drop slightly, Red Hawk continued, "I smelled your fire." He gazed at the meat on the spit. "I'm hungry. The Sioux did not give me very much to eat."

Matt, still angry over having been surprised, looked the Indian over carefully. In spite of the chilly spring evening, the man wore no shirt. There were visible welts tattooed across his back and what appeared to be a bullet wound in his shoulder. It was quite possible that he was telling the truth. Still, it would be wise to remain skeptical. Finally, he motioned toward the fire with his rifle. "Go ahead and eat," he said.

Red Hawk didn't wait for a second invitation. He took the spit from the fire, tore off a hunk of the sizzling meat, and began chewing furiously. After his initial hunger had been satisfied, he paused for a moment and looked Matt up and down. "You're the scout called Slaughter, aren't you?"

Matt seemed surprised. "I'm Slaughter," he answered. "How did you know that?"

"My brother, Spotted Horse, is one of the Crow scouts. He told me about you and the big man who was your friend."

"Ike's dead," Matt replied.

Red Hawk nodded. "I know. They talked about it in the Sioux village. The war chief, Iron Claw, boasted about it."

Matt decided that Red Hawk was probably a friend. He laid his rifle down beside him and joined in the feast. "Iron Claw," he repeated, sounding the name slowly. He figured this was the same man he was trailing, but he wanted to be sure. "This war chief, he rides a paint pony?" Red Hawk nodded. "Has a face like a hawk?" Again Red Hawk nodded. Matt continued, "I'm lookin' for a white girl, and I'm thinkin' she might be in the village you just came from."

Red Hawk's eyes widened with interest at once. "There is a white girl in Iron Claw's camp. She is Iron Claw's captive."

Matt's heartbeat quickened with excitement. "She's alive?"

"Yes."

"How far is this Sioux village?"

Red Hawk paused to think. He had hidden under the bank of the river until dark while the Sioux war parties searched for him. Then, when he felt it safe to leave, he had crossed over the line of hills and walked another day before finding Matt. Considering his weakened condition, and the circuitous route he followed, he guessed that Matt was no more than half a day's ride on a horse.

Matt went to his saddle pack and pulled out a doeskin shirt. "Here," he said, tossing the garment to Red Hawk. "Put this on. You're makin' me cold just lookin' at you." He watched as Red Hawk pulled the garment over his head. "That wound in your shoulder looks kinda tender."

"It's starting to heal now," Red Hawk replied. "It will be all right."

"If you say so," Matt said. "I reckon you don't have to hoof it on foot no more. That little mousy dun don't belong to me. She just decided to tag along. You might as well take her." He remembered one other thing then. "Hell, I've even got a Springfield rifle you can carry."

Since Red Hawk was a Crow, Matt knew for sure that he was an enemy of the Sioux. And since he claimed to be Spotted Horse's brother, Matt supposed that he could trust him. Still, he wasn't ready to put complete faith in the word of a stranger. He decided he'd better keep an eye on his guest.

Matt's cautious attitude was not lost on Red Hawk. The Crow warrior took notice of the care with which Matt placed the Henry beside him when they turned in for the night, Matt on one side of the fire and Red Hawk on the other. Red Hawk rolled up in Matt's extra blanket and went immediately to sleep, his back to the fire and Matt. As for Matt, he remained awake long into the night, keeping a secretive watch upon the Indian.

He awoke with a start when the first rays from the morning sun played across his face. Realizing that he had drifted off, he immediately reached for his rifle. It was not there. "You lookin' for your gun?" He looked up to find Red Hawk sitting next to him, the Henry lying across his lap. "This is a fine gun," the Indian commented. "I heard them talk about you and this gun." He raised it to his shoulder and sighted on a tree several yards away. Then he handed the rifle to Matt. "I could have killed you while you slept, taken the gun and the horses," he said, his sad dark eyes fixed on Matt's. "I am Spotted Horse's brother. He is your friend. I am your friend."

Matt could only stare speechless at the obviously insulted Crow warrior. "I reckon," he finally uttered. "I'm sorry if I offended you." He threw his blanket back and sat up. "I guess I could use a friend, 'specially one that knows where Iron Claw's village is."

Red Hawk studied his new friend's face for a moment before commenting. "It's a big village, many lodges, many warriors."

"I ain't aimin' to fight the whole village," Matt replied. "I just want to get the white girl out, then maybe get a shot at the one called Iron Claw. How 'bout it? You gonna show me where that village is?"

Red Hawk nodded thoughtfully. He had a score to settle with the Sioux war chief as well. Spotted Horse had said that the young white man was a brave warrior. Red Hawk decided he would ride with him. "You give me a horse and a gun, and give me food. I have much to repay."

"You don't owe me anything," Matt replied. "You'd probably have done the same for me."

A partnership was formed, silently, without even as much as a handshake, although Matt would not say how strong it would be until after he had a chance to get to know Red Hawk better.

Matt felt a strong sense of urgency to find Molly. He did not permit himself to dwell upon mental images of what the innocent young girl might be suffering, unable to explain to her captors that she could not speak. Her handicap might serve to infuriate the Sioux even more, leaving them to think her intentionally impudent and simply refusing to speak. In spite of the need for quick action, there was little he could do before nightfall, beyond possibly catching sight of the girl.

As Red Hawk had said, the Sioux village was not far away. They approached it after only half a day's ride. "Better leave the horses here," Red Hawk advised, as he led Matt through a series of deep gullies along the bluffs of the river. "We can get across to the other side and hide in the long grass, but the horses would be seen."

Matt nodded. Looking down across the river, he could see that Red Hawk's account of the camp's size was not an exaggeration. There were at least a hundred lodges arranged in circles among the trees on the far side. A faint smoky haze lay woven through the tops of the cottonwoods, formed by the many cook fires. Matt and Red Hawk had approached the village from the upstream end, since that was the escape route Red Hawk had taken and was closest to Iron Claw's tipi. It was still early in the afternoon, and the camp was busy with the many daily chores of the women while the men visited or worked on their weapons, preparing for the hunt or the warpath.

Moving cautiously, holding his rifle and cartridge belt above the water, Matt followed Red Hawk across the gently flowing river. The Crow had said that he had hidden under the banks of the river, and Matt could see now how that was possible. The bluffs upstream were cut with many deep gullies that ran down to the water's edge, creating a maze of hiding places.

"There," Red Hawk spoke softly and pointed toward a tipi near the center of a circle of lodges. "Iron Claw."

Matt stared at the lodge pointed out. There was nothing to distinguish it from those around it, other than the paint pony tied close beside it. There was no sign of the captive white girl. He studied the terrain between them and the tipi—a distance of at least one hundred yards, about half of that open grass before reaching the cottonwoods. He would have to pass two tipis before reaching Iron Claw's.

"How many people in the lodge?" Matt asked.

"Iron Claw, his wife, his mother," Red Hawk replied. "Maybe not his mother," he added, not certain if the old woman was dead or alive since he had clubbed her with the stick of firewood.

Matt nodded, evaluating his chances of getting into the village without being seen. He quickly realized that his odds were zero during the daylight hours. There were too many people going and coming between the lodges. Still, there was no sign of Molly or the hawk-faced war chief. Matt figured that Iron Claw must be inside the tipi. He could be pretty sure the fierce hostile was in camp, since his favorite pony was tethered beside the tipi. But he was concerned for Molly. What if they had killed her? *Probably not,* he told himself. Iron Claw would not have bothered to bring her back to the village if he intended to kill her.

They continued to watch. The afternoon hours passed with no sign of activity around the tipi. Matt looked over at Red Hawk. The Crow warrior seemed content to lie in the grass, patiently watching the Sioux camp. Matt wondered if his new partner felt the inner turmoil of anxiety that he was experiencing. No more than one hundred yards away were both the man who had killed Ike and the young girl who had saved Matt's life. He told himself to be patient—like Red Hawk appeared to be. "I expect we'd better check on the horses," Matt said.

"I'll go," Red Hawk volunteered, and immediately began to back down the gully that concealed them.

Matt didn't say anything, but moments after the Crow warrior disappeared, he started having worrisome thoughts. What was there to stop Red Hawk from taking both horses and leaving him on foot to deal with the whole Sioux village? Red Hawk had a score to settle, but he was not motivated to rescue the white girl. During those quiet hours watching the Sioux camp, Red Hawk may have been thinking that this was a foolish endeavor he and the white man were contemplating. He had already made good his escape from the Sioux. Why take the risk of being killed or taken captive again? *He was mighty damn quick to volunteer to go back to see to the horses. I should have gone myself.* A few minutes later, he had to chastise himself a second time for having doubted his new partner, for Red Hawk suddenly appeared at the end of the gully. "The horses are okay," he stated simply, and crawled up beside Matt.

Matt nodded and started to reply, but before he could speak, Red Hawk suddenly pointed toward the camp. Matt immediately looked back at the tipi. Having just emerged from inside, Iron Claw stood beside the flap. He stretched his arms and arched his back, much like a cat stretches after a nap. Then he walked over and spent a moment stroking the face and ears of his pony before untying the horse and leading it away.

Just for a moment, Matt was tempted to settle the score for Ike's murder right then while he had an easy target. His hand rested lightly on the trigger guard of his rifle as he fought the urge to raise the weapon and snuff out the life of the savage war chief. He glanced over at Red Hawk, and from the intense frown on the Crow warrior's face, he guessed that they both had the same thought. It served to restore his rational mind. "Wait," he whispered, in case Red Hawk was close to giving in to the temptation.

As they watched, the Sioux warrior led his horse to the edge of the river and stood waiting while the paint drank its fill. Another warrior rode up to Iron Claw and stopped to talk for a few moments before moving on toward the center of the camp. His attention caught by someone else farther downstream, Iron Claw turned to watch the progress of two women as they climbed up from the riverbank.

Matt glanced briefly at the two women, and was about to dismiss them as unimportant when he suddenly realized that one of the women was actually a girl—*a white girl.* He immediately returned his gaze for a long, hard look. *It was Molly, all right.* He had not been certain he would recognize her. It had been some time since he had last seen the young girl who had worked in the hotel kitchen run by her mother. His heart went out to her right away. Carrying two heavy water skins, she staggered along under the constant badgering of the Sioux woman, who controlled her with a noose around her neck. Matt's face instantly flushed with anger, but he held himself in check. There was nothing he could do at this point. He couldn't fight the entire Sioux village, although he was angry enough to be tempted to try it. So he watched the stern Indian woman and her slender white captive until they disappeared into the tipi. "We'll have to wait till dark," he whispered to Red Hawk. "Then I'll go in and get her."

Red Hawk nodded thoughtfully. "That may be a very dangerous thing to do. If anyone sees you, you will be killed on the spot. Maybe we should watch for a few days, and wait for a chance to catch the woman and the girl away from the camp."

Matt could appreciate the Crow warrior's concern, but he didn't like the idea of leaving Molly in the hands of the Sioux for a day longer. Still, he realized that it would not be right to endanger Red Hawk's life with a rash decision, made in a time of anger. He thought about it for a moment before replying. "When it gets dark, I'll go in and get her. You stay with the horses. If I don't make it, you'll probably hear the noise. If you do, then get outta there before they come lookin' for my horse."

Red Hawk shrugged, somewhat chastised by Matt's remark. After a moment, he said, "I came as a warrior, not to hold the horses and run away."

Matt realized then that he had unintentionally insulted the Crow warrior. He quickly explained. "My friend, I didn't mean to insult you. I just meant that, since I decided to walk right into the middle of a Sioux camp and stick my neck out, it wouldn't be right to expect you to do the same. I'm thinkin' that it would be less risky for one man to slip into the camp after dark. And when I come outta there, I'm gonna need to have my horse right handy. That's why I want you to stay with the horses." He could see from Red Hawk's expression that the warrior was not entirely satisfied with the way the plan was laid out.

Red Hawk spoke. "This Iron Claw is a powerful warrior. I have seen this for myself. It will not be an easy thing for one man to fight him and his wife. I think it best if I go with you. I came to kill him, not to hold the horses."

Matt could see that his new partner had made up his mind, and it didn't seem likely that he could persuade him differently. Besides, he thought, Red Hawk was probably right. Matt might have his hands full with two to surprise and overpower—especially if he had hopes of doing it quietly—although he would prefer to have someone keep the horses ready for a quick departure. "Suit yourself, then," he conceded. "We'll just wait till dark."

Several times during the fading afternoon, when someone in the village ventured too close, the two scouts thought they might have to withdraw from the gully. On one occasion, a Lakota girl came within fifty feet of their hiding place, searching the water's edge for greens to add to her mother's cook pot. Matt and Red Hawk froze. A few feet farther and the girl could sound the alarm that would force them either to run for it, or to silence her. Luck was with them, for she found a lush patch of spring greens and filled her basket without even looking their way. Matt was immediately relieved. He had no desire to trade an innocent Lakota girl's life for Molly's.

As the light began to fade, there seemed to be an increase in activity in the camp. It puzzled Matt, for he had expected the village to settle down for the night. "They prepare for a dance," Red Hawk explained. The occasion could be for any number of reasons, he went on. "Maybe they go on war party tomorrow," he speculated.

Whatever the reason, Matt could only feel concern

that it might spoil his chances of slipping into the village. There was nothing to do but wait and watch. A little after sundown, a huge fire was built in the center of the camp. Soon people began to gather around the flames, and a short time later, the monotonous beat of drums filled the river valley. At first, only a few young men danced around the fire as darkness settled upon the riverbanks. It was not long before others, young and old, answered the call of the drums. Holding weapons over their heads, shuffling in a nonrhythmic syncopation, they circled the fire, chanting a singsong appeal to the spirits. Had the occasion not been so sinister, Matt would have been fascinated by the spectacle.

"War dance," Red Hawk decided. He was about to comment further when he suddenly grasped Matt's elbow and pointed toward Iron Claw's tipi.

Iron Claw had emerged from the lodge. The powerful warrior stood for a few moments, looking toward the fire and the dancers. Then he strode purposefully toward the circle to join the celebration. Matt looked at Red Hawk. "Well, that changes things, don't it?" The prospect of catching Iron Claw alone was lost to them at that moment. However, it greatly improved the chances of rescuing Molly and making good their escape.

Red Hawk shrugged. "Maybe the spirits tell us that it is not a good time to kill him." He thought about it for a moment more. "There is still the coyote bitch he is married to." He remembered the vile temper of Iron Claw's wife. She would put up a fight. He was certain of that. As if on cue, the woman appeared at the entrance of the tipi. She paused for a long moment, gazing

at the dance now in full progress, seeming to be struggling with a decision. Apparently having made it, she
took one quick look back inside the tipi. Then she hurried away to watch the dancing.

Matt and Red Hawk looked at each other. Both men
knew that this was definitely a sign from the spirits. "I'll
get the horses," Red Hawk said without hesitation.

"Right," Matt replied, and scrambled up from the
gully. He drew his knife as he ran across the grassy
bank, past the two outermost lodges, crouched slightly
in an effort to keep as low a profile as possible. It was
unnecessary, for he would probably not have been seen
in the dark even if someone had been looking his way.
The distance to Iron Claw's lodge was quickly covered,
and he fell on his knees before the back of the tipi. He
thrust his knife into the wall of the tipi and started hack-
ing away at the tough buffalo hide, but the weathered
hide covering proved to be so tough that his progress
was extremely slow. Impatient, he withdrew the knife,
and ran around the lodge. With his rifle held hip-high
and ready to fire, he plunged into the entrance.

In the gloom of the darkened tipi, he at first thought no
one was there. Then he saw her. She was lying on her side,
her hands and feet bound tightly and tied together with a
length of rawhide rope. Just inches above her shoulder, he
could see the rip in the hide covering where he had thrust
his knife.

Though she was unable to speak, her eyes revealed
the wonder she felt. Thinking at first that it was a hallu-
cination, or at best a dream, she was afraid to believe
her eyes. She had called upon that very image many

times since the tall, sandy-haired scout had ridden out of her life. Many, many lonely nights, when her chores in the hotel kitchen were done and she lay sleepless in her bed, she would gently caress the silver Saint Christopher's medal and concentrate on his features. Only moments before, lying bound and afraid, she had been thinking about him, her eyes closed tight, calling out to him in her mind, so that she had summoned an almost vivid image of him. Then, hearing what she thought was the woman's return, she opened her eyes to discover a vision so real that she thought her mind was caught between a dream and reality. After a few moments, when the vision remained, she realized that it was not a dream or a creation of her imagination. *It was him, her knight in buckskins.* In uncontrolled relief, her eyes filled with tears, blurring the image standing over her.

He went immediately to her, and began sawing away at her bonds. Seeing her tears, he tried to comfort her while he worked to free her. "Molly, it's me, Matt Slaughter," he said, not sure if she remembered him. "Don't be afraid. I'm gonna take you outta here."

She nodded her head excitedly, the only way she could answer him. He cut the rope that held her wrists and ankles linked together, and started to work on the bonds that held her ankles together when she suddenly jerked her feet away from him and began to kick at him frantically. Seeing the panic in her eyes, he looked over his shoulder just in time to see Iron Claw's wife standing in the entrance to the tipi, her eyes wide with surprise. In the next moment, she screamed out an alarm and turned to run. Matt was on her in the blink of an eye, tackling her before she could clear the entrance. With no concern for gender, he hauled the kicking and struggling woman back inside by her ankles. Grabbing anything that she could reach, she threw pots and bowls at him, any object she could throw. When he tried to shield himself with one arm, she jerked away and tried to scramble back out the door. He dived for her again and dragged her back, this time turning her roughly over on her stomach. She continued to wail in shrieks of terror until he sat down hard on her back, knocking the wind out of her. While she struggled for breath, he quickly bound her hands with the rope he had just cut from Molly. Reaching for anything that was handy, he grabbed a blanket and stuffed a corner of it in her mouth to gag her. She tried desperately to spit it out, but he wrapped the blanket around her head several times to hold it. He picked up his rifle, and for a second considered using it to knock her unconscious, but he decided against it. After all, she was a woman.

Working feverishly now, he dragged her over next to Molly and sat on her while he took the rope off of Molly's wrists. With it, he tied the Sioux woman's feet. "Untie your ankles," he said to Molly while he continued to hold Iron Claw's wife down. Molly was quick to do as he instructed, and handed him the rope. He used it to bind the Sioux woman's feet to her hands, just as Molly had been tied.

With the woman immobilized at last, Matt got to his feet and moved to the door of the lodge, half expecting the entire village to be storming in upon him. But there was no one near. The chanting and singing around the fire had drowned out the Sioux woman's cries of alarm. Feeling the cold chill of the night air on the sweat on his brow, he shook his head in exasperation and swore. "Damn," was all he said, looking back at the trussed-up woman. Red Hawk was right—she was a handful. He looked then at Molly. The young girl was on her feet now, and she stood staring at him as if uncertain what to do. "Come on," he said, extending his hand to her. She immediately took it. Seeing another blanket, he picked it up and put it around her shoulders. "Here, put this around you. It's a little cool outside." Then he picked up his rifle again, and led her out into the chill night air.

Outside the tipi, he paused for a few moments to take a cautious look around him. Everyone in the village was apparently attending the dance. The paint pony tied beside the tipi nickered softly when they started to move away from the entrance. Matt stopped. "Yeah, you're right," he said to the pony. "We're gonna need another horse." He untied the horse and led it away, back toward the bluffs where Red Hawk waited.

"Good," Red Hawk commented when he saw them approaching through the dark shadows of the cottonwoods. He climbed up from the edge of the gully where he had been kneeling, and signaled to Matt. When they reached him, he glanced briefly at the slight figure wrapped in the blanket before turning his attention to the paint pony, a prize of much more interest to him. His broad smile shone in the darkness, evidence of the pleasure the sight of Iron Claw's favorite war pony brought. Turning to Matt, he spoke. "You gone a long time. Trouble?"

"No, no trouble," Matt replied. "Let's get goin'." He preferred not to confess that there were moments back in the tipi when he was beginning to wonder if he was going to have to shoot the Sioux woman to subdue her.

Pausing for a brief moment to listen to the sounds coming from the village, Matt was satisfied that no one had discovered the trussed-up woman in Iron Claw's lodge. Taking Molly by the hand then, he followed Red Hawk down a deep gully to the water's edge, where the buckskin and the dun waited. Feeling that she had found the haven she never wanted to leave again, Molly gripped Matt's hand tightly, so much so that he had to pry her fingers loose when he got to the horses.

"Come on," he said gently, and picked her up, preparing to lift her up onto the paint's back. As soon as she was in his arms, she put her arms around his neck and clung close to him. He realized then that the frightened girl needed to feel the safety of his arms. While Red Hawk watched, puzzled by the lack of urgency, Matt held the fragile girl for a few moments.

"Pretty soon, we have company," Red Hawk reminded him.

"Red Hawk's right," Matt said. "We'd best get ourselves outta here."

Molly relaxed her hold on his neck, and Matt started to lift her up, but the paint sidestepped away from them. "Easy now." Matt tried to soothe the skittish pony. It was to no avail. For some reason, the paint did not want the young girl placed upon its back. "We ain't got time for this," Matt grumbled, knowing that at any moment a cry of alarm could go up in the Sioux camp. He turned to Red Hawk. "You wanna trade horses? Maybe that dun you're ridin' ain't got anything against women."

Red Hawk didn't have to think about it. He had been eyeing the paint pony ever since Matt led it from the village. It was Iron Claw's favorite war horse, and would certainly be an object of envy back in the Crow village. Seeing the smile on Red Hawk's face, Matt realized that he should have given him the pony in the first place. It would definitely raise Red Hawk's status with his people. Iron Claw's pony was big medicine. The paint evidently sensed Red Hawk's confidence, for it remained as docile as you please while the Crow warrior jumped upon its back. The mousy dun seemed indifferent when it came to who climbed aboard, so Matt lifted Molly up, and stood back as the pony promptly followed after the paint. There were a good many hours of darkness left, and Matt wanted to make good use of them. He couldn't guess how long it would be before Iron Claw returned to his lodge and discovered his captive gone, but he needed only a little head start to make it impossible to follow them in the dark.

As it turned out, Matt was fortunate to gain more than an hour's start before the Sioux war chief tired of watching the dancers and returned to his tipi. He saw at once that his pony was missing, causing him to become alarmed. Upon first entering the tipi, he thought that his wife was missing as well. The white girl was apparently lying in the same position as when he had last seen her, although it puzzled him somewhat to see her head wrapped with a blanket. *Had his wife taken his horse somewhere?* As his eyes adjusted to the darkened interior of the tipi, he realized that the figure was not that of the slender white girl. Struck with an immediate flush of anger, he knelt beside the woman and unwrapped the blanket.

"Waugh!" An involuntary cry of rage escaped from his throat when he uncovered the angry face of his wife.

She spit the corner of the blanket from her lips and screamed, *"Wasicu! Wasicu!"*

"What?" he snarled. "Where?" Confused by the scene to which he had returned, he looked around him frantically, expecting to be attacked, and still mystified that the white girl was gone.

"A white man came and took the girl," she screeched excitedly as Iron Claw untied her.

"How . . ." he started, but could not finish the question. Her words caused him to recall the image of one particular white man, for he knew at once there was only one who would dare to walk into his camp and take the girl and his pony. Almost overcome by fury, he charged outside and stood for a few moments staring into the darkness, knowing it was futile. When his wife followed him outside, he turned and demanded, "What did this white man look like?"

"Tall," she replied excitedly. "A young man with no hair on his face. He was not a soldier. He wore animal skins. His hair on his head was the color of a mountain lion."

"Waugh!" Iron Claw cried out in agony. It was the white scout who kept crossing his path like a ghost. He cared little for the loss of the white girl, for he had

planned to kill her shortly anyway. But the brazen theft of his favorite pony would torment him until he killed the white scout and tied his scalp to his lance.

His frustration was complete when he thought of the futility in trying to go after Matt before daylight. His other horses were across the river with the pony herd. It would take time to fetch one, giving the white scout even more time to escape. He had no choice but to wait for sunup. He could not track in the dark. "Waugh!" he snarled again, and desperate for some way to vent his frustration and anger, pulled his knife and slashed his chest until his leggings were red with blood. The pain brought no relief for his frustration.

Chapter 8

He hated to wake her. She was sleeping so peacefully, and so soundly. He could only imagine how thoroughly exhausted she must be. He knelt beside her, watching her sleep for a few moments longer while Red Hawk stirred up the coals of the small fire. It had been only a couple of hours since they had stopped for the night, but already the first rays of the sun were filtering through the pines on the eastern slope.

"Molly," he said softly and touched her gently on the shoulder. "We'd best get movin'." He reached down and carefully moved a wisp of golden hair away from her face, wondering as he did how she could sleep with the thin strand tickling her nose.

Very slowly she awakened. Her eyelids fluttered for a moment or two, and then her eyes opened wide to stare unblinking into his. As before, when he had suddenly appeared in Iron Claw's tipi, she was not certain she was not dreaming. He smiled, and she realized that he was not a vision. Then she remembered where she was and returned his smile. "We'd best get movin'," he said again. "We'll take a little time to eat somethin', and then we'll get on outta this valley." He got to his feet. "Looks like you could use somethin' to eat," he remarked, gazing at her slender, pale arms. There were so many questions he wanted to ask her, though he knew she could not answer. How, he wondered, did she happen to be here so far from Nebraska City and the dining room run by her mother? "Where is your mother?" Matt asked. She made several signs, trying to explain. He finally understood that she was trying to tell him that Libby was dead. "I'm sorry," he said, still wondering about the circumstances. It would have to wait. There was little time to linger here.

"Why she not talk?" Red Hawk asked. He had paused to watch Matt and the young white girl, and her strange demeanor puzzled him. It occurred to him that he had never heard her speak when they were both captives in Iron Claw's camp.

"She can't," Matt replied, pointing a finger toward his throat.

"Ahh," the Crow warrior returned, understanding at last the girl's silence. He thought about it for a moment, then, "How you tell her what to do?"

Matt smiled. "You just tell her. She ain't deaf. She can hear. She just can't talk."

Red Hawk nodded, all the while studying Molly as if discovering a new species of people. Then he smiled and said, "She perfect woman" in his broken English.

Matt grinned. "I reckon," he said, turning to look at

Molly again. She acknowledged the comment by pretending to frown.

She pushed her blanket aside and got to her feet, looking around her as if searching for something. Then she made several signs with her hands, which Matt did not understand. "What?" he asked. "I don't understand."

Red Hawk, an interested observer, commented, "She say she need to make water."

"Oh," Matt replied. Turning to his Crow partner, he asked, "How do you know that? Do you understand those signs she's makin'?"

Red Hawk shrugged. "No, but we ride all night, and she don't make water."

"I reckon you're right," Matt replied, feeling a little stupid. He looked at Molly, and she was nodding vigorously. He flushed, embarrassed by his thoughtlessness. Then he pointed toward a thicket of serviceberry bushes. "We're gonna have to learn some kind of sign language," he mumbled, primarily to himself.

Matt was of a mind to take Molly straight to Fort Laramie as quickly as possible. He informed Red Hawk of his intention in case the Crow still had it in his mind to seek his vengeance against Iron Claw. Red Hawk replied that it could wait. In truth, the Crow warrior had taken a liking to the quiet young white man. And he was fascinated by the girl who could not speak. He decided to accompany them to Fort Laramie. He had relatives camped near the fort. He could visit his brother, Spotted Horse. Maybe he would join him and scout for the soldiers again. The decision made, the three set out on a southeast course, intending to cross the south end of the

Bighorns, cross the Powder, and strike the North Platte west of Fort Laramie.

Once they had the Bighorns behind them, Matt let up on the pace. He did not, however, relax his vigilance. They were still in Sioux territory, and while he thought he had left Iron Claw's warriors behind, there remained the possibility of encountering a hunting party from some other village. Although the girl appeared to be frail, Matt and Red Hawk soon learned that was not the case. She gave no signs of weakness or fatigue, sitting astride the dun mare for hours each day as the threesome made their way across a seemingly empty prairie.

Blue sky and an endless prairie. The emptiness was a misnomer, for both Matt and his Crow partner knew the rolling sea of grass was home for a bounty of game—antelope, deer, buffalo, rabbit. A man would have to be dead between the ears to go hungry in such a land of plenty. It was little wonder that the Sioux, the Cheyenne and the Arapaho were upset over the intrusion of white fortune hunters crossing their hunting grounds. The land had once been the home of Red Hawk's people, but the Crow had been driven out by the powerful Sioux tribes. The two tribes were natural enemies, which explained Red Hawk's hatred for all Sioux, and the pleasure he derived from riding Iron Claw's favorite war pony.

After two days with no sign of pursuit, they decided it was safe to stop long enough to hunt for fresh meat, so they camped in a grassy ravine that led down to the Powder River. For the last day and a half they had survived on dried jerky and water, Matt's supply of coffee and salt having long since been depleted. There was plenty of sign that game was about, so Matt strung his bow and prepared to lie in ambush beside what appeared to be a favorite watering hole. At first sight of the bow, Red Hawk immediately became interested. He had not met many white men who had any real skill with a bow.

"You not use gun?" he asked, holding his Springfield up before him.

"Too noisy," Matt replied, testing the tautness of his bowstring. He glanced up at Red Hawk and grinned. "What's the matter? You don't think a white man can shoot a bow?"

"Not worth a damn," Red Hawk replied honestly.

"Well, you can stand behind me with that Springfield, and shoot if I miss with the bow." Red Hawk took him up on it. He was hungry.

As it turned out, Red Hawk did not have to waste a cartridge. They had waited for less than an hour when four deer, all does, came down to the edge of the river to drink. With no wasted motion, Matt suddenly stood up, sighted on a young doe, and let fly his arrow. Shot through the lung, the deer tried to turn and follow her sisters as they bolted away from the water. Halfway up the bank, she stumbled and fell. Matt ran to her and quickly finished her with his knife. Red Hawk nodded his approval, impressed with his white friend's skill with an Indian weapon. Matt supplied him with his extra knife, and the two men skinned and butchered the deer. Molly, through a series of frowns and hand signals, insisted upon doing the cooking, and soon Matt and Red

Hawk were relaxing by the river while Molly roasted the meat.

When his belly was satisfied, Matt sat back and watched his companions eat. It had been a long time since he'd felt it safe to relax his caution to such an extent. Both he and Red Hawk thought it highly unlikely that Iron Claw was anywhere near them, and they had seen no sign of other Indian ponies since leaving the Little Bighorn.

After making sure the men had all they wanted to eat, Molly left the fire and sat down beside Matt to finish her meal. She smiled up at him, contented and secure in his presence, causing him to remember something. He reached inside his shirt pocket and retrieved the small silver medal he had placed there. "Here," he said. "I've got somethin' for you. Maybe it'll take better care of you this time."

She immediately stopped chewing, her eyes fixed upon the medal. She carefully placed the strip of meat she had been eating on a small stone, and wiped her hands on her skirt before taking the medal from him. A tear formed in the corner of her eye as she held the medal in her fingers. Somewhat surprised by the emotional response, Matt reached over, and taking the silver chain, slipped it over her head. "There you go," he said cheerfully. "It looks better on you than it did on that damn Sioux." He was not prepared for her reaction. She suddenly threw her arms around his neck, almost bowling him over as she hugged him tightly. Red Hawk chuckled delightedly. Not knowing what to say, Matt mumbled, "It's all right. Now, finish your food. We can't stay in this place too long."

"You got any kinfolks in Nebraska City?" Matt asked Molly after watching her intently for several minutes. Nebraska City was where he had first met the girl and her mother. She shook her head. He thought about that for a few seconds, then said, "How about back east somewhere?" Again she shook her head and continued chewing on a piece of venison, her eyes trained upon his. "Nobody? Nowhere?" She shook her head slowly, and paused in her chewing. "Well, we've got to find some place to take you." Gazing steadily into his eyes, she slowly pointed a finger at herself and then back at him. Her meaning was unmistakable.

"Whoa," he exclaimed. "You can't stay with me."

With her hands held palms up, she shrugged her shoulders and gestured, her eyebrows arched inquisitively.

"She say, why?" Red Hawk interjected, finding the exchange amusing.

"I know what she's sayin'," Matt snapped, then looking back at her, he tried to explain. "Because you just can't. I have to go places, places I can't take a girl." Again she gestured, obviously asking why. "You just can't," he repeated. Exasperated with the girl's persistence, he looked toward Red Hawk for help, only to be met with a wide grin. The Indian was enjoying his white friend's predicament. Matt answered the grin with a deep-furrowed frown, then turned back to the girl, who had now stopped chewing to stare patiently at her buckskin knight. "Right now we'll worry about gettin' you back to Fort Laramie. We'll worry about what to do next after we get there."

The next two days saw them put a comfortable distance between them and the Powder River. In deference to the lady, Matt did not push for maximum progress, stopping to camp early in the evenings, and keeping an eye out for camping sites that could provide some modest facility for Molly. As for Molly, she quickly became comfortable with her two companions. Red Hawk was impressed with the toughness of the slender young girl, and spent quite some time teaching her words in sign language. She pleased him with her ability to retain almost every word he taught her. Under different circumstances, their journey might have seemed like a pleasant outing.

"One man," Red Hawk said, stating the obvious, for there was no one else in sight.

"Can't tell if he's Indian or white," Matt said, his eyes straining to make out the features of the lone rider they had been watching since he first appeared on the horizon. When Red Hawk first caught sight of him, the man had just appeared from behind a low ridge to the west. Still alert to the possibility of Sioux hunting parties, even though they were only one day away from Fort Laramie, they had decided it prudent to take cover until they were sure he was not an advance Lakota scout.

After a few minutes passed and the rider had progressed to a point that crossed their trail, Red Hawk commented, "White man." Matt nodded, for it was obvious to him at that point also. Dressed in animal skins, riding a mule, and leading another loaded with hides, the man rode slumped in the saddle as if sleeping. From that distance, he appeared to be an old man, for his face was all but invisible behind a bushy gray beard.

"The fact that he's traveling alone in Sioux country doesn't seem to bother him much, does it?" Matt wondered at the boldness of the man, whoever he was.

As they continued to watch, the man abruptly changed directions and turned onto the same trail they followed. Some two hundred yards in front of them, he progressed at a rather leisurely pace, still slumped over in the saddle. It appeared that he had the same destination, so Matt decided they might as well catch up to him. They started out again, Red Hawk in the lead, Matt behind him, and Molly bringing up the rear.

Due to the mules' unhurried pace—it appeared that the stranger had left it to them to set it—Matt and his two companions caught up to the old man within a few minutes' time. When they had closed the distance to about fifty yards, the old man still gave no indication that he was aware of their presence. Matt began to wonder if the old fellow might in fact be dead. A few yards closer, Matt called out to alert him. "We're comin' up behind you!"

"Hell, I know that," was the gruff reply and the only indication that he heard them, for he didn't bother to turn to look behind him.

Matt and Red Hawk pulled up on either side of him and reined back to pace their horses with the mules. Molly continued to follow. "Good day to you," Matt offered in an effort to be neighborly. "Looks like you might be headed for Fort Laramie. That's where we're headin'."

"Figured," the old man replied. "I seen you right off, back behind that low ridge." He barely moved his head to look at Matt. Then he turned the other way, and studied Red Hawk for a few seconds. "Crow," he commented, as if making a judgment. He was a small man, seemingly without a neck, for his bushy head appeared to be pushed back into his shoulders. Matt realized then that the old man had not been sleeping in the saddle, but was bent in the spine, from either old age or disease, or both.

He turned his attention back to Matt again. "I reckon you'd be the feller that's got Iron Claw all riled up. If'n that's so, you'd best be watchin' your topknot, 'cause I hear tell that he's swore to have your scalp."

"Is that so?" Matt replied, finding it interesting that this gray-haired old trapper knew anything about him. "How do you know that?"

The old man snorted contemptuously. "Hell, I been livin' with the Lakota for seven years—Red Cloud's people, though, not Iron Claw's bunch. There ain't much happens in this country that don't get passed around to the other villages. I heared tell that a bunch of soldiers run into an ambush over on the Powder—heared it was Iron Claw's band." He paused to issue a warning. "Don't git too close to that mule there, sonny. He'll take a nip outta that horse." Matt reined his horse over a safe distance. The old man continued. "Iron Claw's a mean Injun. I never had much truck with him."

Something he had once heard Seth Ward telling Ike

suddenly came to Matt's mind, and he asked, "You wouldn't be Cooter Martin, would you?"

The old man jerked his head up to lock eyes with Matt, looking as if he'd been tricked. "I'm Nathaniel Martin," he replied cautiously. "Some folks call me Cooter." He glanced over at Red Hawk, then back at Matt. "Tell that Crow friend of your'n that I've been livin' with Red Cloud's folks, but I ain't no Sioux."

"I reckon you just told him yourself," Matt replied. "He understands American."

Red Hawk grunted in response. "If you were Sioux, I would have shot you on sight, old man."

Matt couldn't help but grin when he heard Red Hawk's reply. "My name's Slaughter," he said. "This is Red Hawk. He's just recently been enjoyin' some of Iron Claw's hospitality, and he ain't particularly fond of the Sioux right now."

"I expect not," Cooter said. "I ain't had no truck with the Crows one way or another, so there ain't no reason for him to be lookin' at my scalp." He turned then to look behind him. "What's she doin' out here?" It was fairly obvious that Molly was out of place, and was there purely by happenstance. Dressed in a torn cotton dress, with a blanket gathered over her shoulders, and riding a mousy dun still showing faint traces of old war paint, she as much as told of her captivity.

Matt explained Molly's presence with them, bringing the first sign of sensitivity from the old man. He turned to speak directly to Molly. "I'm right sorry to hear of your trouble, ma'am. I'd say you was mighty lucky to get away from Iron Claw." He jerked his head back to look directly at Matt again. "No wonder Iron Claw's so riled up over you. You better watch yourself, young feller."

"I aim to," Matt replied, thinking to himself that Iron Claw had something to worry about as well if the two of them should meet. There was still a score to settle with the war chief for his treatment of Ike Brister. The promise he had made over Ike's grave was by no means forgotten, only postponed. Molly had to be taken to safety first. Ike would understand that.

"I expect we'll strike the North Platte before dark," Matt said. "You're welcome to camp with us if you're of a mind to. We've got some fresh meat, and you're welcome to share it."

"Well, that's right neighborly of you," Cooter at once replied. "You wouldn't happen to have some coffee, would you? I swear, I'd love to have some coffee."

"Sorry," Matt replied, "I haven't had any myself for a while."

"Whiskey?" Cooter asked, looking hopeful.

"Nope. We've got some fresh meat, and that's all. One more day oughta see us in Fort Laramie, though." He nodded toward Cooter's pack mule. "From the looks of your pack, you'll be doin' some tradin' when we get there."

"Plan to," Cooter replied. "It's been a spell since I've been to Fort Laramie, so I figured I might as well trade some of my pelts for some coffee and sugar, maybe even a little flour. Livin' with Injuns, a man gets a cravin' for some biscuits after a while."

"Why don't you get down to Laramie more often?" Matt inquired.

"No cravin' to," Cooter answered. "Hell, I wouldn't be goin' there now, but I'm carryin' a message to the soldier chief from Red Cloud."

This aroused Matt's interest. "That so?"

"Yeah," Cooter responded, not reluctant to impress them with the responsibility given him by such an important Sioux leader. "I'm comin' to tell the soldier chief that Red Cloud and some of the others have agreed to come to Fort Laramie to talk about all them white fools that come traipsing through the Powder River country last summer. That country's the Lakota's prime buffalo range."

"That country don't belong to the Sioux," Red Hawk snorted defiantly.

Cooter cocked an eye in his direction. "Well, I don't reckon no Crows is gonna have any say in that, are they? If I recollect rightly, they couldn't hold on to that country when they had it."

Red Hawk made a show of slowly drawing the skinning knife Matt had given him and running his finger lightly over the edge of the blade. "Maybe I might take one old gray scalp to tie in my pony's mane," he threatened.

"Maybe you oughta try," Cooter returned, letting his hand rest on the butt of his rifle. "It might be a harder day's work than you bargained for."

"You talk big, old man," Red Hawk said. "A dog may sleep with wolves, but he's still nothing but a dog."

Matt couldn't help but laugh. He glanced at Molly

and winked, lest she might take the two roosters seriously. "Well, that would suit me and Molly just fine if you two was to kill each other. Then we wouldn't have to put up with either one of you."

Red Hawk and Cooter glared at each other for a moment more before the Crow snorted contemptuously and returned the knife to his belt.

Upon reaching the North Platte, the unlikely foursome made camp. Cooter helped Matt gather wood for a fire. After it was blazing steadily, the men took care of their stock. Signaling with her hands, Molly told them she would take care of cooking the meat.

Cooter watched with fascination as the young girl took Matt's knife and fashioned a spit to roast strips of meat. "She's as handy around a campfire as any Injun woman," he commented after a while. "Can't she make no sound a'tall?"

Matt paused to look at the old man. "You could ask her. She ain't deaf." He glanced over to meet Molly's eye. She nodded her head to indicate she appreciated his comment.

Cooter nodded as well, realizing he had made an assumption. "Beg your pardon, missy," he said, looking directly at her. "I reckon I ain't come across nobody that just can't talk. I mean, usually they's deaf and dumb, 'stead of just one way or the other." She gestured with her hands, dismissing his concern. "I reckon that makes you kinda special," he said, smiling. She returned the smile, then turned her attention to the meat after stealing one more glance at Matt. Cooter noticed. There wasn't much that escaped the old man's eye.

After he had eaten, Matt decided to take a look around the area just to make sure there were no uninvited guests watching from the shadows. "There ain't nobody around," Cooter stated flatly.

"That so?" Matt asked. "How do you know that?"

"Hell, I can feel it. You live in these parts as long as I have, a man gets where he can feel the emptiness."

Matt smiled. "That's reassuring, but I expect I'll take a look around anyway."

"I'll go with you," Cooter said.

Matt picked up his rifle, and paused long enough to reassure Molly. "We'll be back directly. You'll be all right. Red Hawk will look after you." Red Hawk, sitting propped up against a cottonwood to ease his full belly, nodded. Then the two white men disappeared into the shadows.

After making a complete circle around their camp, they paused to stand on the bank of the river where the horses and mules were tied. Cooter had been right. All was peaceful about them. Matt had not expected otherwise, but he preferred to see for himself. He didn't have the confidence in Cooter's senses that the old man had. It was quiet enough on the banks of the North Platte, however. The nights were beginning to warm just a little, with the promise that summer would surely not be long in coming. A gentle breeze drifted across the prairie as a full moon appeared over the distant hills.

"Whaddaya gonna do with the girl?" Cooter asked bluntly. "She got any kin?"

"I don't know," Matt answered. "All I know is that her mother is dead. I guess I'll try to find someone to take care of her at Fort Laramie."

"'Pears to me, she's figurin' on stayin' with you," Cooter said. "She don't never take her eyes off'n you."

Matt shrugged. "She's just scared right now—doesn't have any folks. She knows she can't stay with me."

Cooter almost chuckled. "Man, that young lady ain't lookin' at you like you're her daddy. She's already pickin' out names for the young'uns." When Matt replied that she was only a girl, Cooter did chuckle, amused by Matt's apparent naïveté. "If she was a Lakota, she'd already be married to some young buck, and already have a bunch of young'uns runnin' around."

Matt's immediate reaction to Cooter's remarks was an inclination to tell the old man to mind his own business. But there was something sobering in the old codger's observation—a thought he had not considered until that moment. *Young lady.* Cooter had referred to Molly as a young lady. Matt had looked at her as a child, still remembering her as a shy and strange little girl helping her mother in the hotel dining room back in Nebraska City. Of course she wanted to stay with him. She had already made that known to him. But he figured that was simply because she was frightened and he was the only person she knew in this harsh land. If Cooter was right, then Matt had something more to think about. Rather than dismiss it as an amusing instance of a young girl's adolescence, he chose to give the matter serious thought.

He turned to look toward the campfire, where Molly was kneeling to feed more limbs to the flame. As if feeling his gaze, she looked in his direction. He wished at that moment that Cooter had kept his remarks to himself, for he would now see Molly in a different light, and be forced to examine his own feelings.

He continued to stare at the young woman, knowing that she could not see him standing there in the shadows watching her. It was difficult for him to see her as anything but a frightened girl. There had never been any time in his life for serious thoughts of a woman, and certainly no thoughts of settling down with a woman. His lifestyle would not permit it, anyway. He had joined the army when he was a boy and fought to defend his home in the Shenandoah Valley. After the war, he had been forced to flee the federal soldiers because he took the blame for a murder his brother committed. He never regretted that decision. It was much better that the Union Army pursued him instead of Owen. His brother had a wife and children to take care of. As for himself, he was still an outlaw back east, and there was always the possibility that someday someone might arrive at Fort Laramie and inform the commanding officer that one of his scouts was a fugitive. *No,* he thought, *I've got no business thinking about a wife, even if I was attracted to her.* It occurred to him then that it was awfully strange that he had never even entertained thoughts of a relationship with a woman until Cooter's remarks. The old busybody had planted worrisome seeds in Matt's mind.

"I'll find somebody in Laramie to take care of her,"

he blurted out, surprising Cooter after the long pause in their conversation.

Anxious to put troublesome thoughts out of his mind, he went back to the fire and sat down beside Red Hawk. As soon as he entered the firelight, Molly's eyes were upon him. She picked up the limb she had fashioned for a spit, and held it out, a questioning look on her face. "No, thanks," he replied. "I'm full." She replaced the spit and came over to sit between Matt and Red Hawk. Cooter and Red Hawk exchanged knowing winks.

Chapter 9

Major William H. Evans, Eleventh Ohio Volunteer Cavalry and commanding officer of Fort Laramie, looked up and frowned when the sergeant major informed him of the four people seeking his audience. "What the hell do they want?" he asked when told they were civilians.

"Sir," the sergeant major replied, "it's ol' Cooter Martin. Says he's got a message for you from Red Cloud. There's three others with him. Two of 'em—a white man and a Crow Injun—are a couple of Captain Boyd's scouts. I don't know what they're doin' with Cooter. The other one is a young woman, and I don't know what she's doin' with 'em, either."

Major Evans looked perplexed. "Well, send them in," he said. He had been awaiting word from Red Cloud and High Backbone after messengers were sent asking the chiefs to come to a treaty talk. He had not expected someone like Cooter Martin to speak for the great Sioux leader Red Cloud. But he didn't question it.

"Miss," Major Evans said to Molly in a brief show of

courtesy before turning his attention to the three men standing before him.

"Red Cloud sent me to tell you he's bringing his people in to talk," Cooter said. "He says to tell you he expects the soldiers to close down the trail through the Powder River country." There was a pause while Evans waited for more. "I reckon that's it," Cooter said.

"Huh," Evans grunted. "When is he going to arrive? There are other bands coming in. They'll be here early next month. The commission from Washington will be here then. We need to have Red Cloud here at the same time."

"He'll be here," Cooter replied. "If he says he'll be here, he'll be here." He looked at Matt, then back at the major, as if wondering what more the officer expected.

"All right, then," Evans said, concluding the interview. "We'll be expecting him." He got up from his desk, signaling the end of the meeting.

"Begging your pardon, sir," Matt said. "I was hopin' you might be able to help us find a place for this young lady to stay." He went on to explain that Molly's mother and stepfather had been murdered by a Sioux war party and Molly captured by the Sioux war chief Iron Claw.

Major Evans' demeanor changed immediately upon hearing of the young girl's tragedy. He apologized for not recognizing Molly immediately as the young girl who had passed through recently. "I'm sure we can find a place for you, miss. You can stay with Mrs. Evans and me temporarily until we can find something more permanent." He directed his words back at Matt then. "We wondered about the young lady and her parents after they left here for Montana Territory. They hired a breed named Jack Black Dog as a guide." Matt noticed that Molly's eyes opened wide at the mention of the guide's name. Evans went on. "But he showed up here about a week later, saying that they decided they didn't need a guide and sent him back."

Matt's attention was nailed to Molly's face after seeing her reaction to the mere mention of the half-breed's name. Upon hearing Major Evans' last remark, her eyes almost sparked, her face tensed into a deep frown, and she began shaking her head violently. "What is it, Molly?" Matt pressed. "Ain't that the way it happened?"

She continued to shake her head, even harder than before. Matt continued to probe. "Are you sayin' your guide had somethin' to do with the attack on you?" She nodded then, her eyes wide and excited. But there was more she was trying to tell him. Frowning, she tried to make him understand with gestures. He guessed again. "He ran off and left you. Is that it?" She shook her head, frustrated. Seeing paper and a pen on the major's desk, she pointed at them, her eyes questioning.

"Certainly," Major Evans quickly replied and pushed the ink pot over toward her.

She hurriedly scribbled down a few words and handed Matt the paper.

" 'He was with them,' " Matt read aloud. "Why, that low-down son of a gun—" he started, but turned in mid-sentence to face the major. "Where can I find this Jack Black Dog?"

"I couldn't say," Evans replied. "I think he hung

around the post for a couple of days, then left for who knows where."

"I suspect Jack Black Dog's in Iron Claw's village. That's where he usually hangs out." This came from Cooter Martin. Matt turned to question the old man.

"You know this man?" he asked.

"Shore, I know him—at least know of him. He spends half his time beggin' fer crumbs around Iron Claw's camp. Don't surprise me none that he led this little lady's folks right to ol' Iron Claw."

"The main thing is she's safe now," Major Evans said, "and like I said, she's welcome to stay with my wife and me. I'm being reassigned to another post in June, else she could stay with us longer. We'll find a place, though." He looked again at Molly, whose expression was one of distress. "Don't you worry, miss. We'll take care of you."

"She wanna stay with Slaughter."

Evans turned to gaze at the Crow scout, who until that moment had been content to remain silent. He glanced at Matt, but the sandy-haired scout responded with only a slight shake of his head. Cooter grinned broadly. Not quite sure what to make of it, Major Evans concluded, "I expect it would be a good idea to let the post surgeon take a look at her, after the ordeal she's been through."

When they were outside, Matt questioned Molly. "He said you came through here with your parents. Is that so? I didn't know your father was alive." She shook her head and affected a deep frown. "It wasn't your father?"

Again she shook her head. "Your mother got married again—is that it?" She nodded.

Martha Riddler, wife of assistant surgeon John G. Riddler, was beside herself with empathy for the unfortunate young girl brought in to see her husband. She took over like the natural mother hen she tended to be and insisted, "You can stay right here with us, child—Cora Evans would drive you crazy with her endless prattle." The question of Molly's welfare was settled right then and there.

Matt felt a great sense of relief, knowing that Molly was going to be well taken care of. Martha Riddler had the look of a mother who needed a child to care for. Molly, though grateful for being accepted by the doctor's family, was still distressed that Matt did not choose to take her with him. She would accept his decision without protest, even though she longed with all her heart to go with him. Martha Riddler, compassionate human being that she was, took note of the distress in Molly's eyes and was prompted to reassure her. "Don't you fret, child. You'll be all right with us." She took Molly by the shoulders, held her at arm's length, and added, "First thing we need to do is put some meat on your bones. You look like you haven't eaten in a month."

Molly managed a smile for her before quickly returning her gaze to Matt. "I'll be lookin' in on you from time to time," Matt assured her in leaving.

She nodded, but although he might mean what he said, she was not certain that she would ever see him

again. Her eyes, soft and searching his, did not shed a
tear as he smiled to reassure her. She stood watching
him as he departed, her fingers caressing the small silver medal on the chain around her neck. Her late mother
had often sought to explain the unfairness of life that
would leave an innocent young girl without the ability
to express her feelings. How she longed to cry out to
him that thoughts of him filled her every waking moment! Surely he must know how deeply she felt for him.
How could he not know? Others saw it in her face. Red
Hawk and Cooter had seen it at once. She suspected that
even Martha Riddler had immediately sensed it. She
could only conclude that he, too, knew of her feelings
for him. But he simply did not have similar feelings for
her.

When he had gone, she turned to meet Martha Riddler's understanding smile. "Come, child," the doctor's
wife said. "I'll make us a cup of tea, and we can sit
down and get acquainted."

Looking ashamed and apologetic, Molly motioned
toward her mouth and shook her head. Martha understood what the girl was trying to tell her. "Never you
mind," she said. "There's nothing wrong with silence.
There's too much noise around here, anyway."

Lieutenant Frederick LeVan, upon hearing that the
sandy-haired scout had returned to Fort Laramie, sent
his sergeant to find him. LeVan had been assigned the
duty of leading a patrol to investigate the massacre of
Molly's mother and Franklin Lyons. In actuality, the patrol was little more than a burial detail, but LeVan

wanted Slaughter as a scout. "The man has a head on his shoulders," LeVan told Captain Boyd, "and he's absolutely fearless."

Boyd was reluctant to rehire Slaughter because the man had quit the last patrol to which he had been assigned and ridden off somewhere on some personal business—at least that was the situation as he had interpreted it.

"If it hadn't been for Slaughter's actions, I would have suffered a great many more casualties in that canyon," LeVan insisted. "It's true, he left the patrol, but he went in search of another scout—Brister was his name. You remember, you hired him on with Slaughter. I really couldn't blame him for leaving the patrol. He and Brister were close friends. Besides, the fight was over and we were heading back by that time."

"All right, then," Boyd conceded. "Sounds like you know your man."

"Thank you, sir," LeVan replied, and immediately sent Sergeant Barnes to find Matt. The lieutenant didn't expect to encounter any trouble on the patrol. The murders that had taken place were far too old to even think about pursuing the guilty parties. The entire action was little more than a show of respect to the unfortunate young lady who had lost her family. LeVan suspected that Major Evans preferred not to have any hostile contact with the Sioux just now, on the very eve of scheduled peace talks. His hunch was confirmed by Captain Boyd's parting remarks.

"Fred, Major Evans was clear in his instructions as to the purpose of this patrol. Find the unfortunate victims and give them a decent burial. If you make contact with the hostiles, take whatever action you see fit, but don't go probing deep into Sioux country."

Sergeant Barnes found Matt in the post trader's store, kibitzing with Cooter Martin while the old man bargained with Seth Ward for supplies. "I don't do much tradin' for fur," he heard Seth telling Cooter. "It's hard for me to turn 'em into cash."

"These is all prime," Cooter protested. "You ought'n have no trouble a'tall sellin' them back east."

"Don't let him cheat you, mister," Barnes blurted playfully as he walked in the door. "He'll sell 'em for three times what they're worth."

All three men turned to acknowledge the sergeant. "I wish that was true," Seth replied. "I'm just tryin' to be honest about it. Fur ain't as valuable as it used to be, is all I'm sayin'. I'll do the best I can for you, but I can't take no loss on the deal."

While Cooter and Seth continued to bargain, Sergeant Barnes turned to direct his remarks to Matt. "Well, Slaughter, looks like you got back with all your hair."

"I reckon," Matt said, smiling.

"Did you find Brister?" He didn't have to ask if the big scout was dead. He had already heard that Ike wasn't with Slaughter when he returned.

"I did," Matt replied softly.

"Well, I'm right sorry about the big fellow. I know he was a friend of yours." He shook his head sympathetically, then abruptly changed the subject. "Lieutenant LeVan sent me to fetch you. He wants to talk to you."

"What about?" Matt asked.

"About scoutin' for him. We're goin' out on patrol tomorrow—goin' to investigate the murder of that girl's folks—the one you rode in with."

Matt was surprised. "I figured when I quit up on the Powder that it would be the end of my scoutin' for the army."

"Naw," Barnes replied. "Hell, the lieutenant understands why you left the patrol. Anyway, he asked Captain Boyd specifically for you."

Matt thought about it for only a moment before accepting. "I've still got some unfinished business to take care of, but I can sure use the money."

That settled, Barnes turned his attention back to the bartering going on at the counter. "I reckon you'd be Cooter Martin," he said to the old man. "I've heard tell of you, but I wasn't sure you were real, so I came to see for myself."

Cooter paused long enough to cock a wary eye at the sergeant, not sure if he was being japed or not. "I'm Nathaniel Martin," he said. "I reckon I'm real enough." Turning his gaze back to Seth, he added, "But I don't reckon I'm worth a whole helluva lot."

"I'm trying to do right by you," Seth protested.

They all stood by while the trade was concluded. Then Matt and the sergeant helped Cooter carry his supplies out to load on his mule. "You seem to be in a hurry to leave," Matt commented as he watched the old man tie his packs.

"I been here too long already," Cooter replied. "I can already feel my skin startin' to itch, being around all these dang soldiers." He glanced at Barnes as if about to except him, but said nothing. Turning back to Matt, he said, "I'd like to buy me one of them fancy Henrys like you carry, but I couldn't afford to buy the cartridges for it." Ready to leave then, he reached out to shake Matt's hand. "You watch yourself, young feller. The Injuns is already gettin' to know you and that *spirit gun* of your'n. Igmutaka, that's what they're callin' you. Mountain lion. You've already sent a few of Iron Claw's boys to hunt with the spirits. It'd be big medicine for the man that kills you."

"I'll be careful," Matt said. "You'd best watch yourself as well."

"I always do," Cooter replied. He looked around then as if searching for someone. "Where's that Crow you was ridin' with?"

"Red Hawk's gone up to the Crow camp to see his family," Matt answered.

Cooter winked as he said, "Tell him he ain't a bad feller in spite of bein' a damn Crow."

"I'll tell him," Matt said. "You watch your topknot."

The old man nodded, and climbed aboard his mule. Without another glance in their direction, he gave the mule a kick with his heels and started back toward Powder River country. Matt stood for a few moments watching him depart, then followed Sergeant Barnes back to report to Lieutenant LeVan.

*   *   *

"Molly," Martha Riddler called, "there's a young man here to see you."

Molly appeared at the door a few moments later, a dish towel in her hand. Martha stepped back to let her come out on the porch. She did not miss the glimmer of excitement in the girl's eye when she saw Matt.

Matt reached up quickly and pulled his hat from his head. "I just thought I'd drop by to see how you were makin' out," he said.

She smiled shyly and nodded. Martha spoke for her. "She's doing just grand. Aren't you, honey?" Molly smiled broadly then and, looking at the doctor's wife, nodded again. "We've just cleaned up the supper dishes, or I'd invite you to sit down with us," Martha said. "There may be some coffee left in the pot, if you'd care for a cup."

"Oh, no, ma'am," Matt quickly replied. "I don't wanna intrude. I just dropped by to tell Molly I won't be by for a few days." He turned his full attention upon Molly then. "Looks like I'm goin' back to work for the army. I'm goin' out on a patrol with Lieutenant LeVan in the mornin'—should be back in a week or so."

Molly responded with a slight frown, but then quickly recovered to force a smile. Remembering her lessons while on the trail, she made the sign for Red Hawk, accompanied with a questioning look. Matt understood.

"Red Hawk's visiting his people," he said. "He ain't goin' on this one with me."

Martha tilted her head in mock surprise. "My

goodness," she said, laughing, "you've turned this child into an Indian."

"That's Red Hawk's doin'," Matt replied. "I don't know much more sign than she does." He turned to gaze at Molly for a long moment, feeling self-conscious about the sudden silence. Finally, unable to think of anything else to say, he blurted, "Anyway, I just wanted to see you before I go."

Molly could only gaze into his eyes until he glanced away to look at Martha again. "I'm beholdin' to you, Mrs. Riddler, for takin' care of Molly. She's kinda special to me." As soon as the words left his lips, he wished he could recall them. *Why the hell did I say that?* he thought. He glanced quickly at Molly in time to see her eyes grow wide with surprise. "Well, I'd best be goin'," he mumbled, and turned on his heel. He could feel both women's eyes on his back as he strode away.

"Well, I guess we can bury what's left of them," Lieutenant LeVan said. "The buzzards didn't leave much." He stood over the remains of Libby Donovan Lyons, her dress tattered and torn, evidence of the buzzards' greedy banquet, her bones already starting to bleach in the summer sun. One side of her skull was crushed. He could only speculate as to whether that blow was what killed her, or the shattered breastbone that indicated a bullet hole. Several yards away lay the remains of Franklin Lyons. A neat hole in the middle of his skull bore evidence of his execution. "He must not have even known it was coming," LeVan speculated. He looked around for Sergeant Barnes. "Sergeant, let's get a grave dug—might as well put them both in the same hole."

Matt stood looking at the broken wagon wheel for a few minutes longer, picturing in his mind what had taken place there, and how terrifying it must have been for Molly. He had known her mother, Libby, but the buzzards had not left enough of the poor woman to recognize. *Jack Black Dog,* he thought, and tucked the name away in the back of his mind. In the event he ever crossed paths with the breed, there would be a reckoning.

After the grave was covered, LeVan decided to follow the trail farther north to scout the low ridges for signs of any increased Indian activity. There was no way to tell for sure, but Spotted Horse felt strongly that this was the work of Iron Claw, as Cooter Martin had speculated. On the morning the patrol left Fort Laramie, Major Evans had reminded the lieutenant that the Sioux were coming in to talk to a delegation from Washington within a couple of weeks. It was Washington's hope that the Sioux chiefs would agree to allow peaceful traffic along the Bozeman Trail. In view of this, Evans suggested that LeVan should not be too diligent in searching for the parties guilty of the attack on the wagon. Having already been advised of the major's position on the issue by Captain Boyd, Levan was clear on what was expected of him. Still, it stuck in his craw. As far as he could tell, this business with Libby and Franklin Lyons had nothing to do with the impending treaty talks. Iron Claw was nothing more than a bloodthirsty criminal, and as such, he should not be tolerated by either red man or white. In all likelihood, Iron Claw would not attend the talks, anyway. And while LeVan was not reluctant to ignore the letter of the law, he would not completely disobey. Consequently, he decided to have a look around the head of the Powder in case Iron Claw was lingering in the area.

"What are we gonna do if we find Iron Claw and he's got as many warriors as we got jumped with before?" Sergeant Barnes whispered to Matt.

"Run like hell, I reckon," Matt replied. He didn't really believe the lieutenant expected to find any Sioux in the area. It was his feeling that LeVan just enjoyed being in the field and away from the post.

Chapter 10

"Damn," Parker Boyd uttered softly when he read the paper just handed to him by Lieutenant James O'Connor. "I can't believe it. Are you sure this is the same man?" he asked, handing the paper back.

"It's him, all right," O'Connor replied smugly, reading the article.

Matthew Scott Slaughter, approximately twenty-five years of age; height, over six feet; weight, approximately one hundred ninety pounds; hair, light brown or blond; eyes, blue. Last seen in Oklahoma Territory—believed to be traveling with an older companion named Ike Brister.

"Hell," Boyd snorted, "that could describe any number of outlaws passing this way." As chief of scouts, Boyd was reluctant to lose a man as capable as Slaughter had proven to be.

"That's true," O'Connor conceded, "but he's the only

one who calls himself Matt Slaughter and was traveling with Ike Brister." He laughed. "I'd have more respect for him if he had at least had enough sense to change his name."

"I still can't believe it. He just doesn't fit the mold of a murderer."

"The army doesn't take kindly to a Johnny Reb murdering one of its officers." O'Connor was thoroughly enjoying the turn of events. He was still smarting from the rebuke he had received after Ike Brister had been killed. This notice just received from Omaha, alerting all posts to be on the lookout for more than a dozen fugitives, might have been carelessly discarded, like similar notices before. As luck would have it, however, O'Connor was killing time in the adjutant's office, and just happened to casually scan the names. The name Matthew Scott Slaughter jumped out at him at once. Slaughter was wanted by the army for killing a Captain Harvey Mathis in Virginia, in June 1865. It was almost too good to be true! O'Connor had immediately volunteered to take charge of a detail to arrest the fugitive.

"This isn't going to make Fred LeVan any too happy," Boyd said. "He puts a lot of stock in Slaughter. It still doesn't seem possible."

"I don't doubt it a bit," O'Connor insisted. "If you'd seen the way that man handles that Henry rifle he carries, you wouldn't either."

"Are you going to arrest him as soon as he gets back with LeVan's patrol?"

"I could," O'Connor answered. "But I don't think I'll wait for him to get back. I think I'll take a detail out to meet the patrol. I wanna make sure nobody has a chance to warn him."

Lieutenant O'Connor was justified in his decision not to wait for LeVan's patrol to return to the post, for word of the wanted poster soon spread throughout the fort. "Oh, my goodness," Martha Riddler sighed, hardly able to believe what her husband told her. "That nice young man . . ." she began. Then, "Molly will be devastated." She frowned as she pictured the impact the news would have upon their houseguest. "Are they sure, John? Maybe they have the wrong man."

"They're pretty sure it's him," the doctor replied. "I was as surprised as you. It just shows you that it's hard to judge a person, but there are a lot of men out here who are running from a past back east. Lieutenant O'Connor is taking a patrol out in the morning to intercept LeVan."

"I still think there must be some mistake," Martha murmured, unwilling to believe she could have been so wrong in her assessment of Matt's character. She gave it a few more moments' thought before shaking her head and saying, "We'd best not let Molly know about this. She'll find out soon enough as it is."

Just inside the door, about to join Martha on the porch, a shocked young girl stood paralyzed, her hand on the doorknob. As Martha had expected, Molly was devastated. She felt her knees weaken beneath her, and she thought at first that she might faint right there in the living room. Almost in a trance, she withdrew her hand from the doorknob and backed away from the door. This could not be true, she told herself. She was having a nightmare. Not until she bumped against the kitchen door did she gain control of her senses again. *What must I do?* she wondered, knowing that she must do something to help him, but feeling totally helpless. There was only one possible way, she decided, and with no second thoughts, she hurried out the back door.

"Yes, ma'am," the soldier on stable duty replied, finally understanding Molly's gestures. "It's the mousy dun yonder against the rail, ain't it?" She nodded her head. "I'll get her for you. It's kinda late to be goin' for a ride. You want me to throw a saddle on her?" Molly shook her head no. When the private put a bridle on the mare and brought her to the gate, Molly smiled her thanks, stepped up on the fence rail, and jumped over onto the pony's back. Perched there, she waited while the soldier opened the gate.

It was a little more than a mile down the river to the Crow village, and the sun was sinking low by the time she arrived. The Indian women were tending their cook fires, preparing the evening meal. Each one stopped to stare at the young white woman as she rode her pony through the camp, searching right and left as she passed by them.

She could feel the tension tightening her throat as she came to the end of the camp without sighting him. Fighting an attack of panic, she turned her horse around and began to ride back through the scattering of tipis. Then she saw him. Red Hawk had come out of his mother's lodge when he heard the old woman comment that there was a strange white girl riding through the camp.

"Molly," Red Hawk called to her, and walked to meet her. "Why are you here? Are you looking for me?" She nodded anxiously and slid from her pony's back. "What's wrong?" he asked. She made the sign for mountain lion, which he had taught her to make when she referred to Matt. "Slaughter?" Red Hawk responded. Before he could ask another question, she signed *danger*. "Danger," he said. "Slaughter, danger— is Slaughter in trouble?" She nodded. Yes.

There followed a lengthy guessing game, during which several of Red Hawk's friends wandered over to satisfy their curiosity. Soon the spectators joined in the game, watching Molly's frantic attempts to sign out her message, then trying to guess her meaning. Finally, when she was about to give in to her despair, Red Hawk put it all together. "Slaughter in trouble—soldiers come to kill him. You want me to find him, warn him?" She breathed a long, weary sigh and nodded her head slowly with exaggerated motions.

"I go," he said, and prepared to leave at once. In a matter of minutes, he was ready to ride. Before setting out toward the Powder River, he rode with Molly back to the fort, partly to see that she got back safely but also to see if he could find out more about what trouble his friend was in. After escorting her to the surgeon's house, he went to see Seth Ward. Seth usually knew everything that went on around the post, and he did not disappoint on this occasion.

"Seems like your friend killed an army officer back

in Virginia, and Lieutenant O'Connor is headin' out in the mornin' to arrest him."

Red Hawk considered that for a few moments before commenting. "If he killed an officer, the officer musta needed killin'. Too bad." Seeing no need to tell the post trader what he proposed to do, Red Hawk promptly took his leave. His brother, Spotted Horse, had told him where the patrol was heading, so Red Hawk knew where to look for Matt.

Back at the surgeon's dwelling, Martha Riddler looked in the spare room where Molly slept. Molly was not there. "Well, where on earth has she disappeared to?" Martha asked aloud. She was not on the front porch, and not in the kitchen. Martha was about to become concerned when she heard a light footfall on the back-porch steps. She went immediately to see if Molly was all right. "Goodness gracious, child," she said cheerfully, "I didn't know what happened to you." She was about to go on making idle chatter, but the look on Molly's face caused her to pause. "Is something wrong?" Molly shook her head no, but Martha could read the distress in the young girl's eyes. "You heard, didn't you?"

Molly slowly nodded her head, dropping her gaze to her feet. Martha stepped up and put her arm around her young charge's shoulders. "Oh, darlin', you don't seem to get anything but bad news, do you?" Molly raised her head to meet Martha's gaze, her eyes glistening with tears. Martha studied her face before commenting. "Merciful heavens," she sighed. "You really are in love with him, aren't you?" It wasn't necessary for Molly to answer. Martha pulled her close and hugged her tightly. Molly submitted willingly, seeking the comforting shoulder she needed. "You poor girl, you've really got it bad," Martha said. After a few moments, she whispered, "I like him, too. There must be some mistake."

Spotted Horse sat motionless, watching the lone figure as it crossed over a low rise. Still some distance away, the rider had a familiar look about him, and Spotted Horse thought he recognized the paint pony as the one that had once belonged to the hated Sioux war chief Iron Claw. Wondering what would bring his brother riding out this far alone, he remained hidden in the shadow of the cottonwoods. When at last the rider approached close enough to confirm that it was, indeed, Red Hawk, Spotted Horse prodded his pony and moved out into the open grass. Red Hawk, startled by the sudden appearance of a horse and rider, jerked hard on the paint's reins before realizing a second later that it was his brother.

"If I was a Sioux," Spotted Horse shouted, "you would be dead." He rode down the slope to meet Red Hawk. "What are you doing here?"

"I came to warn Slaughter. He's in trouble."

"What do you mean? What trouble?"

"They say he killed a soldier before he came to Fort Laramie. Lieutenant O'Connor is on his way to arrest him before the patrol returns."

Spotted Horse thought about it for a moment. It didn't seem likely that Slaughter would kill one of his own people unless the man deserved it. "Maybe it happened in the great war between the whites."

"Maybe," Red Hawk said. "Where is the patrol?"

Spotted Horse turned to point behind him. "There, on the other side of that ridge. They stopped by War Woman Creek to eat and rest the horses." Turning back and pointing toward the north, he said, "Slaughter is somewhere beyond those hills." With no further discussion, the two Crow brothers set out toward the hills to find him. Like Red Hawk, Spotted Horse never considered Matt's actions, whatever had occurred, to be anything but justified. He had read the courage in Slaughter's eyes. A man like that did not kill without justification.

Matt recognized Red Hawk's paint pony as he watched the two Indians approaching, and he was surprised to see him. When last he had talked to the young warrior, Red Hawk had said he was going to lie around his mother's tipi for a few days and get fat. He gave his horse a gentle nudge with his heels, and the buckskin responded immediately. "I see you found somebody," Matt joked when he pulled up before the two brothers. "He musta got lost to wind up out here."

Ignoring the tease, Red Hawk blurted out, "O'Connor is coming to arrest you! You must run!"

"Whoa!" Matt replied, taken by surprise. "What are you talkin' about? Arrest me for what?"

Red Hawk went on to relate the events as he had discovered them. "The girl, Molly, came to find me," he said. "It was she who heard them talking about you. She heard them say you killed a soldier. A paper came with your name on it, and they're sending Lieutenant O'Connor to get you."

So the day has finally arrived, he thought. Enough time had passed since he'd left Oklahoma Indian Territory to give him a sense that he had been forgotten as far as the army was concerned. Captain Harvey Mathis—that was the officer's name he was supposed to have killed. There had never been a day since that he had regretted taking the blame for his brother's fit of rage that resulted in the Union officer's accidental death. There had been minor thoughts of regret that he was saddled with the unearned label of *murderer*, but he would never have reversed his decision, even if given the choice. Owen had a wife and children, a farm to work in order to provide for them. It would have been a total tragedy for them to lose him. At the time of the incident, Matt had been young and free, with no family to worry about and no desire to work a farm. He honestly thought he could disappear on the western frontier. He had been unconcerned to the extent that he didn't bother to use an assumed name. *Well, I was wrong,* he thought.

"How far behind you?" Matt asked.

"Don't know," Red Hawk answered. "Maybe day, maybe half day—don't know for sure."

Matt didn't say anything more for a few moments while he considered his options. He turned and looked toward the northwest, toward the hills and the Bighorns beyond. He thought of the mountains where he and Ike had spent most of the winter trying to avoid Iron Claw's war parties. Maybe, he thought, it was time for him to move on through the Powder River country, up to the

Yellowstone, and over to Virginia City. His promise to Ike returned to his mind. Could he ever be at peace with himself if he allowed Iron Claw to go unpunished for the brutal murder of his friend? There were other reasons to remain within a few days' ride of Fort Laramie—other promises he had made.

"So Molly went to find you and sent you to warn me?" he said, after his lengthy silence.

"Yes," Red Hawk answered. A wide grin formed on his face, and he added, "She still wanna go with you. I don't think she give a damn how many officers you killed."

Matt's expression remained impassive, although inside he could not deny a definite stirring of his blood. "I don't reckon that'll ever happen," he stated firmly. "I guess I'd best not hang around here much longer. I better be gone when O'Connor gets here."

"Where will you go?" Spotted Horse asked.

"Ain't made up my mind for certain—maybe Montana Territory. Right now, I'm just thinkin' about findin' me a place close by to hole up for a few days till I decide." He looked at Spotted Horse and shook his head in apology. "Tell Lieutenant LeVan that I'm sorry I had to run out on him again."

"I'll tell him."

"Red Hawk, my friend, I'm obliged for the warning. Tell Molly I'm obliged to her, too."

"I will," Red Hawk replied. "You want me to bring her to you? She'll come."

"No! Hell, no!" Matt quickly responded. "I don't

want you to bring her out here. Just tell her I said thanks."

Red Hawk shrugged indifferently. It was his friend's decision to make, but the Crow warrior saw no reason for Matt to be alone when he could have a woman to do for him.

"He what?" Lieutenant LeVan demanded when he overheard Spotted Horse talking to Sergeant Barnes.

Barnes shook his head thoughtfully, then turned to face the lieutenant. "Spotted Horse says Slaughter's took off—says he told him to tell you."

"Jesus Christ!" LeVan fumed. "Again? He's deserted my patrol for the second time?" He was instantly irritated, mainly at himself for misjudging the man. He had just vouched for Matt's character when he lobbied for rehiring him as a scout.

"Looks that way, sir," Barnes replied. He nodded his head toward the Crow scout. "Spotted Horse says you'll know why pretty soon."

"What does he mean by that?"

Barnes was about to ask Spotted Horse when he was suddenly interrupted by a warning call from the picket on the south bank of the creek. "Rider approaching!" It was followed a few minutes later by, "It's Zeb Benson!"

Perplexed as he was upon hearing that Slaughter had quit him again, LeVan put his irritation aside for the moment, replacing it with curiosity about the veteran scout's sudden appearance. He and Barnes turned toward the sentry on the south bank and waited. In a few minutes, the familiar form of Zeb Benson topped the rise beyond the creek and waved an arm once before riding down to cross over.

"Howdy, Lieutenant," Zeb offered in casual greeting, pulling up before LeVan and Barnes.

"What are you doing out this way, Benson?" LeVan asked.

"Lookin' fer you," Zeb replied as he swung a leg over and dismounted. He looked around him, taking in the soldiers at rest. "Looks like you boys ain't workin' too hard. Maybe I could find me a cup of coffee."

"You found me," LeVan said, impatient to hear why Zeb was looking for him, and not willing to wait out the crusty old scout's dallying. "Out with it, man!"

Zeb blinked, surprised by LeVan's departure from his usual lack of emotion. He glanced around him again, searching the bivouac. "Where's Slaughter?" he asked in response.

"He lit out about an hour ago," Sergeant Barnes answered for the lieutenant.

"That's right," LeVan said. "He's gone. Now why were you looking for me? Or did you ride all the way out here just to wonder where Slaughter was?"

Zeb grinned. "As a matter of fact," he said, taking his time in spite of the lieutenant's impatience, "I'd best go back and fetch Lieutenant O'Connor. He's about a mile behind me, with half a dozen soldiers." Zeb had been instructed by O'Connor to remain silent regarding the purpose of his mission so as not to give Slaughter warning. The news that Matt had already gone put his mind at ease, for he had decided to warn him in spite of O'Connor's orders. In the short time he had known

Slaughter, Zeb had come to think of him as a man you could count on. He might have killed an officer in Virginia, like they said. Zeb wasn't concerned about it—didn't care whether he did or did not. Most likely, he had his reasons. After all, Slaughter had worn Confederate gray during the war back east. If Zeb had been back east during the conflict, gray would have been the color he would have worn, too.

He nodded to Spotted Horse and Red Hawk, who were standing aside and watching. Both of the Crow brothers' faces were expressionless, devoid of any sign of emotion. It occurred to Zeb then that Red Hawk had not been with LeVan's patrol when it left Fort Laramie. Understanding immediately, he fixed his gaze upon Red Hawk's face and nodded slightly again. Then he turned back to LeVan. "My orders is to keep my trap shut, find you, and go back to get Lieutenant O'Connor," he said, climbing back into the saddle. "He'll be here directly." With that, he wheeled his horse and went back the way he had come, leaving LeVan shaking his head in bewilderment.

"Tell 'em they can build fires if they want to," LeVan finally said to Sergeant Barnes. "We might as well just stay where we are and wait for O'Connor."

"Yes, sir," Barnes answered.

In a short time there were several small fires crackling with dead cottonwood branches as the men took the opportunity to boil some coffee. LeVan sent Spotted Horse and Red Hawk out to scout the area north of the creek, since that was the most likely direction from which any Sioux war party might come. He didn't expect to encounter any hostile activity because most of the bands had agreed to come in for the peace talks. But he made it a habit to act with caution until he knew for sure there was no need. The ambush he had ridden into in that narrow canyon was still fresh in his mind. He didn't intend to let it happen again. He had lost some men on that day—would have lost a good many more had it not been for the action taken by Slaughter. "Damn!" he swore when reminded of the scout. "How could I have been so wrong about a man?"

Although Zeb Benson had said O'Connor was about a mile behind him, almost an hour passed before the scout returned with the six-man detail and Lieutenant James O'Connor. LeVan got to his feet, emptied the last swallow of coffee from his cup, and waited while they crested the low ridge on the far side of the creek. "What's up, Jim?" he greeted O'Connor.

"Fred." O'Connor returned the greeting, looking anxiously about, expecting to spot Slaughter. Zeb had not deemed it necessary to inform the lieutenant that the man he had come to arrest had already departed. Not seeing Slaughter, O'Connor dismounted. "I've been ordered to arrest your man Slaughter, and take him back to Fort Laramie to stand trial," he stated.

"Stand trial?" Levan exclaimed. "For what?"

"Murder," O'Connor replied. "Back east in Virginia—he killed a U.S. Army officer in a scuffle over some land or something." He continued to look around him, searching for the fugitive. "Anyway, I was sent to get him. Where is he?"

"Well, no damn wonder . . ." LeVan muttered, realizing that it had been no coincidence that Slaughter had deserted just before Red Hawk appeared. He almost laughed at the irony of it, knowing how much Jim O'Connor disliked the young scout. Seeing O'Connor's puzzled expression as he waited for an answer, LeVan rubbed his chin thoughtfully and replied, "Looks like you're too late. I was just told no more than an hour or so ago that Mr. Slaughter has deserted the column. Unless I miss my guess, I expect he's heading straight into Sioux country."

"Damn the luck!" O'Connor swore. "The murdering son of a bitch's luck is gonna run out pretty soon, and I aim to be right there when it does."

"Well, he's gone from here. What are you planning to do? Go into hostile territory after him?"

"Damn right I am!" O'Connor exclaimed. "I aim to see that man in irons."

"With six men?" LeVan replied.

O'Connor looked surprised. "With your patrol we'll have twenty-one and scouts."

LeVan reacted immediately. "Oh, no, mister. This is as far as this patrol is going. We're heading back to Laramie. I'm already farther north than I was ordered to go."

"Under the circumstances," O'Connor sputtered, "I think my orders would supersede yours."

"Like hell they would. I'm not taking a column this size into that country. Dammit, Jim, we almost got our asses fried with a lot more troops than we've got here— or don't you remember that little fracas over by the Powder?"

O'Connor flushed slightly at the mention of that ill-fated patrol. He was still smarting from the display of panic he had suffered. "The man murdered an officer," he protested weakly. "My orders are to bring him back to Laramie for trial."

"Look, Jim," LeVan said, his tone deadly serious now, "I know how much you hate Slaughter. But taking a small patrol into the Powder River country isn't a healthy thing to do right now—and it damn sure isn't a wise one."

O'Connor's flush deepened, this time fueled by anger as it began to sink in that Slaughter was going to get away. There was no uncertainty in LeVan's tone. If he was going to try to follow Slaughter, it was going to be with no more than the six men he'd brought with him. Deep down, he was reluctant to venture into hostile territory with so few, but he registered one last feeble protest. "The Sioux have already sent word that they're coming in to talk. They won't attack a patrol now."

LeVan shook his head slowly back and forth, as if confronting an unruly child. "Tell that to the folks we just buried back there." He paused for a moment, watching O'Connor's silent battle with himself. Then he made the decision for him. "We'll sit here a little longer, so your men can have a chance to have some coffee and rest the horses. Then we'll start back to Laramie."

"Begging your pardon, sir," Sergeant Barnes said. "There ain't a whole lot of daylight left, and we've got good water here—might be a good idea to go ahead and camp right where we are. If I recollect, there ain't no water for a good ways back the way we come."

LeVan thought about it. He squinted up at the cloudless sky for a few moments before deciding. "Maybe you're right, Sergeant." He paused for a moment more. "All right." He finally gave the order. "Tell the men to make camp—but, Barnes, get the scouts out."

"Yes, sir," Barnes replied, and went to tell the men.

Turning his attention back to O'Connor, LeVan said, "If you want to take your detail and go looking for Slaughter, it's your decision to make. We'll be right here till morning. But at sunup I'm heading back to Laramie."

O'Connor had no real desire to venture deeper into Sioux country without LeVan's support, but he again protested. "Dammit, Fred, my orders were to arrest Slaughter and bring him back. How's it gonna look if I don't do that?"

LeVan was weary of the discussion. He was rather sharp in his reply. "Your orders were to intercept my patrol and arrest Slaughter. If he isn't riding with my patrol, you can't be expected to arrest him. Your orders didn't say to chase him all over hell and back, did they? You did what you were ordered to do. Slaughter's gone—nothing you can do about it." He watched O'Connor's reaction for a few moments. "Dammit, man, it's damn near dark already, and I doubt you could find him in broad daylight if he didn't want to be found." He shrugged and sighed. "Cheer up. The Sioux will probably kill him."

Separated from the patrol by a good five miles and two steep ridges, Matt guided the buckskin into a stand of pines that crowned a low ledge overlooking a sharp bend in the river below. It had been his intention to cross over to the other side of the river and continue up into the Bighorn Mountains—thinking to possibly find one of the old camps that he and Ike Brister had used. That plan was delayed, however, by the necessity to avoid riding up on two Sioux scouts who were watering their ponies near the lower end of the ledge. Not certain that the two Indians had not seen him, he drew his rifle just in case he had to defend himself. But the warriors' attention had been focused on a couple of antelope some fifty yards downstream. He took the opportunity to slip into the trees before they became aware of his presence.

After tying his horse to a pine bough, he made his way down to the edge of the ledge, where he had a clear view of the two hostiles. *I hope to hell you two aren't going to linger there all day,* he thought. He had to assume that O'Connor would be tracking him, and he preferred not to waste any more time than necessary. The two scouts appeared to be in no hurry, however, and were evidently not tempted to stalk the antelope. *Well, I can't sit here much longer,* he decided after watching them for almost half an hour. There was no other choice but to backtrack and go around them. He was about to make that decision when he saw the war party appear at the top of a slope about a quarter mile from the river.

One of the scouts below him jumped on his pony's back, rode out onto an open flat beside the river, and wheeled the pony around in a circle, waving a rifle over his head. He continued until he got a response from the slope. The war party proceeded down the slope, heading directly toward the scouts.

Well, that's just grand, Matt thought. *They're heading right for me.* He took a moment to consider his options. He could go back the way he had come and take a chance on meeting a patrol led by Lieutenant O'Connor. He could backtrack a quarter mile or so and make a wide circle to avoid the war party. The problem with the second option was that he was presently holed up in the only spot that offered real concealment. Even if he made a wide circle, there was the chance that he might be spotted before he reached the cottonwoods that grew along the river, even in the fading light. *Of course, I could just take off straight north till I strike the Yellowstone, but I don't know what's between here and the Yellowstone.* According to what Spotted Horse had told him, there were several large Sioux villages in that area. After no more than a few seconds' thought, he decided to stay put and let the Sioux war party pass—and hope none of the warriors would find any reason to ride up through the stand of pines.

That's too damn big to be a hunting party, he thought, as the line of warriors descended the slope and approached the shallow river crossing. He did a quick count and estimated the party to be at least a hundred strong—all wearing paint and stripped down for battle. He didn't have to guess what their objective was. He figured that the two scouts had probably been following LeVan's column of soldiers and were waiting to guide the war party to them.

He shifted his body slightly when he felt a pine root

pressing against his stomach. When he looked back at the advancing war party, he suddenly tensed. There was no mistaking the hawk-faced warrior who rode up to take the lead. *Iron Claw—I should have known,* he thought. Images of Ike Brister's mangled body hanging between two trees came rushing back to fill his mind. He reached back and clutched his rifle, his first thought being to rid the world of the evil savage. Bringing the Henry up to bear on the unsuspecting warriors, he settled the front sight squarely upon the chest of the menacing war chief. For a long moment, he fought to maintain his self-control as he held the sights on his target. His finger, resting lightly on the trigger, seemed to go numb, losing all sense of touch. In less than a heartbeat, it could be over. Ike Brister's killer could be sent to hell with only an ounce more pressure from his trigger finger. Fate stepped in to intervene, though, for in that moment of indecision, Lame Deer pulled up beside Iron Claw, blocking Matt's line of sight. This was the second time he had had the murdering savage dead in his sights and failed to pull the trigger.

He lowered the rifle slowly until it rested upon a small rock before him as a cool head replaced the fury that had seized him a moment before. That one shot might have settled the score for Ike, but it would have surely brought the entire war party down upon him— and hundred-to-one odds meant certain death, even to a man with a Yellow Boy Henry rifle.

There'll be other chances, Ike. I'll see to it. With that solemn promise, he backed a few inches away from the rim of the ledge and watched the war party approach.

Within seconds, the riverbank below him was filled with ponies crowding each other for water. Amid the noise of the grunting, snorting ponies, the snort of curiosity that came from his own horse in the trees behind him went unnoticed by the throng of warriors. After a quick glance toward the thicket where he had tied the buckskin, Matt returned his gaze to the milling swarm below him. He watched as Iron Claw consulted with the two scouts who had awaited him. Pushing his horse up through the mob of ponies, a rider joined in the parlay with the scouts. At first glance, Matt thought it was a white man dressed in buckskins. Upon closer observation, he decided the man was most likely a half-breed. The name Jack Black Dog instantly struck his mind. Iron Claw paused briefly to listen when the breed spoke, registering a deep scowl upon his face that seemed to imply irritation. Then with a toss of his head, the war chief dismissed the breed's comments and resumed his parlay with the two scouts.

Watching the animated conversation and the many gestures toward the direction he had come from, Matt confirmed what he had figured—the scouts were telling Iron Claw about the army patrol he had just deserted. *Uh-oh,* he thought. *LeVan's patrol is in for a helluva surprise.* There was no doubt in his mind that the Sioux war party meant business. At least one hundred strong, they were painted for war, and LeVan was leading a fifteen-man patrol. Matt had no idea how many men O'Connor could add to the total, but it was unlikely his detail was more than fifteen. Upon further observation, Matt realized that the war party was well armed, with more than half carrying rifles of various makes, most of them single-shot, although he spotted several Sharps cavalry carbines. *I sure as hell don't have to worry about O'Connor now,* he thought. *He's going to be up to his ass in redskins.* The thought of the arrogant young lieutenant surrounded by a horde of screaming savages brought a modicum of satisfaction, he had to admit. But there was not a moment of indecision on his part when it came to his moral duty. There were also innocent lives to consider, one of which was that of Lieutenant LeVan. He was just going to have to take a chance on being able to warn the soldiers without being taken prisoner himself—by O'Connor or Iron Claw. There was a chance that he might lead the hostiles away from the army column if he used himself as bait—and if he could eventually lose them, he could get back to LeVan and warn him. The big buckskin gelding had demonstrated his power and stamina several times before this. With a sizable enough lead on the swift Indian ponies, Matt was confident that Ike could hold his own for an indefinite time.

The only question before him now was how much time he had before the column arrived. If O'Connor was coming after him, they might not be far behind, riding right into Iron Claw's war party. With that thought to worry him, he backed away from the ledge and retreated to the pines where he had left his horse. Untying the buckskin, he led the horse up through the pines toward the top of the ridge where the trees thinned out. Crossing the crest of the ridge, he paused to take a quick look behind, expecting to see Sioux scouts appear at any minute. He could still hear the war party, but they were evidently still watering their ponies. He took another moment to stroke the big buckskin's neck before climbing up in the saddle. "Ike, boy, don't let me down now," he said, addressing the gelding by the name he had given him. Before him, he faced nothing but open prairie with no apparent cover for several miles. Off to the northeast, there was a line of low hills. He decided that he would try to lure the Indians in that direction. At least there was no cavalry patrol in sight as yet. Glancing at the sky then, he realized that the light was fading fast. It would not be long before the prairie would be cloaked in darkness. *One hour before hard dark,* he thought, wishing it was less. He patted the buckskin's neck again as he climbed into the saddle. It was going to be a race.

Holding the horse to an easy walk, he started down the east side of the ridge. His intention was to go easy on him until he was discovered by the war party, hoping to get as much distance as he could before calling on Ike to run for it. Once he had descended the slope, still without any sign of the war party, he kicked up the pace a notch, letting the buckskin lope comfortably through the tall spring grass, taking an occasional look behind him. The minutes passed, each one gaining additional ground as he increased his lead. He figured he had put almost half a mile behind him when he heard the first distant cry of alarm. The race was on. "All right, boy," he said softly. "They've spotted us—it's up to you now."

*   *   *

"There!" Two Bears shouted to the warriors behind him and pointed toward the distant figure fleeing in the fading light. "A scout!"

Iron Claw pulled up beside him and scowled as he stared after the rapidly disappearing figure. It angered him that the war party had been discovered before he could strike the soldier column. "After him!" he ordered immediately. "We have to catch him before he gets back to warn the soldiers! He must have followed our scouts back to us." He glanced accusingly at the two young warriors who had scouted the column of troopers.

"The scouts said the soldiers were camped on War Woman Creek," Jack Black Dog said, "not in the direction that man is riding."

Iron Claw jerked his head around to glare at the half-breed. He didn't like Jack Black Dog, primarily because of his impure blood but also because he traveled freely among the white people. He didn't trust the breed, and he was always inclined to question anything Jack Black Dog told him. He was further irritated by Jack Black Dog's incessant whining about the white girl's rescue from Iron Claw's tipi. Jack Black Dog had wanted the girl. Iron Claw had no use for her, and would have killed her but for the satisfaction he derived from knowing of Jack Black Dog's lust for her. "It is obvious that the soldiers have left War Woman Creek, and are now somewhere north of there." He held Ike's Spencer high over his head and motioned toward the galloping horse in the distance. "After him!"

"You're making a mistake," Jack Black Dog insisted.

"He's just leading us off somewhere so the soldiers will have time to get away."

Iron Claw's eyes blazed with anger as he told the insolent half-breed, "Go where you choose! You are no longer welcome here." He wheeled his pony and started out after the white man at a full gallop.

Feeling the sting of Iron Claw's rebuff, Jack Black Dog's temper flared, and had it not been for the condemning glances of the warriors who filed out after the angry war chief, he might have been tempted to put a bullet in Iron Claw's back. *There may be other times,* he thought as he watched the huge war party ride away without him. *There are other villages,* he said to himself, and turned his pony toward the west. As he rode away, his thoughts returned to the young white girl. She was rightfully his. Iron Claw had had no right to keep her. He had delivered the girl's parents to Iron Claw's war party, and this had been his reward. Feeling betrayed, he thought about the girl's fragile being, and the milky white skin he had caught glimpses of beneath her skirt. He was obsessed with thoughts of knowing her entire body. It was a pleasure he had promised himself when he had first led Franklin Lyons out of Fort Laramie. It was an obsession he had no intention of abandoning.

Chapter 11

The broad-chested buckskin gelding seemed to sense the importance of the race he ran. Matt bent low over the big horse's neck, leaning forward to balance his weight over Ike's withers as he sped across the prairie. Ike felt solid under him, his hooves pounding a relentless beat upon the prairie floor, never breaking stride over gullies or rises. Flying so recklessly over the ground, their flight could come to a fatal ending with the sudden appearance of a prairie dog hole, for there was no time for caution. Behind them, the war party had taken up the chase, and when Matt looked back, it seemed like the entire Sioux nation was coming after him. Looking ahead, he wondered if he had overestimated the buckskin's ability, for the hills he sought refuge in now appeared farther away than he had first thought. Still the big horse answered the call, his hooves pounding the grassy plain in steady rhythm with the solid beat of his lungs taking air in measured breaths. The buckskin gelding had never before been pushed to the limit of his capacity. *This might be the day,* Matt thought.

At last there appeared to be some progress in cutting down the distance, for the hills began to inch closer to him. Looking back periodically, he determined that Ike was holding his own with the Indian ponies—with two exceptions. Two of the warriors were racing out in front of the others and were gradually gaining on him. Matt looked ahead toward the hills again. It was hard to guess whether he would be able to reach them before the two warriors closed the gap. Everything depended upon the buckskin's stamina. He couldn't say how long the horse had been running at full gallop—maybe four or five minutes. It seemed longer, and he feared Ike might founder if he didn't let up soon. He felt sure the buckskin could last as long as the ponies chasing him, even though he carried the extra weight of saddle and pack.

He heard the crack of a rifle, followed almost immediately by a second shot. Although the bullets fell short of the galloping buckskin, they told Matt that the two warriors were closing within range of their rifles. "Come on, boy," he whispered softly, "just stay with it." The horse seemed to respond to his encouragement, reaching out with his neck on each stride as if pulling the hills to them. Another rifle shot rang out behind him. This time a puff of dirt jumped up beside him. The quick Indian ponies had pulled within rifle range.

Soon the two warriors would be raining a steady shower of lead upon him, and there was no place to take cover. Out on the open plain, he was totally exposed and at their mercy. Still the buckskin chewed away at the distance, his head bobbing slightly with each stride. Suddenly Matt felt a stinging blow as a bullet ripped through his shirt and creased his shoulder. "Come on, boy," he pleaded, wondering if the warrior's next shot would cut center. But the next shot fell short again.

He looked back to see one of the warriors suddenly pull up and stop. Seconds later, the other one did the same. Some one hundred yards behind them, the rest of the war party began to slow as well, and Matt realized that the buckskin had won. "Hod damn!" he blurted out. "You did it! You ran the bastards right into the ground. I ain't never been so proud of a horse in my whole life."

He pulled back on the reins until Ike settled into an easy lope, and they continued toward the hills, which were now looming up before them, the first one no more than two or three hundred yards away. He heard several rifle shots sing out in frustration as the powerful horse, still blowing and gasping for air, gained the cover of the trees that formed a dark ring around the base of the hill. As soon as he was out of sight of his pursuers, he slid off of Ike's back and started up the slope on foot, leading the horse. He had not had time until that moment to take a look at the slash on his shoulder where the bullet had grazed him. In spite of a slight stinging, he deemed it not worthy of wasting time, and continued up the slope.

Willing at first, the big buckskin followed for a few yards, then hesitated, his powerful lungs laboring for air. Matt paused, puzzled by the horse's reluctance to continue. "What is it, boy?" he wondered as the horse stopped, head down with his muzzle almost touching the ground. As Matt watched, bewildered, Ike pulled his back legs up under him as if trying to take weight off his front legs, while still grunting for air. Horrified, Matt realized that the buckskin could not breathe.

He looked back toward the prairie. The Sioux war party was still following him, walking their ponies after the unsuccessful attempt to overtake him. He figured he had a quarter of an hour's leeway at best. He glanced up toward the tops of the trees. Long shadows had now vanished, replaced by a solid gloom in the pines where he stood. The sun had long since departed, leaving the forest in total darkness. Turning back to his disabled mount, he tried to soothe the stricken animal. "Come on, boy," he pleaded, holding Ike's head in his arms. "Take it easy. It'll come." The buckskin rolled his eyes, confused and frightened. Matt knew at that moment that the big gelding was finished. He had broken his lungs. Still Matt was reluctant to admit it. He was at a loss as to what he should do to help Ike. He quickly loosened the girth strap and pulled the saddle off. Ike gazed at him with wide and mournful eyes. Seconds later, the horse's knees buckled and he went down on his chest.

"Get up, boy," Matt pleaded. "You gotta stay up on your feet." He knew that once the horse went down, he was finished. With no time to waste, he tried to pull the horse back up, but his efforts were to no avail. Ike was foundering, suffocating from lack of breath. The gelding had given his all, everything he had in him, and Matt was sickened by the thought of losing him and the heartbreaking choice left to him.

"I'm sorry, boy," he said, pulling his pistol. Holding

the weapon next to the horse's head, he hesitated, reluctant to pull the trigger. The two of them had been through so much together, it was almost too much for him to bear, but Ike was suffering. Over his shoulder, he heard the war party approaching the foot of the hill. There was no more time. The buckskin had given his life to outrun the Indian ponies. It would be a senseless waste of the big horse's sacrifice if Matt allowed himself to be caught now. He pulled the trigger.

Taking only what he had to have to survive, mainly his rifle and cartridges, his bow and quiver, he hurriedly looked around for a place to hide his saddle. He was not afforded the luxury of a lot of time, but he didn't like the idea of leaving his saddle for the hostiles to find. The only place that offered any potential was a shallow gully that cut a groove between two boulders. He didn't hesitate, throwing the saddle as far as he could manage into the deepening shadows. *Maybe they won't see it in the dark,* he thought. Then with nothing but his weapons and flint and steel, he set off up through the pines, pausing briefly only once to try to set the place in his memory. *I'll play hell trying to find this place again,* he couldn't help thinking. *I might have just thrown my saddle away.*

Arriving at the bottom of the slope, Iron Claw directed his war party to spread out and proceed with caution. He had witnessed on too many occasions the danger in charging recklessly after the white devil with the gun that never rested. There was no doubt that this scout they had chased across the prairie was the very devil who had killed many of his people. He was certain, after hearing Rising Moon's description of him, that it was also the same devil who had blatantly walked into his tipi and taken the white girl. Iron Claw was tormented by the thought that the white man could continue to frustrate him. The man they now chased could be no other. He recognized the big buckskin horse the white man rode. Igmutaka, some had named him. Mountain lion. Iron Claw could almost feel the mountain lion's rifle being trained upon him from somewhere in the darkness above him. The sensation caused no fear in the war chief's heart, only anger—anger at the realization that the white man had led the war party away from the army patrol, anger that he had not listened to his own scouts, with no choice but to chase after the hated white man instead, and anger because the irritating half-breed, Jack Black Dog, had warned him that he was being led in the wrong direction. He knew that he must not fail in killing the white Igmutaka to prove that his medicine was stronger than that of the hated white man. Already aware of some muted comments from a few of the warriors, expressing doubts concerning their leader's medicine, he was desperate in his resolve. If Igmutaka escaped this time—and killed more of his warriors—the village might lose all confidence in him. His thoughts were interrupted by a cry of discovery in the darkened forest.

"Here!" a warrior cried out. "Here is his horse!"

Iron Claw hurried to follow the voice. Upon arriving at the dead gelding, Iron Claw's heart immediately soared. *He is on foot!* "Comb these trees," he commanded.

"He cannot have gotten far." He divided his war party into three groups, directing one third to search the woods around the right side of the hill, one third to search around the left, and the rest, led by himself, to search straight up toward the top. With so many warriors, he felt confident that they would flush their quarry.

No more than seventy-five yards above the mass of warriors, weaving his way slowly through the trees, Matt climbed up through the pines and rocks. Moving at a trot whenever the slope permitted, he dared not stop to catch his breath. Below him, he could clearly hear the shouts as one warrior yelled something to another. They had already found the buckskin's carcass. He had to move fast, but his progress was impeded somewhat by the necessity to carry a rifle and all of his extra cartridges, and further hampered by the bow and quiver slung on his back by the bowstring.

Suddenly the pines ended, and he found himself in a meadow at the top of the hill. Moving steadily upward, breathing hard from the exertion, he left the cover of the trees. It was fully dark now, for which he was truly thankful. Without pause, he headed straight up to the top of the hill, anxious to cross over to the opposite side and feeling vulnerable to a shot from the trees below him—even though it was a moonless night and he would be very hard to see from any distance at all.

Once he gained the very top of the hill, he paused only briefly to look back on the meadow behind him. He couldn't be sure, but it didn't appear that the war party had worked their way through the trees as yet. He hurried down the other side, almost at a trot, afraid of taking a tumble if he tried to go any faster. Upon reaching the ring of trees again, he had to slow to a walk in order to see where he was going.

The slope was steep, the ground beneath the pines matted with pine needles, making the footing treacherous in places. As a result, he was forced to be more careful in the darkness. Being more careful meant more time, and he worried that his pursuers might gain on him. His hope was that he could leave the war party searching around the hills for him in the dark while he struck out across the prairie on foot. He still had it in his mind to warn Lieutenant LeVan. He desperately needed a horse, but he felt he had no choice but to make an attempt on foot to reach the patrol before morning. As near as he could figure, War Woman Creek was probably around thirty miles away.

About to leave the cover of the trees, he was suddenly stopped by a sound to his right. Cocking his head to listen, he tried to identify the rustling noises, realizing an instant later that it was the sound of many warriors moving through the brush near the bottom of the slope. Another moment passed and he heard the same sound off to his left. *They've already circled the base of the hill!* He had not expected them to cover the distance so quickly. In a few minutes, if he remained where he was, they would converge on him. He didn't like his chances in a footrace on the open prairie, so he reconsidered making a run for it. The only way open to him was to go back up the slope. If he could get to the clearing again before the rest of the war party came up from the other side, there was a chance that he could move across the ridge to the adjoining hill.

He didn't wait to explore further options. Back up through the pines he ran, taking the steep slope in long, powerful strides. When he reached the meadow above the tree line again, he paused, gasping to fill his lungs with air. With no hostiles in sight, he forced his aching legs to sprint along the ridge to the second in the line of hills. Over a grassy knob, dotted with small boulders, he sprinted until he reached the cover of a thick clump of sage. Unable to push his weary legs farther without rest, he dropped down on the ground long enough to calm his breathing. While he knelt there, his lungs straining for air, he heard Iron Claw's warriors as they reached the top of the hill behind him. He tensed, preparing to run again, but the hostiles continued over the top of the hill and down the slope, just as he had at first. They were on foot, which told him that their horses had been left at the bottom of the first hill. *Too damn far away for me to try to work back and steal one of them,* he thought.

Feeling like a fox with a pack of hounds after him, he got up again and ran farther along the ridge. At this point, he decided to change his plan. Instead of trying to get to War Woman Creek to warn the soldiers, he would find a place to hide. It was obvious to him now that Iron Claw was determined to track him down, so the longer he could keep the warriors occupied with searching for him, the better the chances that the soldiers would be long gone. *Unless,* he reminded himself, *Lieutenant O'Connor is still hell-bent on coming after me.*

*   *   *

"He is gone from here," Gray Bull said after searching every bush on the hill. It had been hours since they had seen the white scout disappear in the trees. "Maybe there is some truth in what some say about the white mountain lion's medicine."

"Nonsense!" Iron Claw retorted angrily. "He is here. He must have slipped by us and crossed over to the next ridge." There was already too much grumbling among the warriors that too much time had been wasted on this one man—that while they stumbled around in the dark, the army patrol might be getting away, and with them, the opportunity to capture guns and ammunition. "We must pay homage to the memory of our brothers who have been killed by this man," Iron Claw insisted.

Lame Deer said nothing for a few moments, but he agreed with Gray Bull. The white man had obviously managed to slip by them, and they might spend the rest of the night trying to find him in these hills. He was reluctant, however, to question Iron Claw's wisdom. Finally he spoke his opinion. "What Gray Bull says may be true. I say we should forget this white devil and attack the soldiers before it is too late."

"He is here," Iron Claw insisted. "He must have crossed the ridge back there." He pointed toward the ridge bridging the two slopes. Realizing that he was losing the confidence of his warriors, he offered a compromise. "We will search that hill. If he is not found, then we will give up."

Lame Deer saw the anger in Iron Claw's eyes, even in the dark. "I will go back and get my pony, and circle around to the edge of the hills to make sure he does not come out on the other side."

Two Kills spoke up. "I'll go with Lame Deer."

Upon reaching the bottom of the second slope and the edge of the trees, Matt paused before heading out across the open prairie. He looked up at the deep sky hanging over the rolling land, a dark canopy sprinkled with a million tiny stars, but no moon. He took a moment more to make sure of his bearings. Confident of the direction, he started out, then abruptly stopped when a solitary Lakota warrior suddenly appeared out of the darkness.

Matt instinctively dropped to one knee. His rifle ready, he remained stone still, uncertain if the rider had seen him at the edge of the trees. When the Sioux showed no sign of having spotted him, but continued to slow-walk his pony along the tree line, Matt started to cock his rifle. He needed a horse, and fate had provided one. Having second thoughts then, he carefully laid his rifle down beside him and took his bow from his back. *No need to bring the rest of the party down on me,* he thought.

Moving silently to a better position on the other side of a small pine, he notched an arrow and drew it back. Once again, he had to pause when another rider appeared, following the first. With no choice but to remain still right where he was, with his rifle on the ground on the other side of the tree, he watched anxiously, wondering how many more warriors were following. When the second rider passed by, trailing the first along the edge of the trees, Matt moved back to pick up his rifle, thinking he might have a passel of Indians on his hands within a few minutes. Once again it was time for decisions. He considered the wisdom in retreating into the forest to try to find a place to hide, and if necessary, to stand off the war party. Or should he continue with his original thought, to set out on the open prairie on foot? If that was his decision, it was absolutely critical that he should slip through the Sioux scouts circling the hill without being detected. He didn't like the idea of being chased by a hundred hostiles, like a hare running from a pack of hounds, even in the dark. Equally unattractive was the picture of being surrounded by the same mob of warriors in the pine forest. *I need a horse.* The thought hammered away at his brain.

As the second Sioux rider faded into the darkness, Matt waited. When, after a considerable lapse of time, no more riders appeared, he realized that there were only two to contend with. There was no longer any decision to be made. He needed a horse. The only problem was that he had to do it quietly without alerting the main war party. With his rifle in one hand and his bow in the other, he started out after the two scouts.

Lame Deer reined his pony back, unsure if he had heard something moving in the trees. Listening, he squinted his eyes, trying to look into the dark woods, wondering if he should call out to Two Kills, some thirty yards before him. He waited while Two Kills faded into the darkness ahead. After a few moments more, he decided it was nothing. He had just started to nudge his pony forward when he thought he heard the sound of something running behind him. Too late, he turned to look as Matt vaulted up on the horse's back behind him. Before he could defend himself, he was locked in a powerful death embrace with his head jerked violently backward and his throat laid open with one vicious slash of a skinning knife.

Matt continued to hold the dying warrior until he felt the life drain from his body. Then he released him to slide off onto the ground at the pony's feet. Startled, the horse sidestepped away from the body. Matt held it firmly with the reins, calming the frightened animal with his hand. The pony recovered in seconds, responding obediently when Matt turned it and rode back a dozen yards to retrieve his rifle and bow. He had the horse he needed, but there was still the matter of the other scout.

Two Kills was not sure. It had sounded like a low grunt and then nothing more. He reined his pony to a stop and waited, listening to see if the sound was repeated. He turned his pony and started back to meet Lame Deer. In a moment, he saw the horse and rider materialize in the darkness. Lame Deer appeared to be sitting unusually upright on his pony's back, as if straining forward in an effort to see in the dark. In the next second, as the two horses converged, he suddenly realized that the figure was not that of Lame Deer. It was the white Igmutaka, with bowstring fully drawn, the arrow aimed directly at him. In that terrible moment Two Kills had no time to react. The arrow struck him full in the chest. At such close range, the force drove the arrowhead all the way through and left it protruding out of his back. Stunned, he was helpless to act beyond grabbing for his pony's mane to try to remain upright. His rifle dropped harmlessly to the ground. The cruel shaft of the arrow felt as large as a tree limb, tearing at his ribs and organs. He tried to cry out a warning, but could not speak. As the two ponies passed, Matt reached out and shoved the mortally wounded Two Kills off the horse's back. Pulling his pony to a halt then, he turned around and returned to finish off the dying man.

Two Kills attempted to get up on his hands and knees, but each movement of his body produced excruciating stabs of pain as the arrow shaft tore at his insides. He had managed to crawl no more than a few feet before the white scout was standing over him. He sank back to the ground, helpless to resist his passage into the spirit world. Looking up at Matt, he whispered through bloody lips, "Igmutaka," and waited for the end. One quick slash across the Lakota's throat, and his suffering was over.

Matt shook his head in apology as he watched the last breath escape. "Sorry I couldn't have put a bullet in your brain," he said softly. "It'da been quicker, but I couldn't chance the noise." Getting to his feet, he looked down at the body. "Igmutaka," he repeated. He had heard the word before. Then he remembered— igmutaka, mountain lion. It was the name Cooter Martin had said the Sioux had given him.

Once he was certain the warrior was dead, he wasted no more time. He jumped back on Lame Deer's horse, but then hesitated in a moment of indecision. He could feel the strong muscles of the Indian pony beneath him, ready to respond to his command. And thoughts of his own survival surfaced in his mind. *I don't owe that patrol a damn thing,* he thought. After all, he reasoned, he had led Iron Claw's warriors in a chase that had surely given the soldiers ample time to get out of harm's way. *I've got my own butt to look out for.* He turned the pony to face the east, looking along the line of low hills. There couldn't be more than an hour or two of darkness left. *Ah, hell,* he thought, *if it was just O'Connor . . .* He left the thought to trail off behind him, and turned the pony back toward the south.

He caught up the reins of Two Kills' pony and, leading it, started out across the darkened prairie. He drove the horses hard, his uppermost priority to put as much distance as possible between himself and the large war party combing the hills behind him. LeVan's patrol had been resting at War Woman Creek when Matt had left them. In all likelihood they had moved on, but since he couldn't guess where they might have headed, he set out straight for the creek. It was his hope that the patrol had already turned around and headed for home. If not, daylight would find them facing about one hundred angry Sioux warriors.

Reasonably sure that he couldn't miss the creek if he rode straight south, he pushed on, riding as fast as he could for as long as he could. He rode through the waning darkness until the horse began to weary. Then he changed over to the other horse, took the bridle from Lame Deer's pony, and left the exhausted horse behind. In less than a mile, he determined that, of the two, this was by far the stronger pony, and he was glad then that he had saved it till last, for this would be the horse he would keep. A paint like the horse he took from Iron Claw, his new mount was broad-chested and solid. Whether or not it would prove to be a worthy replacement for the buckskin was another matter. He had no desire to complain. It sure beat walking.

Sunup found him crossing a wide, flat meadow that led up to what he was certain was War Woman Creek. However, he wasn't sure if the army patrol was upstream or downstream. While he tried to decide which way to go, he walked the paint up to the creek to drink. He reminded himself that it was entirely probable that the cavalry patrol had moved on and was no longer at the creek at all. He hoped for their sake that was the case, but since he had come this far, he'd might as well be sure.

Chapter 12

"Dammit, Jim, why don't you forget about the man?" Lieutenant Fred LeVan exclaimed, exasperated with his fellow officer.

Lieutenant O'Connor struck a defiant pose, his prominent jaw jutting out to match the petulant frown on his face. "I've got my orders," he insisted. "Slaughter's a murdering savage, and I intend to see him in irons."

"I told you last night that I'm going back to Laramie this morning," LeVan reminded him. "You're a damn fool if you go looking for him with no more than six men." He glanced at Zeb Benson, who was standing close enough to eavesdrop on the conversation between the two officers. "What are the scouts reporting, Benson?"

Zeb nodded his head several times as if priming his vocal cords to act. "Lot of sign," he finally replied. "They said there's been a heap of Injuns in these parts—most likely huntin' parties." He watched O'Connor's face for his reaction, then added, "Spotted Horse said they ain't cut no sign of a shod horse, if you're a'-thinkin' Slaughter's still around."

O'Connor made no reply for a few moments while he studied the craggy scout's face. Finally, he shook his head, disgusted. "I don't know why you all seem so damned determined to let that murderer go free," he said. "Well, I've got my orders, and I intend to carry them out."

"Lots of sign meaning lots of Sioux, and no shod horse." LeVan repeated Zeb's comments. "How do you expect to find Slaughter when you have no idea where to look for him?"

O'Connor began to realize how ludicrous his intentions were, and consequently how stupid he must appear to the men. He tried to extricate himself from the embarrassing situation he had insisted upon stumbling into. "I just think I want to satisfy myself that he has indeed vanished into Indian territory. I'll have a little look around before I give up."

"Suit yourself," LeVan said as O'Connor did an about-face and strode off to join his six-man detail. He noted the look on Zeb Benson's face. The old scout didn't look any too pleased with O'Connor's decision.

"Want me to mount 'em up?" Sergeant Barnes asked as soon as O'Connor had crossed the creek.

LeVan just stared at the sergeant for a long moment while he made up his mind. O'Connor was too damn stubborn for his own good. It might teach him a lesson if he got his ass chased back to the fort by a bunch of bloodthirsty hostiles. Still, LeVan felt responsible to the men in O'Connor's detail. "Ah, hell," he replied at last, "we'll wait around here for a couple more hours before we start back." *Maybe the damn fool will satisfy his ego by then and come on back,* he thought.

"Damn!" Matt swore when he saw the thin veil of smoke that betrayed the presence of the cavalry patrol. They were still encamped on the bank of the creek. *They should have been gone,* he thought, unless they remained because of him. O'Connor probably brought orders for LeVan to assist him in his search. From the look of the smoke that lay lightly in the cottonwoods, he could guess that the patrol was in bivouac. He realized that if he simply rode in to warn them of the Sioux war party heading their way, he would more than likely be placed in irons for his trouble, and he had no intention of letting that happen. Instead, he would try to find Red Hawk or Spotted Horse.

Moving up the creek to a position a hundred yards or so from the bivouac, he dismounted and tied his horse in the trees. Then he made his way along the creek bank on foot until he could see the soldiers taking their ease around their tiny fires. He paused then to look over the camp. There were sentries posted. He could see the picket posted closest to him, sitting with his back against the trunk of a tree, evidently focusing upon the camp in case Sergeant Barnes started his way. *It's a damn good thing I'm not Iron Claw,* he thought. *I could walk right into this camp before they even knew I was here.* He wondered if the scouts were out. His desperate ride across the prairie to warn the soldiers might have been unnecessary if LeVan had scouts out between here and the hills to the north. But from the looks of the lounging troopers, he thought he could dismiss that possibility.

Leaving the clump of berry bushes he had used for cover, he moved closer up the bank, to within forty yards of the picket. The soldier still showed no sign of awareness. Matt knelt in the dark sand, searching. Then he spotted what he was looking for. A short distance from the soldiers, Red Hawk sat next to a large cottonwood, a tin cup in his hand. The dilemma for Matt at that point was how to call out to his friend without being heard by anyone else.

He looked at Red Hawk, then back at the sentry, only ten or fifteen yards from the Crow scout. Even a loud whisper would be heard equally well by either man. *Damn,* he thought, exasperated, thinking about the war party that might be arriving at any minute. He considered the situation for a moment more. Then he went back to the Indian pony to get his bow and returned to his position under the bank of the creek. Notching an arrow, he drew the bowstring and aimed carefully.

Red Hawk sat up straight, surprised by the sudden chunk of the arrowhead burying itself in the tree trunk above his head. Thinking at first that someone had thrown a rock at him, he glanced up, and was startled to see the still quivering shaft of an arrow. Immediately alarmed, he jumped up, preparing to alert the patrol. But something about the arrow caused him to hold his tongue. The shaft bore the marks of the Cherokee nation. The only person he knew who had arrows with those markings was Slaughter. He dropped down on one knee, his rifle ready, but still he gave no alarm. All was quiet in the trees that lined the creek. He scanned the bushes with his eyes, only to be startled again with the solid *chunk* of a second arrow a foot above the first. This time he was sure the arrow had come from the creek below the camp. Something told him the arrows were not meant to harm him, but were to alert him. It had to be Slaughter.

Playing his hunch, the Crow scout stood up, pulled the arrows from the tree, and walked toward the creek. As he passed the sentry, he made a casual comment that he was going downstream to relieve himself. "All right," the picket replied, smiling. "I won't shoot at'cha when you come back."

Once he was out of sight of the sentry, Red Hawk hurried along the bank, searching from one side to the other, certain that his friend was there. As he approached a thick clump of berry bushes, Matt stood up and beckoned to him. Red Hawk couldn't help but grin, but the smile immediately left his face when he remembered the trouble Matt was in. "The soldiers look for you," he blurted. "Why did you come back?"

"To save your hide, I reckon," Matt replied. Then he wasted no time telling Red Hawk about the Sioux hell that was about to descend upon the patrol. "You've got to tell LeVan to get the hell outta here, and I mean right now." Matt impressed the message upon his friend. "I don't know for sure how much head start you've got. I wore out two horses gettin' here, so you've got a little gap, but tell LeVan not to dally."

"Maybe lieutenant wanna fight them Sioux," Red Hawk suggested.

"He'd be a damn fool if he did," Matt replied. "Tell him there's as many warriors in this bunch as there were in that box canyon where he got ambushed before."

"I'll tell him," Red Hawk said. "What you gonna do now?"

"I'm headin' for South Pass, maybe Wind River country—somewhere where nobody's lookin' for me." He stepped back to take another look toward the camp. "I don't see Lieutenant O'Connor. I thought you told me he was comin' to arrest me."

"O'Connor and six soldiers were here. He went to look for you. He wants you bad. He says he's gonna hang you."

"Damn," Matt muttered. "Which way did he go?" When Red Hawk pointed in the general direction from which he had just come, Matt said, "Hell, he might be headin' for Iron Claw's bunch." He paused to think about that for a moment. O'Connor was not riding in the same general direction Matt would take if he, in fact, intended to go to South Pass. He looked Red Hawk directly in the eye. "You tell LeVan to get his ass outta here," he emphasized. "Don't wait around for O'Connor to come back." It would just have to be tough luck for the brash lieutenant. There was no sense in endangering the lives of the rest of LeVan's patrol. Now Matt had done all that his conscience demanded. The rest was up to the soldiers. He had no further obligation to them, and certainly none to O'Connor. "O'Connor rode out with six soldiers, you say?"

"And Zeb Benson," Red Hawk replied.

"Zeb's with 'em?" This threw a different light on his thinking. He took a long look back toward the prairie he had crossed during the night, as if expecting to see Iron Claw appearing on the horizon. He liked Zeb Benson. If he had any real friend except for the Crow scouts, it was Zeb. He fought the temptation to be free of the army's problem. *Hell,* he reasoned, *I warned them. It ain't up to me to chase after the strays.* It was unlikely that they would ride into an ambush after they had failed to find him—not with Zeb along. Still, it would be a whole lot better if Zeb knew about the large war party beforehand so he could avoid it altogether. Matt pictured Zeb riding unsuspecting into a trap. "Ah, shit." He finally caved in to his conscience once again. "You tell LeVan that I'll go after O'Connor and warn him to cut south to the Platte, so he can quit worrying about him."

The issue settled, Red Hawk turned to depart. "You watch out, Slaughter," he said.

"Yeah, I will. You take care of yourself." Once again, the two friends parted.

Fred LeVan was amazed. "Slaughter was here?" he demanded, finding it hard to believe. "Here? Just a few minutes ago?" He thought the Indian had fallen asleep and had been dreaming.

Red Hawk nodded his head. "He said Iron Claw was coming to attack us. He said we better get our asses back to Fort Laramie pretty damn quick. Many warriors, too many for this patrol."

The lieutenant stroked his chin thoughtfully. What if what Red Hawk said was true? His patrol would be in a helluva lot of trouble if Iron Claw was riding against him with a war party the size of the one Red Hawk claimed. On the other hand, he knew that Red Hawk was very fond of Slaughter. There was always the possibility that he had simply made up a story, hoping to persuade LeVan not to pursue his friend. But the scout had to know that LeVan had no intention to join O'Connor's search for Slaughter.

Having been close enough to hear the exchange between the officer and Red Hawk, Spotted Horse looked out through the trees toward the open prairie in the direction O'Connor had taken. "There!" he suddenly exclaimed, pointing toward the distant mountains. LeVan turned to follow the direction indicated just in time to glimpse a rider moments before he disappeared on the horizon.

At that distance, it was hard to tell who the rider was. It could be Slaughter. LeVan decided that he had been warned, and he decided to act upon it. Then he hesitated again, remembering O'Connor.

Red Hawk anticipated his next question. "Slaughter rides to warn O'Connor," he said. "He said for you to go right now."

"He said he was going to warn O'Connor?" LeVan found that hard to believe. "Are you sure that's what he said?"

"That's what he said," Red Hawk insisted.

LeVan thought about that for a few moments, wondering if he could believe it. In the end, he decided he had to make the decision that was best for the greatest number of troops under his command. "Sergeant Barnes," he barked, "mount 'em up!"

Barnes, who had been listening to the conversation, responded at once. "We gonna chase after him?"

"Hell, no," LeVan snapped. "Get 'em mounted. We're getting our asses back to Fort Laramie." He had a lot of faith in Matt Slaughter, feeling that he had judged the man's character correctly after all. Barnes winked at Red Hawk as he turned to obey the lieutenant's order.

"Damfool business, this," Zeb Benson mumbled to himself as he guided his horse up the side of another empty ravine. He turned to look behind him to make sure the officer and six enlisted men were following. "I was a damn fool to come on this damn patrol," he continued to lecture himself. "Out here where Sioux warriors is thicker'n fleas on a yard dog. Might as well wear a big sign sayin' 'Easy pickin's—scalp me, scalp me!'" He glanced back at the lieutenant again. "I swear, if we get jumped by a big war party, I'm gonna shoot that arrogant son of a bitch myself. I shoulda never come on this little party." Even though he scolded himself for a poor decision, he knew he'd had to come because he believed that Slaughter deserved a head start, and he had planned to warn him.

Zeb had scouted for the army, on and off, for more than eight years. Even though he was approaching his fifty-fifth birthday, as near as he could recollect, his eye and instincts were as sharp as those of a younger man. But on this particular morning, his mind was elsewhere as he grumbled to himself about the foolishness of his mission. Otherwise, he most probably would never have ridden into the ambush.

Private Enrico Trintini rode at the rear of the single file of six troopers that followed the lieutenant and Zeb Benson. Trintini always brought up the rear. Unable to speak proper English, having enlisted in the army to obtain citizenship, he felt it his place to be last. Three more years in the army and he would be free to go where he pleased in this new land. He would go back east and open a shoe repair shop like his father had in the old country. Those plans were canceled in one split second with the impact of the rifle ball that cracked his skull.

Startled, Zeb's horse flinched at the sharp crack of the rifle, and the old scout jerked around in the saddle in time to see Trintini topple over and drop to the ground. Snapped immediately out of the daze into which he had allowed himself to be drawn, he yelled out to O'Connor, "This way! Follow me!"

O'Connor's initial reaction to the rifle shot had been to go back the way he had come. Consequently, he found himself facing the remaining five troopers who had been following. In the narrow confines at the top of the ravine, his retreating action created a jam of horses as two more shots rang out from the tall grass on both sides. Two more troopers slid from their saddles.

"Don't go back!" Zeb shouted. "This way, dammit!" He kicked his horse into a gallop, knowing their best chance was to race forward, and possibly escape the trap before it closed upon them. The three remaining troopers followed his lead, almost knocking O'Connor out of the saddle in their haste to escape the deadly rifle fire.

Wild-eyed and flustered, O'Connor managed to turn his confused horse around and follow the three troopers. "Ride like hell!" Zeb shouted back over his shoulder, all the while whipping his horse for all he was worth.

Galloping recklessly over the lip of the ravine, the lieutenant just managed to clear the top of the hill before the Sioux warriors closed in from both sides. With bullets snapping around him like furious wasps, he plunged down the slope after his men. In the lead, Zeb pushed his horse for all the speed he could get out of the frightened animal. In full flight, and with no time to consider choices, he headed straight for the first cover he could see. A dry gully that ran like a gash across the base of a small hill offered the only immediate protection, and Zeb wasted no time plunging into its scanty sanctuary. "Get them horses back behind us," he ordered, taking command of the confused soldiers. "I can't tell how many there was, but I reckon we'll soon find out."

On his hands and knees, the lieutenant crawled up beside Zeb. "We can't stay here," he whined, his voice trembling in fear. "We've got to get back to the patrol."

Already agitated by the fact that he had allowed himself to be caught in such a desperate situation, Zeb had scant patience for O'Connor's fear. That their situation was indeed desperate there was little doubt. They were pinned down in a dry gully with a dozen hostiles surrounding them—at least that was the number he estimated—three green troopers, two of them barely able to speak English, and an officer scared out of his gizzard. Answering O'Connor's fearful remark, Zeb informed him none too gently, "We ain't goin' nowheres for the time bein'. Set foot outta this gully and you'll get your ass peppered properly." He looked past the lieutenant to give directions to the men. "You there," he commanded, pointing to one of the soldiers, "get up on the other side of that rock near the top of the gully." He sent the next man to cover the opposite side. The third trooper was positioned to watch for any attempt to get to the horses. With the three in place as best he could deploy them, he turned back to O'Connor. "All right, Lieutenant, you and me'll keep our heads down and wait right here in the middle, me on this side, you on that one." O'Connor meekly obeyed.

They waited. There had been no more shots fired since they had reached cover in the gully. "Go easy on that water, soldier," Zeb warned when the trooper watching the horses reached for his canteen. "What's your name?"

"Private Smith," the soldier answered.

Zeb grunted, certain that Smith was not the name he had been christened with in the old country. "Well, Smith," he said, keeping his voice calm and compassionate, "we might be pinned down here for a helluva long time, so you'd best make that water last." The trooper nodded and capped the canteen.

Gray Bull pulled the ammunition belt from one of the dead soldiers and looped it over his shoulder. He took a moment to inspect the Sharps carbine, then grunted his satisfaction. Three Horses pulled the tunic from one of the other corpses and tried it on. It was a little small for him, but he kept it on while he proceeded to take the scalp.

"They were lucky to get away," Gray Bull complained, "but they didn't get far."

"Igmutaka was not with them," Three Horses said. "The one with the soldiers is an old man. Maybe we should forget about them and go back to the others."

"They have guns and bullets," Gray Bull protested. "I say we should kill them all and take the guns. There are only five of them."

What Gray Bull said made sense to the rest of the scouting party. They were twice as many as the soldiers pinned down in the gully. And while Iron Claw seemed bent upon killing Igmutaka, the main purpose of the war party was to attack the army patrol to gain guns and ammunition. This lust for the white scout's death had become a sickness in Iron Claw's head, and it appeared that the sickness was getting worse. Gray Bull held no fondness for Jack Black Dog, but he agreed with the half-breed that it was a waste of time to have chased after Igmutaka. He believed the patrol had camped at War Woman Creek, just as their scouts had reported. Who could say where the soldiers were now? Too much time had been wasted. Gray Bull and Three Horses had at least persuaded Iron Claw to send out scouting parties to the east and west while the main body of warriors continued on to War Woman Creek. If the army patrol moved in any direction other than returning to Fort Laramie, one of the smaller scouting parties should find them. "Come," he called out to the others. "We will kill the rest of them."

Zeb looked up at the noonday sun. It was going to get pretty warm in this sunbaked gully. *Too bad I couldn't have picked one with some shade trees,* he thought, glancing around him at the open land. "But there wasn't none handy," he muttered to himself.

"What?" O'Connor asked in a loud whisper.

"I said keep your eyes peeled," Zeb replied without looking back at the lieutenant. Suddenly one of the troopers behind him fired off a shot. Zeb turned quickly in response. "Where?" he blurted, looking for a target, only to be met with a blank stare on the face of Private Smith.

"I thought I saw something there," Smith replied sheepishly as a large lizard scurried back to cover behind a rock some thirty yards behind them.

Zeb shook his head solemnly, realizing at that point that it was going to take a miracle if they were to survive this day. "Ever'body," he announced, "hold your fire till you see a damn Injun. There ain't no tellin' how long we're gonna have to set in this damn hole. Till dark, most likely. Then maybe while they're tryin' to sneak in, we can sneak out." He paused, then added under his breath, "If the Good Lord sends that miracle."

They waited. It seemed like a long time with no sounds to indicate that the hostiles were even there. In reality, it was no more than a few minutes, while the Sioux warriors positioned themselves in a half circle above the gully, using an outcropping of rocks for cover. The first hostile fire came almost in a volley, kicking up soil on the grassy rim of the defile. The soldiers crouched low, trying to keep their heads below the edge.

"They're spread out amongst them rocks," Zeb said, having been the only one with an eye at risk. He looked back at the soldier he had posted near the horses. "Try to keep them horses quiet," he said. "They're already gettin' nervous."

The soldier nodded, even though he was more interested in keeping himself from being exposed. Balled up in an almost fetal position against the side of the gully, he made no move to quiet the nervous mounts. Zeb was about to emphasize the importance of keeping the horses safe when another volley sent dirt showering down upon them. The shots came too close to the fidgety horses, kicking up a pebble that struck Zeb's mount in the side. The startled animal scrambled up out of the gully. Before Zeb could get back to stop them, the other horses followed in panic.

He called out frantically to his horse, but the frightened animal galloped away, seeking safety, followed by the army mounts, their empty stirrups flogging away at their sides. "Damn," was all he could mutter, realizing that the small detail of soldiers was most certainly doomed. The Sioux would fire away at them until they tired of it and decided to overrun the gully. *Well,* he thought, *ain't nothing to do but make 'em pay dearly for this old scalp.*

The afternoon wore on, the sun directly overhead now as the Sioux warriors contented themselves with occasional shots at the gully to keep the troopers pinned down. They allowed the soldiers' horses to remain loose, obviously tempting the trapped men to make an attempt to recover them. But no one of the cornered troopers was willing to expose himself to the hostiles' rifle fire. Finally, Gray Bull became weary of the waiting game.

"The soldiers are not coming out of there until they run out of water," he said impatiently. "And I don't want to wait that long. We must make them come out and fight."

Down in the sunbaked gully, his face almost in the dirt, Zeb watched the rocks. As he stared at the rugged hillside, he caught sight of a figure, crouching as it ran, moving quickly among the rocks toward the trees that formed the base of the slope. Zeb squinted extra hard, straining to pick up any further movement of the man. In a few seconds, the warrior was on his feet again, darting from rock to rock. Zeb turned to look beyond the rocks, where a scattering of pines dotted the slope. There was little doubt what the hostile had in mind. Zeb turned back to the lieutenant.

"One of 'em's tryin' to work around us to come up the gully behind us. If he does, he'll be shootin' right down our backsides. I'm gonna try to cut him off. You crawl up here and keep your eyes peeled."

O'Connor hesitated, unwilling to position himself too close to the edge of the gully. "We're badly outnumbered," the lieutenant declared, his voice halting and shaky. "Maybe we should try to negotiate a surrender."

Zeb, already poised to move out after the hostile, had to pause when he heard O'Connor's remark. "Whose?" he questioned. "Ours or theirs?"

Catching the sarcastic tone in the scout's reply,

O'Connor tried to regain a modicum of authority. "I'm thinking about the men. If we continue to resist, they'll overrun us and kill us all. I think there's a chance that, if we give them our weapons, they may agree to let us go."

Zeb couldn't believe his ears. "Why you yellow—" he began, but was unable to find profanity enough to finish the insult. "They want our rifles, all right. And it looks like they stand a damn good chance of gettin' 'em. But they damn sure intend to take our scalps along with 'em. You go on out there and talk to 'em if you think you can trade your gun for your life. Me and the boys here are gonna take a few of the son of a bitches with us to hell." He turned toward the three troopers, who looked as fearful as the lieutenant. "Smith, get up here and keep your eye on them rocks—one of 'em shows his face, bust him." With one last look of disgust for O'Connor, he scrambled off toward the head of the gully.

Near the end of the gully the trench became quite shallow, forcing Zeb to crawl almost flat against the ground. Each time he stuck his head up to see where he was going, the dirt around him was peppered with rifle bullets, causing him to quickly duck again. It left little time to try to catch sight of the warrior making his way from tree to tree now. When Zeb had crawled as far as he could without exposing himself, he placed his rifle on the ground in front of him and waited.

Just as he had figured, the hostile suddenly appeared, running now toward the head of the gully. They saw each other at the same time. Zeb was quicker, his bullet splitting the Indian's breastbone. He ducked down again immediately as a hailstorm of lead spattered the ground around him. Afraid to turn around for fear his rump would be too appealing a target, he hugged the ground and shoved himself backward until he could breathe easy again. There was a short pause, and then the firing resumed. But this time there was something different about it. Puzzled, he cocked his head to listen. Then it dawned upon him—three shots in rapid succession, a short pause, then three more—and he recognized the sound of a Henry rifle. *Slaughter!*

"Glory be!" he blurted out, for there was not a sweeter sound on this earth. Even before he had time to slide back down the gully to a place deep enough to get up on his knees to look, the Henry barked four times more. There were other sounds now as the Sioux returned fire haphazardly while scrambling to escape the deadly fire that had descended upon them. He thought he even heard Private Smith's carbine a couple of times.

By the time Zeb reached the deepest part of the gully where the others waited, he saw the hostiles in full flight, their ponies galloping over the crest of the hill. Looking back toward the top of the hill, he spotted their rescuer. With the afternoon sun almost directly behind him, he stood like a dark avenger, his features blurred by the bright sunshine. He paused there for a few moments before casually ejecting an empty shell from his rifle. Then, satisfied that the hostiles showed no signs of regrouping, he walked down through the rocks, checking each of the four bodies for signs of life.

"Slaughter." Zeb muttered the name, still astonished

by the man's sudden appearance on the hilltop. They had been goners for sure. Of that, Zeb had no doubt. Although he had had every intention to make it extremely costly for the Sioux warriors, the outcome would have been inevitable. Without realizing it, at that moment Matt had acquired a friend for life.

Satisfied that the four bodies posed no further threat, Matt turned and climbed back up the hill, disappearing over the top. To one who might be a believer in things supernatural, it would almost seem that Igmutaka had suddenly come from the sun, and had now disappeared into it once more. Zeb started to call out to him to wait, but held his tongue, figuring Matt was just going to get his horse.

He turned his gaze back to the troopers, who were just now confident enough to leave the protection of the gully. He blinked away green spots appearing before his eyes from staring directly at the sun moments before. The spots danced from one pale trooper to another, each one realizing they had been given a second chance. The spots gradually faded away as his gaze settled upon the flushed face of Lieutenant O'Connor. The lieutenant was no doubt thinking about the surrender talk he had made, realizing the image it had formed of his valor, and regretting the fearful outburst. The thought of it prompted Zeb to grunt contemptuously.

"Well, the man you wanna hang just pulled our bacon outta the fire," Zeb commented as O'Connor crawled up from the gully. "Seems to me like the ledger oughta be balanced. He shot one officer, and saved the life of another'n. That oughta make him about square with the army."

O'Connor's flush deepened. No longer facing immediate death, he sought to regain his authority. "He's still wanted for murder. It is our duty to take him back for trial."

"Shit," Zeb grunted in disgust, finding it difficult to believe the man's lack of gratitude. He just stared at the lieutenant for a long second before finally remarking, "You know, Slaughter knows you came lookin' to arrest him. He didn't have to come save our behinds, but he did. Don't that tell you he ain't the kinda man that murders somebody in cold blood?" He glanced from the lieutenant to the faces of the three troopers, then back at O'Connor. Out of patience with the brash young officer, he said, "It was probably some rock-headed officer like you, anyway."

O'Connor recoiled, insulted. "How dare you get insolent with me," he fumed. "I'll have you court-martialed. You'll never work as a scout again!"

Zeb was just before inviting the insufferable officer to embrace his backside when Slaughter suddenly rode out of the trees at the base of the hill, causing them all to turn to look. Forgetting the lieutenant for the moment, Zeb turned and strode forward to meet him. "By God, partner, you're sure as hell a sight for sore eyes!"

Matt couldn't help but mirror the grin on Zeb's face. "Zeb, how the hell did you get yourself holed up like this?"

"Just dumb-ass luck," Zeb replied. "Rode right into an ambush. I reckon I was caught settin' on my brains."

"Well, you'd best not linger here any longer," Matt said. "You'd best head straight south from here, then cut back toward Fort Laramie. There's a helluva big war party headin' toward War Woman Creek. LeVan's already headin' home." He glanced beyond Zeb toward the others. "Red Hawk said you went out with six soldiers and the lieutenant."

"Yeah, we lost three of 'em in that ambush," Zeb replied as O'Connor and the enlisted men walked up to join them.

"I suppose we owe you a word of thanks," O'Connor said begrudgingly. He suffered the pain of it for a brief moment before his next remark. "I assume you've come to give yourself up."

If the remark startled Matt, it did not show in his face. His expression never changing, he replied softly, "I reckon not. I came to warn you about a war party led by Iron Claw. Then I reckon I'll be on my way."

O'Connor stiffened. "Then I guess I'll have to inform you that you are under arrest. I'll ask you to hand over your weapon."

"Afraid I can't do that, Lieutenant," he said, cradling his rifle across his saddle.

"Then, by God, I have no choice but to have you taken by force," O'Connor flared. He took a step back, and ordered his men to arrest him.

There was no immediate response to the lieutenant's command. The three troopers stood dumbfounded, none anxious to make the first move. Zeb was the first to act. He stepped over to stand beside Matt's horse, his rifle held ready before him, and turned to face the soldiers. "I reckon I gotta stand with Slaughter in this fight," he informed them. He threw a quick glance up at Matt, and asked casually, "Where's that buckskin you usually ride?"

"He's gone under," Matt replied, equally as casual. "I rode him to death."

"That's a shame. I liked that horse."

"So did I."

O'Connor was mortified, unable to believe the casual exchange between the two. He turned to the soldier standing nearest him. "Pull him off that horse!" he commanded.

In response, the private took one fearful glance at the two scouts, then backed away. The other two made no move to raise their weapons, choosing to stand mute. O'Connor was beside himself with anger. "By God," he blurted, "I'll have you all court-martialed when we get back!"

"You do, and I'll have to tell the court about you cowarding on your belly back there like a yeller dog, wantin' to trade our rifles to them Injuns if they'd let us go," Zeb said.

"It would be my word against yours," O'Connor replied. "The word of an officer against that of a piece of civilian trash."

"I got three witnesses," Zeb said.

O'Connor turned to examine the faces of his soldiers. To a man, they all nodded in agreement with Zeb's statement. The lieutenant realized then that the conspiracy was complete. Still he would not surrender without a feeble attempt to bluster. "We'll just see about that," he threatened. "You men will live to regret this day." Then he spun on his heel and stalked back to catch his horse. The three troopers fanned out to round up the other mounts.

"Is he goin' to cause trouble for you?" Matt asked.

"I doubt it," Zeb said. "He's all full of piss and vinegar right now, but you shoulda seen him when them Sioux was peppering us back in that gully. I think he'll keep his mouth shut about it and hope I do the same. Besides, none of the four of 'em could find their way back without me." Changing the subject, he asked, "Where are you headin'?"

"Don't know for sure. Kinda thinkin' about Wind River country, but I haven't made up my mind."

"I swear, I've half a mind to go with you." Then abruptly changing the subject again, Zeb asked, "Did you really shoot that damn army officer back in Virginia?"

"Nope," Matt answered honestly, feeling no need to volunteer anything further on the matter. "You'd best get goin' now."

Zeb nodded, then extended his hand. "You watch your scalp, Igmutaka," he said with a grin. "Maybe we'll meet up again."

"Maybe so," Matt said, taking Zeb's hand. "You take care of yourself." He turned the paint's head west and was soon lost from their sight.

Chapter 13

"They were here," Iron Claw muttered softly, not really talking to anyone. Stirring the ashes of one of the small fires, he made a guess as to how much of a head start the patrol had on his war party, a war party with tired ponies and frustrated warriors. "Half a day, maybe," he decided, knowing that they could not catch the soldiers before they reached Fort Laramie. He was to return to his village with nothing more than a few rifles. It would be a shameful return. *Slaughter!* He cursed the name, for it was he who had covered the distance to War Woman Creek in time enough to let the soldiers escape. His brooding thoughts were interrupted by a cry from one of his warriors.

"Gray Bull comes!"

Iron Claw looked west along the creek bank to see Gray Bull and Three Horses making their way toward them. There were warriors missing, which immediately concerned Iron Claw. Was there to be no end to the bad news? He hurried to meet the scouting party. Before he could question Gray Bull, Three Horses blurted out, "Igmutaka!" Iron Claw's warriors crowded around the small scout party, anxious to hear. When Gray Bull related how the white man called Slaughter had appeared out of the sun and killed four of their brothers with his *spirit gun*, there were many gasps and foreboding groans among the crowd of warriors. Iron Claw clenched his teeth, biting off the cry of frustration that threatened to escape his throat. There followed a great deal of grumbling and angry discussion, and it was the general feeling that there had been too many bad signs from the start of the raid.

Iron Claw did not try to persuade the others to continue. Though frustrated and angry, he knew that he had lost the confidence of his warriors. His medicine had not been strong enough to overcome that of the hated Igmutaka. The war party would return to the village. Now there was no doubt but that he must kill this mountain lion. Only then would he regain the confidence of his warriors.

The object of Iron Claw's loathing was making his way west toward South Pass, still undecided as to what he should do. He thought it best to skirt the southern end of the Bighorns, since that area was getting a little hot for him. Maybe, he thought, if he laid low in the Wind River country, or the Bitterroots for a while, things might cool off a bit, and then he might have a better chance to pay Iron Claw a little visit. Riding through the rolling meadows of summer grass with the mountains rising up ahead, their peaks still crowned snowy white,

Matt felt a sense of peace. There was a feel about this country that struck deep in his soul, a feeling that he was returning home even though he had never ventured past the Bighorns before this day. He remembered how Ike had talked about the Wind River country, and he had promised himself that he would see it firsthand.

The thought of Ike reminded him of the vow he had made to exact vengeance for Ike's death. Iron Claw was behind him now, and seemingly far away, and there had already been so much killing. It caused him to wonder, to question his own sanity, and he paused to examine his motives. Had he turned into a heartless, conscienceless killer—like the mountain lion the Sioux had likened him to? Then he thought of Ike's body when he had found it suspended in the trees by the river, and the image of Iron Claw's snarling face formed in his mind. Before he realized it, the muscles in his arms tensed in response, and he knew that he would never rid his mind of his vow.

He tried to clear his thoughts of such deep and sobering obligations by concentrating on a brace of antelopes bounding across a grassy ridge a few hundred yards off to his right. Like free spirits, they seemed to bounce across the earth, darting this way and that, barely touching the ground at all. For some reason he could not explain, the sight of them brought the young girl, Molly, to mind. At this distance, the antelopes seemed silent, floating effortlessly over the prairie, reminding him of the willowy movements of the slight and silent girl. For a moment, he felt regret for what might have been, but now seemed unlikely. There was no time to dwell on it, however, for in the next instant, a rider emerged from the ridge, his head and shoulders rising up from the crest and finally the horse beneath him.

Matt immediately jerked the paint's head toward a small ravine that looked deep enough to conceal him and his horse. Sliding the Henry from the saddle sling, he dismounted and moved quickly to the top of the ravine where he could watch the rider. He realized then that there had been a reason for the antelope to be so excited. Thinking the rider an Indian at first, he hugged the ground, using the knee-high grass along the ridge as cover. The rider seemed to be alone, for there was no sign of another. Matt intended to lay hidden and let him pass. On his present line of travel, the rider would pass by him at about seventy-five yards at the closest point. Matt watched as the rider came closer. Something about the Indian looked familiar. Suddenly it dawned upon him—it was Cooter Martin.

Still, Matt did not make known his presence. Cooter was as much a Sioux as most of the warriors. It might not be a good idea to hail the old trapper until he was certain there was no one with him. After Cooter had reached the closest point and there was still no one else in sight, Matt stood up and called out to him. The old man reined his pony to a stop immediately, then turned the animal toward Matt.

"Damn," Matt exclaimed when Cooter approached. "In all this big country, how in hell could I run into you? That's one helluva coincidence."

"Howdy, Slaughter," Cooter replied casually and

stepped down. "Weren't no coincidence a'tall. Hell, I've been lookin' for you."

"Lookin' for me?" Matt questioned. "What for?" Before Cooter had time to answer, he added, "How the hell did you find me, anyway?"

"Weren't hard to figure," Cooter answered. "That no-good half-breed Jack Black Dog turned up at Red Cloud's camp t'other evenin'. He was talkin' about your little set-to with Iron Claw." The mere mention of the name of Jack Black Dog caught Matt's full attention at once. Cooter went on. "We heared tell of that fight you was in with some of Iron Claw's boys this mornin', too."

"How'd you hear about that?" Matt asked, since it had only just occurred.

"Injun telegraph," Cooter replied. "Hell, word passes quicker among Injun tribes than it does on the government wire. Last time I seen you, you was fixin' to do some scoutin' for the army, but Jack Black Dog was goin' on about the white ghost, Igmutaka, raisin' hell with Iron Claw's boys. You were the only mountain lion I knew about, so I figured you musta quit the army and was tendin' to business on your own. When I bumped into you and that little gal, and that Crow, you was askin' me about the Wind River country. I just kinda got me a hunch that you might be headin' that way now, so I took a chance you'd be following the old settlers' trail over South Pass. Figured if I seen you, I'd see you. If I didn't, I wouldn't."

Matt laughed. "Well, I reckon you seen me."

"I reckon," the old man agreed. "I figured there was

somethin' you needed to know." He paused to watch the reaction in Matt's eyes. "Red Cloud's bunch is on their way to Fort Laramie to the treaty talks—and Jack Black Dog is goin' with 'em."

Cooter was right. The news that the treacherous half-breed had the gall to return to Fort Laramie was of more than casual interest to Matt. He said nothing for a long moment while he thought of the man who had killed Molly's mother and stepfather and abducted Molly. When finally he spoke, his voice was soft, his words measured, "That man ain't fit to live on God's earth." Then he looked Cooter in the eye accusingly. "Why does a great chief like Red Cloud allow a low-down murderin' devil like Jack Black Dog to live with his village?"

Cooter shrugged. "Don't many folks in Red Cloud's camp know much about Jack Black Dog in the first place. Besides, what would they have against him? It ain't likely they would be mad at him for killin' white folks, now is it?"

Matt nodded thoughtfully. "I reckon not," he agreed. "But after Molly made it back to tell 'em, the army knows about the son of a bitch now. As soon as he's spotted, he'll be arrested."

Cooter shrugged again. "Son, there's gonna be thousands of Sioux, Cheyenne, and maybe Arapaho camped around Fort Laramie for them talks. It ain't likely anybody's gonna spot one half-breed that don't wanna be spotted in all that crowd. On top of that, ain't nobody gonna be lookin' for Jack Black Dog." He nodded his head for emphasis. "I reckon that's the reason I come lookin' for you. I don't think Jack Black Dog's got it outta his head about that girl, Molly. I thought you'd wanna know about that." He hesitated for a few moments, watching Matt's reaction to his words. Anticipating the question, he volunteered, "I'd shoot the bastard myself, but I've been livin' with the Sioux for too long—they might not understand. Hell, there's even some folks in Red Cloud's band that claims Jack Black Dog as kin."

Matt thought about it for a long moment. His first reaction to Cooter's statement was to question the old man's reasoning. In his opinion, Cooter should have shot the evil half-breed on sight, kin or no kin. But after a moment's reflection, he saw the old trapper's point of view. "Well, you were right about me headin' to the high country. I'm glad you found me. I don't know if that damn half-breed is crazy enough to go after Molly in the middle of a fort full of soldiers or not. He just might be. I reckon it's somethin' I can't take a chance on. The problem is, I'm takin' a helluva chance on goin' back to Fort Laramie myself." He went on to tell Cooter about the warrant for his arrest for murder. "But," he concluded, "I don't see that I've got much choice in the matter."

"I'm supposed to join Red Cloud at Laramie," Cooter said. "We can ride back together. 'Course, I don't recommend ridin' into Red Cloud's camp together—you ain't exactly welcome in a Sioux camp—so we'd best split up before we get there."

"I'm obliged to you," Matt said. "I expect we'd better drop down toward the Sweetwater, though. Iron

Claw's boys might still be on my tail, and they'll most likely shoot first and ask questions later. If they see you ridin' with me, they might figure you've gone back to being a white man."

Cooter smiled at that. "I expect you might be right. Iron Claw ain't never been too fond of me in the first place. If me and Red Cloud wasn't friends, Iron Claw would most likely already be sportin' my scalp on his lance." He paused to scratch his beard while he thought about Red Cloud's treacherous cousin. "Iron Claw's Oglala, same as Red Cloud's mother, but they don't share much love for each other. Right now, they're farther apart than ever since Red Cloud's goin' in to talk peace with the soldiers."

Chapter 14

Major James Van Voast, Eighteenth Infantry, looked up from his desk and frowned at his clerk. "Who is he?"

"He's one of the civilian scouts," the corporal replied. "He came in with that lieutenant and three troopers who got cut off from Lieutenant LeVan's patrol."

"Well, what's he want?" The major's mind was fully occupied with a peace commission from Washington and the ominous prospect of several thousand Indians camped around the post. Having just arrived at his new assignment this very month, he was not familiar with any of the personnel, especially the civilian scouts.

"He says he just wants to talk to you a minute. He was looking for Major Evans."

Van Voast's first inclination was to tell his clerk to send the man to the chief of scouts, but he reconsidered. Maybe the man had something important to say. "All right. Tell him I'll see him in a few minutes."

Zeb nodded in response to the clerk's message from

the major. He stood there, shifting his weight back and forth from one foot to the other while the clerk returned to the preparation of the morning report. After a few long minutes had passed with no word from behind the closed office door, Zeb broke the silence. "Where's Major Evans? I ain't never heard of Major Van what's his name."

"Van Voast," the corporal said. "Major Van Voast just replaced Major Evans as post commander."

"Van Voast," Zeb repeated. "What kinda feller is he?"

The corporal shrugged indifferently. "I don't know—he's an officer." He returned his attention to the ledger in front of him, not really interested in conversation with the rough-looking old scout rocking impatiently from foot to foot. He was spared further questions when the door to the office opened and Major Van Voast appeared.

A short, stocky Dutchman with a close-cropped beard, the major stood in the doorway while he looked Zeb over. A painful frown spread across his face as he asked, "There was something you wanted to see me about?"

"Yes, sir," Zeb replied respectfully. "My name's Zeb Benson. I'm ridin' scout for Lieutenant LeVan. You know him?"

"I've met the lieutenant," Van Voast responded impatiently, anxious to get back to his desk. "If you have some sort of grievance with Lieutenant LeVan, you should take that up with Captain Boyd."

"Oh, no, sir," Zeb quickly replied. "I got no grief with Lieutenant LeVan. He's most likely the best officer you've got on the post. That ain't what I come to see you about."

"Well, what is it you came to see me about? Out with it, man! I've got a couple of thousand savages and a peace commission to worry about, and right now I'm damn busy."

"Yes, sir," Zeb humbly replied, wishing that Major Evans was still there. "I was just wantin' to say something about one of the scouts, name of Slaughter. Lieutenant O'Connor was sent out to arrest Slaughter for something they say he did back east, and I was hopin' you might use your authority to cancel them orders for his arrest."

Van Voast made no effort to conceal his exasperation. "Now why in the world would I want to do that?"

"'Cause Slaughter has saved your soldiers' bacon on more than one occasion, and it would make no damn sense a'tall to send a man like him to jail. Even if he did kill somebody back east, he's done more'n enough to make up for it."

The major threw a furtive glance at the corporal as if confounded that the clerk had interrupted his work to talk to this backwoods lunatic. Looking at Zeb again, he concluded the interview. "Mr. Benson, was it? This is something to take up with the post adjutant's office. If there's a warrant out for this Slaughter person, there must have been a damn good reason. I see no chance in hell of ignoring it. That's not the way things are done in the army. Now, if you'll excuse me, I've got important issues to address." With that, he turned on his heel and returned to his desk, closing the door behind him.

Zeb looked at the corporal, who shook his head and offered a faint sympathetic smile. Feeling as if he had just made a fool of himself, Zeb nodded his head and turned to leave. It had been a rather naive attempt for a pardon, he realized, but he'd felt that something should be said in Slaughter's defense. It was probably a waste of time, anyway. Slaughter was most likely riding the high country, heading up into the Wind River Range, or maybe over to the Absarokas. *Damn,* he thought, *I wish I was with him. I never was worth a shit anywhere but in the woods,* he complained to himself as he took his leave. Outside the post commander's office, he cut diagonally across the parade ground, past the end of the infantry barracks, headed for the post trader's store. Maybe Seth Ward would stand him to a drink.

It was almost dark when Matt and Cooter paused to water their horses in a small stream that emptied into the North Platte River. "There's a sizable camp up ahead, judging by the shine of them campfires in the trees," Cooter remarked. "Could be Red Cloud's village. I'll ride in and see who it is."

They approached to within a hundred yards of the camp, and then Matt dismounted near a little clump of willows while Cooter went on. While he waited, Matt passed the time by checking the paint's hooves. He had thought the horse had recently shown a tendency to favor its left front hoof, and he feared that it may have split it. The horse had been challenged to do some hard riding over the last several days, and there had been little opportunity to give it much attention. Upon close inspection, however, he could see no sign of injury. He decided that what he had perceived to be an injured hoof was, in fact, just a characteristic peculiar to the horse's gait. Thinking back, he realized that the tendency surfaced only during a fast walk or lope. At a full gallop, there was no sign of the irregularity. Though he was relieved, he still took the moment to admonish himself for not paying more attention to the paint's welfare.

He took the stallion's muzzle in his hand and stroked its face gently. It was a good horse, he thought—maybe not as stout through the chest as the buckskin he had just lost, but possibly a wee bit faster, and a little smaller. "I reckon it's time I gave you a name," he said. He thought for a minute. "I think I'll call you Buck. Whaddaya think about that?" He playfully rubbed the paint's neck. "Is that all right with you? Buck? I think it suits you." The horse responded with a gentle whinny, which Matt interpreted as approval.

In a few minutes' time, Cooter loped up to the willows. "That's a Cheyenne camp. They said Red Cloud's camp joins theirs down the river a ways. So I reckon I'll ride on in." He sat looking down at Matt for a few seconds. "What are you gonna do?"

"I'm not sure," Matt replied. "I can't go with you, and I damn sure can't ride in to Fort Laramie. I reckon I'm just gonna have to lose myself in the crowd of soldiers and Indians somehow till I can find Jack Black Dog." The thought occurred then that there was one place where he might find refuge. "I guess I'll ride on down to the Crow camp."

Cooter nodded, understanding Matt's predicament.

"Well," he finally said, "good luck to you, Slaughter. I hope ever'thin' turns out for the best. If you was to happen to settle up with Jack Black Dog, I don't reckon there'd be many Sioux lodges in mournin'."

He had never before seen so many Indians in one place. Riding toward the fort, he passed camp after camp of Sioux and Cheyenne, as well as some Arapaho. In total numbers, there had to be thousands, enough to annihilate the few hundred soldiers presently manning the fort. He couldn't help but think of the difference it would make if the various tribes ever united into one great army instead of dividing as they did, even into separate bands within a tribe. Looking at the many campfires flickering among the trees near the river, he could hardly believe that only a few hours earlier he had been running for his life from these people. It caused an eerie feeling, although no one seemed to pay any attention to him as he rode by.

Red Hawk's people had been camped east of the fort when last he visited his friend, about halfway between the fort and Horse Creek, the treaty grounds for the peace talks back in '51. Zeb had been there for that treaty, and had once commented on it. "A big powwow with a helluva lot of promises," Zeb had said, "and in the end, it didn't settle a damn thing." Zeb speculated that this new peace conference wouldn't fare any better. The government was going to try to persuade the Indians to quit attacking prospectors and settlers using the Bozeman Trail. "Any fool can tell you the Sioux ain't gonna agree to that. Hell, it runs right through their best huntin' grounds." A faint smile traced Matt's lips when he thought of the grizzled old scout. *He's probably standing at the bar right now, trying to talk Seth Ward out of a free shot of whiskey,* he thought. It caused him to smile, but only for a moment before worrisome thoughts returned to his mind.

Approaching the fort, he kept to a wide circle around the complex of buildings, lest he chance upon someone who might recognize him. The odds of that were small, but there was a chance, and he wouldn't be of much help to Molly if he was locked up in the guardhouse. Thoughts of Molly brought a frown to his face, reminding him of the uncertainty of his mission, and the lack of a definite plan to protect her.

In all common sense, it would seem that the safest place for the young girl would be right where she was — in the midst of a fort full of soldiers. Yet he had a bad feeling about the half-breed renegade he searched for. Cooter had commented that Jack Black Dog was crazy. He thought the half-breed was obsessed with the "white bird with no song," and crazy enough to try to steal her. Jack Black Dog had often been to Fort Laramie, had been employed as a scout on occasion. He could probably move freely about the fort without being challenged. *Hell,* Matt thought, *I could probably ride right through the middle of the place myself without anybody noticing.* He would have been even more worried had he known that Major Evans was no longer the post commander and the new commander knew nothing about the accusations made against Jack Black Dog — and for that matter, was far too occupied to give them consideration in any case.

Matt tried to form a picture of Molly in his mind as he had last seen her, but it kept fading away, to be replaced with that of the dangerous half-breed. He considered riding into the fort to the doctor's house, but he could not be sure how the surgeon and his wife would react. They must surely know of the warrant for his arrest. He wasn't particularly concerned with what Martha Riddler thought of him, but he found it of utmost importance to him that Molly should know the truth about the murder he was wanted for. Several times he reined the paint to a stop, then circled the outbuildings of the military post while he tried to decide whether or not to go to her. Finally he convinced himself that it was best to find Red Hawk and ask him to carry a message to Molly.

Red Hawk was surprised to see his friend riding through the circle of lodges in the Crow camp just below the confluence of the Laramie and Platte rivers. Knowing the risk Slaughter was taking in being there, he strode forward to signal him. At almost the same time, Matt spotted the pony stolen from Iron Claw tied outside one of the lodges, and headed toward Red Hawk's campfire.

"Come inside," Red Hawk said while quickly glancing around to see if anyone else in the camp had noticed the white man. There were several women tending their cook fires, but none appeared to pay much attention to the buckskin-clad rider. Wasting no time, he took the paint's reins and hurried Matt inside. Matt and Red Hawk's mother stared at each other, dumbfounded, for a few moments until the Crow warrior followed him inside. After explaining to the old woman who their unexpected guest was, he turned back to Matt while his mother made an effort to find some food to offer. "What are you doing here?" Red Hawk asked. "The soldiers still look for you."

"I know," Matt replied. "I don't wanna make trouble for you, but I need your help." He went on to explain why he had returned to Fort Laramie, and his concern for Molly's safety.

"Jack Black Dog no good," Red Hawk said after he heard of the half-breed's obsession with Molly. "He maybe crazy enough to try to steal her. What you want me to do?"

"I can't take a chance on goin' into the post," Matt replied. "I want you to go to her, and warn her not to go anywhere by herself, to stay close to the doctor's house, at least until the treaty talks are done and the Sioux clear outta here."

Red Hawk agreed immediately. "I'll go at once," he said. "If I see that mad dog, maybe I kill him for you."

"Just warn Molly to be careful," Matt said. "Meanwhile, I'll try to see if I can spot Jack Black Dog."

"How you gonna do that?" Red Hawk asked, more than a little skeptical that Matt could get close enough to Red Cloud's camp to do so.

"I don't know," Matt answered honestly. "I guess I'm countin' on some luck." In truth, he had little hope beyond a chance encounter with the half-breed. "If he's really after Molly, he'll be snoopin' around the post. Maybe I'll get a chance to spot him."

Red Hawk shook his head, unconvinced. "Maybe soldiers get a chance to spot you," he said. "It's best I keep my eye out for Jack Black Dog."

"It ain't your chore to do," Matt said. "That breed is a dangerous son of a bitch. There's no call for you to get in the middle of it."

Red Hawk drew back as if insulted. "Molly my friend, too," he said indignantly.

Matt couldn't help but recall the same reaction not long before when he had asked Red Hawk to hold the horses while he went into Iron Claw's camp to rescue Molly. "I reckon you're right," he said. "Maybe you can keep an eye on her while I scout around the Sioux camp, and maybe spot him outside the fort—maybe when he ain't got too many friends with him."

"Jack Black Dog ain't got many friends, even in Sioux camp."

"You may be right," Matt said.

"Where you gonna camp?" Red Hawk asked.

"Looks like nobody much is camped up the Laramie River. Most all the Indians are along the Platte. So I guess that's where I'll go." He stopped to recollect. "You know where that little double-fork creek joins the river just past those high bluffs about a mile down from the Platte?" Red Hawk thought for a few seconds, then nodded his head. "Well, I'll look for a place close to that creek."

Chapter 15

Finished with the supper dishes, Molly folded her dish towel and carefully put it away. After she threw the dishwater out the back door, she placed the pan on the shelf beside the stove. Then she turned to attract Martha Riddler's attention. With a signal that had become familiar to the doctor's wife, she indicated that she was going for a walk. Martha smiled and nodded.

Molly took a walk almost every night. And while she never let on, Martha knew that the young girl's walk usually led to the chapel. She suspected that Molly's prayers were most likely for the safety of a certain sandy-haired outlaw. It was a sad thing, a dream that had very little chance of ever coming true. Martha found it hard to believe that the young man she had met would be capable of committing the crime he was charged with, but there was apparently enough evidence for the army to pursue him. She shook her head sadly as she watched the worried young girl go down the front steps and turn in the direction of the chapel. So much sadness in such a nice young girl's life—it hardly seemed fair.

Molly was not a religious person, having been raised by a mother who had very little time, and no inclination, to attend church services. But she felt a peace inside the little whitewashed chapel. There was never anyone there in the evening, and it was never locked. Seated on one of the hard, backless benches in the dim quiet, she could think about the things that were most important to her. And foremost among these was the one person she longed to see more than anyone else in the world. She would often find herself far away in the mountains on the horizon, drifting along winding game trails, looking out over high cliffs to isolated valleys below—mentally seeing the places she imagined he saw. Sometimes, she would suddenly realize that she had been away from the house too long, and she would have to scurry back before Martha became concerned.

They said he had murdered an army officer in Virginia and, like many other outlaws, was on the run in this untamed country. She knew that should matter to her, but she could not—would not—believe he was capable of cold-blooded murder. There had to be some mistake. She knew in her heart that she could not feel this longing for such a man. Every night she prayed to God to watch over him, to hear her prayers even though she had not been the Christian she should have been for all her young years.

As on most evenings, the chapel was empty on this night. Molly pushed the door open and peeked in to make sure. Satisfied that she was the only lonely soul seeking solace, she went in and closed the door behind her, then stood there for a few moments while her eyes adjusted to the dim evening light. Then she went to the front bench and sat down. For a few minutes, she simply gazed at the wooden cross behind the raised pulpit. Far from ornate, it was a rather crude symbol, constructed by one of the post carpenters. But it served to encourage the proper atmosphere for soulful meditation. After a short reverie, she silently recited her standard plea for God to watch over her knight in buckskins.

Her mind wandered again to the high places where she dreamed of going with him. Then she thought about the night he had suddenly appeared to rescue her from Iron Claw's tipi. She pictured him when he had sat before the campfire at night on the journey back to Fort Laramie, making conversation with Red Hawk and Cooter Martin. Cooter had said the Sioux called Matt Igmutaka, mountain lion. She could understand the reason, but even if he was as fierce and deadly as they claimed, she knew that this mountain lion possessed a compassionate heart. She suddenly felt an ache in her soul and a feeling of despair, for she longed so desperately to see him again.

She permitted her mind to dwell on what could never be for longer than she had intended, for she realized then that it was getting quite dark in the chapel. Anxious to get back before Martha began to worry, she got to her feet and hurried toward the entrance. Stepping out the front door, she paused to look toward the parade ground. It was almost deserted, with only an occasional soldier or two crossing on his way to Seth Ward's bar or back to the barracks. It was already too dark for anyone to notice her standing before the chapel.

Turning to look over her left shoulder, she could see the soft, rosy glow of campfires hovering over the closest Indian camp—a band of Oglala Sioux, Dr. Riddler had informed her. They were more than a mile away, yet the sky glowed with their fires. She involuntarily shivered when she thought about the thousands of savages that surrounded the fort. Pushing that thought from her mind, she turned and started across the parade ground, in a hurry now to get back to the house.

Walking briskly toward the officers' quarters, she picked up her step a little. She had never had any fear of the dark, but she suddenly felt very alone, as if sensing that something was wrong. She had reached the center of the darkened parade ground when she heard a soft footfall behind her. Startled, she almost turned to look, but told herself she was letting her imagination run away with her. She hurried on, certain now that Martha would be standing on the porch looking for her. *There it was again!* This time she knew it was not her imagination. Someone was behind her, and was closer than before. Frightened, she spun on her heel to face him. In the dim light, she was unable to identify him at first, but she could see that he was an Indian. Her heart fairly leaped into her throat. Moments later, she exhaled a great sigh of relief. It was Red Hawk.

"You must not go out alone no more till Sioux are gone," he said. "Slaughter sent me to tell you, you're in danger."

Slaughter, she signed excitedly. *Here?*

Red Hawk nodded, then said, "Slaughter's here, but can't come to you—soldiers get him."

Where? She wanted to know, unaware of the pounding of her heart.

"He's camped on the Laramie. He told me to find you. You got to be careful. Jack Black Dog's lookin' for you."

Jack Black Dog. The name instantly brought chills to her spine. Well aware of the savage half-breed's insane lust for her, still she could not believe he was crazy enough to risk coming after her in this place. An image of his leering face came immediately to her mind, causing her to shudder involuntarily when she remembered his insistence that he would one day possess her. How, she wondered, could the treacherous half-breed think he could come for her with soldiers all around?

Anticipating her question, Red Hawk said, "Cooter Martin said Jack Black Dog is crazy in the head—said he aims to take you back."

Molly shook her head in frantic despair. The thought of Jack Black Dog stalking her brought back the terror she had felt when her mother and stepfather were blatantly shot down before her eyes. How could this nightmare continue? She remembered the breed's threats and his sneering, lecherous stares when she was Iron Claw's captive. It seemed he was always close by, watching her whenever she was taken outside the war chief's lodge.

"Don't worry," Red Hawk said, in an effort to reassure her. "Me and Slaughter, we'll get him. You just stay close to the doctor's house like Slaughter said."

Her fear overshadowed by the thought that Matt was

near, she repeatedly signed his name. When Red Hawk appeared puzzled, she signed that she wanted to see him.

Red Hawk cocked his head to one side, obviously uncertain about the wisdom of her request. "Slaughter said you stay close to fort."

Showing a spark of anger as she became frustrated with her limited knowledge of sign language, she tried to convey her thoughts to the Crow warrior, but he was clearly confused. She pounded her chest adamantly, then pointed to him, then back at herself while signing Matt's name. Finally, after she repeated the motions several times, the meaning of her frantic gestures dawned upon him, and he asked, "If I don't take you to Slaughter, you gonna go by yourself?" With a great sigh, she nodded her head. "I don't know . . ." He hesitated, thinking of Slaughter's instructions to him. She placed her hand on his arm, her eyes pleading with him. Finally, against his better judgment, he relented. "Tomorrow," he said. "I'll meet you at the stables when the sun is straight overhead."

Chapter 16

True to his word, Red Hawk was waiting at the stables when the sun approached high noon the next day. He would have already had Molly's horse saddled but for the two troopers on stable duty. The peace talks had started that morning, and since he was not well known to the soldiers, they looked upon him with a suspicious eye. Neither of them had been at Fort Laramie for longer than a month, so consequently, to them Red Hawk was just another Indian. Their heads had been properly filled with warnings that Indians, no matter the tribe, were constantly looking for opportunities to steal horses. After several attempts to persuade the soldiers that the mousy dun belonged to a young lady who was staying at the surgeon's house and that she would soon be there to ride it, he gave up and sat down by the stable door to wait.

He didn't have to wait long. He had no sooner settled himself comfortably when he saw Molly walking hurriedly toward the stables. He didn't get up right away, for she was still some hundred yards away, striding purposefully past the cavalry barracks. Watching her now, he thought back to the first time he had seen her. Frail and frightened, like an injured rabbit, she had clung to Slaughter, her arms clasped tightly around his neck, while he carried her from Iron Claw's tipi. Red Hawk shook his head, thinking of that night. She was still slight in appearance, but he had learned that she was made of a tough moral fiber that could prove to be troublesome. For evidence of that, one had to look no further than this very morning.

The realization of that caused him to have second thoughts about having agreed to take her to Slaughter. Slaughter had specifically stressed that Molly should stay close to the surgeon's house, and he would most likely be angry with Red Hawk for allowing her to ride down the river to find him. He would have to explain that she was determined to go, with or without him. *"Waugh,"* he growled, wishing he had not told her where Slaughter had camped.

She waved a greeting to the Crow scout when she saw him by the door. He nodded in response, got to his feet as she swept past him, and followed her into the stable to the two troopers mucking out stalls. Upon glancing up to see the lady, both soldiers pulled themselves to attention. "Ma'am," one of them greeted her.

"She say she want her horse," Red Hawk spoke for her. Molly nodded in confirmation. The trooper looked from the Indian to the young lady, then back again at Red Hawk. "The gray pony in the pen," Red Hawk said. "Like I already told you."

Still not sure if he should permit a civilian to take a horse, the private stated his concern. "Well, we can't just let everybody come walking up and ride off with a horse. You understand that, don't you, ma'am?" She nodded her head. "Have you got a saddle?" She pointed toward the tack room. He hesitated for a moment, exchanging glances with the other soldier, who had paused to witness the exchange. His partner shrugged indifferently.

Before the first soldier could say more, Molly turned and walked directly to the tack room. Both troopers hastened to follow her. Inside the tack room, she walked down the line of saddles, stopping before the one that belonged to the mousy dun. Placing her hand on the saddle, she stood patiently waiting.

Seeing that he was to have little choice, the trooper pulled the saddle and bridle from the rail. "Yes, ma'am. I'll saddle him up for you."

The other soldier stood next to Red Hawk, watching the young lady follow his partner out to the corral. "She don't waste a lot of words, does she?"

"No," Red Hawk replied and turned to follow.

With many in the garrison gone to the treaty grounds, the post presented an unusually quiet scene as the young white girl and the Crow Indian scout rode away from the stables, passing behind the cavalry barracks and the officers' quarters, angling toward a bend in the Laramie River. Upon reaching the river, Red Hawk followed the north bank west as it wound its way into the mountains. After less than an hour's ride, they approached a point where a creek cut between the high bluffs to empty into the river.

Red Hawk held up his hand to halt the girl behind him. "He said he would camp somewhere close to the fork in the creek." There was no obvious evidence of a camp, so Red Hawk began to scout the banks of the creek, working back up into the bluffs. After a short time, he called out to Molly, "Here." When she caught up to him, he pointed to a thick stand of willows. "He camp here, but he's gone now."

Disappointed, she hurried up to him, looking toward the willows he had pointed out. There was evidence of a small fire in a tiny clearing. She pushed on across the creek, and dismounted to look for any sign that might tell her where he had gone. Red Hawk slid down from his pony and walked to the edge of the creek, where he stood watching Molly as she felt the ashes of the fire. He was somewhat relieved that Slaughter was no longer there. He would take Molly back now. He should not have brought her out there in the first place. He opened his mouth to tell her that, but was unable to voice the first word.

Hearing a sharp intake of his breath as he suddenly sucked air into his lungs, Molly turned to witness the brutal execution. Attacked from behind, Red Hawk struggled helplessly as Jack Black Dog held him with one hand across his neck, while the other hand thrust a long skinning knife deep into his side. Holding the mortally wounded Crow locked securely in the death embrace, Jack Black Dog continued to work the blade around in his side, tearing away at his victim's organs.

Feeling the life drain from the body, he withdrew the knife, then thrust it in again and again until there was no resistance left. Then he stepped back and let the body drop.

Driven almost out of her mind by the horrifying scene playing out before her eyes, Molly felt the blood drain from her brain. The ground beneath her feet seemed to be spinning, causing her to stagger against a willow trunk. Strange grunting sounds registered in her ears, but she did not recognize them as her own attempts to scream. She gazed terrified into the leering face of Jack Black Dog until it, too, began to spin, and she slid down the tree trunk to the ground, unconscious.

It was toward the shank of the afternoon when her eyes fluttered open and she returned to her senses, only to find her hands bound tightly together and a six-foot rawhide rope tying her wrists to a tree. The reality of her situation struck her with devastating impact. The horror she had witnessed had not been a nightmare! Red Hawk's body was lying where it had dropped, a lifeless lump on the creek bank, and she at once felt the sorrow of having been responsible for his death. Unwilling to look at him longer, she turned her head away, only to look directly into the grinning face of Jack Black Dog.

"Well, little bird," he sneered, "did you have a nice little nap?" He was seated cross-legged a few feet from her, obviously waiting for her to awaken. He reached out to touch her ankle, laughing when she quickly snatched it away. "Oh, I don't reckon you'll be so sassy when I get through with you." Delighting in her obvious contempt for him, he continued to torment her. "You caused me a helluva lot of trouble, but I told you I'd getcha before it was over. I'm fixin' to have me a little look at what you got under that skirt. I'm a fair man, though. If you don't want me to, all you got to do is say no." He chuckled gleefully at his obvious joke. "Little bird with no song," he crowed, "just say you don't wanna be with me, and I'll let you go." He leered at her, his foolish grin spread across his wide jaw. "What's that? Did I hear you say somethin'? I reckon not, so I guess we'll have us a little fun." Then the grin faded completely away, replaced by a threatening scowl. "I'll keep you alive as long as you please me. If you don't, I'll carve you up and eat you for supper."

Molly was close to choking on the terror filling her throat. She was certain she could not endure what his leering, evil eyes promised. Trying desperately to think of something that might delay the attack upon her, she could not force herself to rational thought. Her mind was reeling with the horrible thought that she was about to have her virginity ripped from her body by a foul and evil demon. Horrified, she tried to make herself urinate, hoping that if she fouled herself, it would dissuade him—at least for a short time—but she found that she was too terrified to force it.

Growing weary of verbally tormenting her, and ready to know the pleasure that had dominated his mind, he got up and started untying his buckskin trousers. *It was going to happen!* She tried to shrink from him, but he grabbed her ankles and dragged her back toward him. In a fashion more akin to the butchering of an animal, he set himself upon her, forcing her ankles apart, wedging his body between her legs. With her wrists tied over her head, she did all she could to resist, causing him to hesitate long enough to slap her roughly several times before renewing his assault. She finally reached the point where she could resist no longer, and she felt her mind slipping away from consciousness. Suddenly, he stopped pressing forward. Confused and dazed, she opened her eyes, startled to find his head being forced backward, his face a painful grimace. He released her at once, reaching up with both hands in an attempt to capture the hand that grasped his hair.

Slaughter was almost blind in his rage. He had never before experienced fury like he felt at that moment. The one thought in his mind was that he wanted to totally destroy this vile beast, and he wanted to do it in the most painful way possible. With a death grip on the half-breed's scalp and a knee planted firmly in his back, Matt continued to force the head back until Jack Black Dog screamed out in pain. He did not stop until he heard the sharp crack of the breed's back, and he knew that he had broken his spine. Still enraged, he dragged the limp body away from Molly and stood staring down into Jack Black Dog's face. He realized that the treacherous half-breed was still alive, although obviously paralyzed, for he stared up at him with eyes wide with terror. With no feeling of compassion, Matt reached down and drew the knife Jack Black Dog had used to kill Red Hawk. He held it before the helpless breed's face to let him get a good long look at the blade. Then he methodically drew it across the breed's throat.

Several long moments passed before the storm inside

him abated, as he stood staring down at the corpse. Finally he regained his senses to the point of rational thought, and he went immediately to calm Molly. Still in a state of shock, she involuntarily jerked away from him when he knelt down to untie her wrists.

"Molly," he said softly, "it's me, Matt. You're safe now. It's over."

Recognizing his voice, she relaxed. Tears began to fill her eyes as she was able to once again focus, seeing his face plainly now. The tears multiplied until she finally broke into deep sobs of relief. As soon as her wrists were free, she threw her arms around his neck and pulled herself tightly to his chest.

He knew at that moment why he had been overcome with rage before. She was all that really mattered in the world to him. "It's all right, darlin', I'll take care of you. I promise not to let anything else happen to you."

The thoroughly shaken young woman continued to hold on to Matt for some time before allowing him to leave long enough to take care of the dead. Finally, she became calm enough to sit down and wait while he dragged Jack Black Dog's corpse away from his camp and dumped the hated breed over the edge of the bluff. Next, he rounded up the horses. Wrapping Red Hawk's body in a blanket he found behind Jack Black Dog's saddle, he lifted his friend up and laid him across the saddle. "I've got to take Red Hawk back to his people," he told Molly. "I at least owe him that." His intention was to take the body to Spotted Horse, along with Red Hawk's and Jack Black Dog's horses. It was risky, he had to admit, but not as risky as riding into the fort. Perhaps it would have been the wise thing to do to simply ride out and leave the army and the Sioux behind him, but he felt directly responsible for Red Hawk's death, and obligated to return the dead warrior to his people to be given a proper burial.

With Red Hawk securely bound across his saddle, Matt returned to the fire. "Can you ride now?" he asked Molly. She didn't answer at once, but simply stared up at him, her eyes questioning. "I reckon I'd best get you back to the doctor's house. Do they even know you left the fort?" She responded then, shaking her head slowly. "Well," he repeated, "I'd best get you back. They'll be worried about you." She did not move, her eyes wide and following his every motion.

He suspected what she might be thinking. He had said some things in the heat of the moment, things that had come out uncontrolled in the depth of his compassion for her, things that could not necessarily be. He had promised to take care of her. She might have interpreted that to mean she would now go with him to the mountains. Thinking back on that moment when he first saw Jack Black Dog forcing his body between her legs, he became insanely furious again. At that moment, she had been the most precious thing in his life. Now, he was confused, his feelings mixed up in his head, and he didn't know what to do about her. One thing was clear—he couldn't take her with him. With that thought, he made up his mind.

"You'll be all right now that Jack Black Dog is dead. I'll take you back to the stables to leave your horse. You can walk back to Dr. Riddle's house from there. It wouldn't be too smart for me to take you to the house. I might wind up in irons." She continued to stare at him, the disappointment apparent in her eyes. "We can take Red Hawk's body to the Crow camp on the way back to the fort."

She dutifully got to her feet, and permitted him to give her a boost up onto her horse, her gaze straight ahead now. Once before, she had asked to go with him. She would not shame herself by asking again. To him, her stoic acceptance of her situation was worse than when she had stared accusingly at him. *Dammit,* he thought, *I got no reason to feel guilty. I did what I came back to do. The murdering son of a bitch is dead, and Molly's safe. That's all a man can do.* It still gnawed away at his conscience, and the emptiness he suddenly felt inside would not go away.

Chapter 17

They left the small Crow camp in mourning for the death of Red Hawk. Spotted Horse was grateful to Matt for bringing his brother's body home. He, like Red Hawk, had counted Slaughter as a close friend, and knew the tall white scout was grieving the loss. If he blamed Molly for Red Hawk's death, he showed no indication.

"The soldiers still mean to arrest you," Spotted Horse said when he walked beside Matt's horse to the edge of the Crow camp.

"I know."

Spotted Horse turned his head briefly to gaze at Molly before remarking, "It is dangerous for you to go to the fort. Do you want me to take the woman back?"

Matt shook his head. That would have definitely been the smarter choice, but he felt obligated to Molly to return with her to the fort—at least as far as the stables, since he had told her he would do so. "I 'preciate the offer," he said, "but I guess I'll see Molly home."

Spotted Horse slowly nodded his head as if considering Matt's answer. Then he stepped back from the horse. "You be damn careful, Slaughter."

"I will." He nudged the paint with his heels, leaving the Crow camp to bury Red Hawk. Molly followed along behind him on the mousy dun.

Dr. John Riddler looked up from his desk, surprised to see his wife at his office door. He was about finished for the day, and would have been home within a few minutes, so her visit was even more curious. She never came to the hospital, even when she was sick. He put the daily report aside and waited to hear the reason for her rare visit. "John," Martha Riddler began, "I'm worried about Molly."

"Oh?" the doctor replied. "Why is that? Is she sick?"

"No, it's not that. She left the house a little before noon, and I haven't seen her since. It's just not like her to be gone this long without letting me know where she is."

The doctor was not overly concerned. "I'm sure she's wandering around the post somewhere. Maybe she went to the sutler's store."

"All afternoon?" Martha questioned. "Besides, Molly doesn't ever go to the trader's store unless I send her for something." She frowned as she thought about it. "I even walked over to the chapel to see if she was there."

"I'm sure she's just gotten distracted somewhere," Riddler said and got up from his desk. "I'm about ready to quit for the day. I'll be home in a few minutes." He walked his wife to the door just as the first notes of mess call sounded out across the parade ground. "She'll probably be there when you get back," he assured her.

As they stepped outside the building, Lieutenant O'Connor rode by. He reined his horse to a halt, and exchanged greetings with the doctor and his wife. "Say, Jim," Dr. Riddler said, "the missus here is looking for our houseguest. You haven't seen her, have you?"

"No. I've been down at the peace talks all day," O'Connor replied. "On my way back to the stables now."

"Maybe Molly went over there to see that horse of hers," the doctor remarked. "If you see her, tell her we're wondering where she is."

"I'll be glad to," O'Connor said.

Private Darren Murphy reported for duty at the stables as he had the previous three evenings—the extra duty a punishment tour for drunkenness. He arrived at the stables a few minutes before Lieutenant O'Connor rode in. With one arm resting on the handle of a hay rake, he offered a somewhat indifferent salute to the officer as O'Connor dismounted and led his mount inside. Like most of the men in his company, Murphy had very little respect for the arrogant lieutenant, especially in light of the officer's recent performance under fire. His disgust for O'Connor was further intensified by the insulting fact that O'Connor was Irish, the same as he.

O'Connor, aware of the disrespect being exhibited, was of a mind to take the private to task for his lack of courtesy. "Soldier!" he barked. "You'd best snap to attention when an officer enters the building."

"Yes, sir," Murphy drawled and made a halfhearted stab at coming to attention.

O'Connor was just before launching into a tirade when two riders approaching the corral caught his eye. Without another word, he handed his reins to Murphy, and moved quickly to a window, not willing to trust his eyes. He stood peering out the window for a long moment, scarcely able to believe his good fortune. *Slaughter*— the man who had managed to frustrate his attempts to arrest him—was riding right into his arms.

Murphy stood puzzled by the officer's strange actions until O'Connor glanced briefly at him and motioned frantically for him to lead his horse to a stall. When the private finally led the horse away, O'Connor drew his revolver and made his way toward the front corner of the barn, the closest point to the corral gate, where the riders seemed to be heading. Upon reaching that point, he knelt there just inside the stable door and waited. As the two horses came closer, he could feel his heart pounding inside his chest, and he had to shift the pistol to his other hand briefly in order to wipe the sweat from his palm. Recalling a mental picture of Slaughter's Henry rifle in action, he had second thoughts about what he was about to do. Glancing back toward the rear of the stables, he thought to signal Murphy to come forward, but the private was in the tack room.

Maybe I should wait until I have a proper arresting party under my command, he thought. Then an image came to mind of Private Murphy regaling the enlisted men with tales of Lieutenant O'Connor hiding behind the door until Slaughter had gone. *Damn the murdering dog!* He fumed, unable to make up his mind.

"Don't see anybody around," Matt said as he reined the paint up before the corral gate. "Must be inside. I'll unsaddle your horse, and you can get on back. They must be worried about you." He dismounted and went to help Molly down.

His back pressed against the wall of the stable, Lieutenant O'Connor inched closer to the door, his palm wet again as he grasped the handle of his revolver. With his heart almost choking his throat, he peeked cautiously through the crack in the door. The first thing that caught his eye was the Henry rifle sitting securely in the sling of an empty saddle. Shifting his gaze quickly, he saw the broad back of the tall scout as Matt stood waiting to assist the young lady to dismount.

His mind a whirlpool of irrational thoughts of loathing and fear of this man of the mountains, O'Connor was gripped by indecision. His hatred for the man who had humiliated him in front of his men overcame any sense of military duty at that critical moment when Slaughter was at his mercy. The temptation was too great. Slowly he pushed the barrel of the revolver through the crack of the door where the hinges were nailed. His hand was shaking so badly that he had to steady it with the other one. Still the barrel of the revolver bobbed up and down uncontrollably.

The sudden report of the pistol shattered the silence

of the stable, causing both horses to bolt. Molly grabbed the saddle horn and held on desperately to keep from being thrown. Matt dropped to the ground, a bullet in his back. Seeing the tall scout fall, O'Connor was stunned for a moment, unable to move. When he realized that Slaughter was actually helpless, he cocked the pistol again, but before he could pull the trigger, the stable door slammed against his hand, causing him to drop the revolver. Confused and stunned, he looked up to see Private Murphy scrambling to his feet after having just thrust his shoulder into the door. There ensued a race then to get to the pistol on the ground. Murphy got to it first.

Horrified, Molly fought to control her horse long enough to slide down from the saddle and rush to Matt's side. On her knees beside him, she tried to stop the blood that was already beginning to spread across his back. Unable to stem the flow that soon soaked his shirt, she looked around her, frantically seeking help from someone. Murphy came to her aid while a stunned Lieutenant O'Connor staggered back against the side of the stable to stare helplessly at the still body on the ground.

"We need some help here," Private Murphy yelled to a couple of soldiers heading for some off-duty relaxation at a gambling parlor off post. They had stopped when they heard the report of the revolver. One of the two responded immediately, and his friend followed after a moment. "Bring that handcart yonder," Murphy instructed. "We've gotta get him to the hospital."

"Excuse me, ma'am." One of the soldiers took Molly gently by the arm. "I need to get in here." He knelt down to take hold of Matt's shoulders. Murphy and the other soldier carefully lifted the wounded man and placed him on the cart.

With Molly hurrying tearfully along beside, the two enlisted men started pushing the cart toward the hospital just as the guard detail marched up to post the stable guard. Murphy left the others to explain what had just happened to the sergeant of the guard. He climbed on Matt's horse and sped off at a gallop to alert the surgeon.

Seeing the guard detail, Lieutenant O'Connor seemed to recover from the stupor that had immobilized him seconds before. He rushed up to the sergeant and blurted out, "That man's a murderer! He's under arrest!" His eyes wide with excitement, he then pointed to Murphy galloping away. "And he assaulted me when I was trying to carry out my orders!"

The sergeant took a moment to consider the lieutenant's words. Like most every man on the post, he was well aware of O'Connor's cowardice in the field, and the fact that the lieutenant had retreated from an ambush, leaving his men to fend for themselves. "Yes, sir," he answered calmly, taking note of the officer's empty holster and the fact that Murphy had had a revolver stuck in his belt. "I'll notify the officer of the day as soon as I finish posting the guards."

O'Connor was not satisfied. "The man's a dangerous murderer," he insisted. "It was me or him."

"Well, sir, he don't look too dangerous right now, does he?—what with him being shot in the back and all. It don't appear like he's liable to run off anywhere. I expect you'd best let me take care of it."

*   *   *

"You poor darling," Martha Riddler murmured when she found Molly sitting in a chair beside the door of Dr. Riddler's surgery. "I heard about what happened." She opened her arms to receive the distraught young woman, and Molly came immediately to her. Her skirt and blouse covered with Matt's blood, she pressed close to the older woman and released the flood of tears that she had been holding back. Martha well understood the pain the girl was experiencing. There was no doubt that Molly was hopelessly in love with the untamed young scout. And she could see nothing but heartbreak and disappointment for the girl. Matt Slaughter was wanted for murder by the army. Like Molly, Martha wanted to believe the army had made a mistake. It just didn't seem fair. The girl had had nothing but tragedy all her life.

After a few minutes, Molly seemed to relax from the sobbing that had at first racked her body, and she pulled away to try to regain her composure. "Has John been out to tell you anything yet?" Martha asked. Molly shook her head. "I'll see if I can find out what's going on," Martha said, her voice gentle and comforting. "You wait right here."

"Dammit, I'm busy," John Riddler scolded when he heard the door open behind him. "I've got a patient on the table."

"It's me, John," Martha responded. "How is he?"

When the doctor realized who had entered the room, his tone softened. "Oh . . . Martha. What are you doing here?" Before she could answer, he glanced at the orderly assisting him. "Hold that lamp over to this side a little more. I can't see a damn thing for all this blood."

"Molly's outside, sick with worry," Martha said. "How is he?"

He paused to consider the blood now on his wife's dress for a brief moment before answering. "He's damn near dead is all I can tell you. He's lost a lot of blood, and I can't seem to stop the bleeding. The good news, if there is any, is that it doesn't appear any of the vital organs were hit. All the bleeding is coming from the wound—doesn't seem to be any in his lungs or heart." He paused to wipe the perspiration from his forehead. "I'm going to have to leave the bullet in there. I'm about to kill him trying to get it out."

"Is he going to live?"

"Hell, I don't know—if we get the bleeding stopped, maybe. If he makes it through the night, then I guess he'll probably recover."

It wasn't much in the way of encouragement to give Molly, but neither was it entirely discouraging. The young girl wanted to stay there all night, but Martha finally persuaded her that she could see Matt in the morning, that her husband would pull him through. She fervently prayed that she was not giving the girl false hope. As they were leaving the hospital, the sergeant of the guard met them at the door with one sentry. Martha paused to confront the sergeant. "Is that really necessary?"

"Probably not, ma'am, but the officer of the day thinks we'd best be cautious. He is a wanted man."

*   *   *

Matt was alive the next morning, but so weakened by the loss of blood that he didn't care much whether he lived or died. Molly was there almost constantly, although he wasn't aware of it for the first two days. Gradually his strength returned, and on the third day he woke up feeling tired and hungry. He opened his eyes, to be met with the wide-eyed questioning gaze of Molly. Much to her relief, he smiled at her, and attempted to sit up. She was quick to respond, springing from her chair to help him.

"What the hell happened?" he mumbled, his words only barely discernible through parched lips. He was pretty sure he had been shot, but he had no idea by whom. He may have been told sometime during the past couple of days, but if he had been, he didn't remember.

Molly, though she tried, could not, of course, tell him. She made several motions in an effort to convey the information, but none that made any sense to him. It wasn't hard to figure out that he had been shot. The part that puzzled him was why he was simply shot on sight, instead of an attempt being made to arrest him. He wanted answers, but at the moment, he had a more urgent problem to solve. Studying his eyes, Molly guessed the problem. She pointed to the bedpan on the floor beside the bed, a question in her eyes. He looked down at the innocuous object, realizing only then what it was for. Preferring to get up and stagger to the hospital sink behind the building, he started to throw the sheets back, only to discover he had nothing on but a gown. He flushed in his embarrassment, further mortified by Molly's benevolent smile. "Gimme the damn pan," he said, "but you're gonna have to leave the room." Smiling broadly, she did as she was bid.

Intent upon completing his awkward endeavor, he was unaware of the person stepping quietly inside the door until startled by the booming voice. "Hod damn, I didn't know you could ride one of them things. Be careful it don't throw you."

The sudden outburst almost succeeded in doing just that. "Dammit, Zeb," Matt fumed, "don't you know a closed door means you oughta knock?"

"Molly told me you was takin' a piss," Zeb said, laughing. "Where'd that girl learn to talk sign like that?"

"Red Hawk," Matt said, smiling when he remembered.

"'Course, I thought you was standin' in the middle of the bed to do it. I reckon there ain't no sign language for one of them bedpans."

At Matt's insistence, Zeb slid the offending bedpan under the bed. Then he proceeded to enlighten Matt on the circumstances of his injury. Matt listened, feeling more frustration than anger. He was more angry at himself than he was at Lieutenant O'Connor. "That was mighty damn careless of me," he said. "I should have checked to see if there was anyone around."

"Hell, how could you know that little weasel was hidin' in the barn? Wouldn't surprise me a'tall if that little son of a bitch caught one in the back hisself, next time he's in a skirmish. And I expect he'll have a chance before the summer's over. Red Cloud and the other chiefs has done pulled out of the treaty talks, and said they was gonna fight anybody tryin' to use the Bozeman

Trail. Anybody with a thimbleful of brains wouldn't hardly expect him to agree to lettin' whites cut through his best buffalo ground. But the thing that killed the treaty right quick was a whole passel of new soldiers pullin' in here day before yesterday from back east. There's a colonel in charge—Carrington, I think I heard somebody say—and he claims his orders are to march on into Powder River country, staff old Fort Reno, and set up two more forts along the Bozeman. They said Red Cloud got madder'n hell—he told 'em that the army has already sent troops to build forts, and he ain't agreed to nothin' yet."

Zeb paused in his diatribe, and lowered his voice, changing the subject completely. He looked over his shoulder as if concerned that someone might hear. "What are you aimin' to do?"

Matt didn't understand the question. "About what?" he asked.

"About the army fixin' to ship you back east to stand trial."

The question brought Matt back to the reality of his situation, which he had been too incapacitated to think about until that moment. He didn't have to spend much thought on it to express his intent. "I reckon I don't plan to go back," he said evenly.

"That's what I figured," Zeb said. "Can you ride?"

"I don't know. If somebody could help me get on a horse, I could give it a helluva try."

"Doc says your insides is all right. The bullet didn't cut into none of your organs. Let's see if you can stand up." He moved close to the bed to give Matt a hand. "Be quiet about it. There's a guard outside the door."

Matt nodded and very gingerly eased his legs over the side of the bed. With some help from Zeb, he sat up, a low grunt the only indication of the pain it caused. He rested there for a minute before attempting to stand up. Then, with a nod to Zeb, he pushed on up to stand unsteadily by the bed, one hand on Zeb's shoulder for support. "Hell," Zeb snorted, "you're ready to run with the antelopes."

"Not quite," Matt said, "but I reckon I could ride if I had to." As he was about to say that he might be a little more likely to walk in another day, the door opened and Molly returned to the room. Startled to see Matt standing, she opened her eyes wide as if she were about to speak. Then she frowned and placed her hands on her hips like an irate mother hen. There was no mistaking her meaning.

"Don't go gettin' all in a fuss," Zeb said. "He's just tryin' out his legs. He's been lazin' around in that bed too long, anyway."

She shook her head as if perplexed, and moved to help Matt back into bed. He allowed it, but only because he once again realized that he was wearing nothing but a gown. "Zeb's right, Molly. I can't lay around in this bed."

"Can you ride by tomorrow night?" Zeb asked.

Matt didn't hesitate. "Yeah, I can ride." He studied the old scout's face for a long moment before asking, "What are you thinkin' about?" Before Zeb could answer, he said, "I can't let you get involved in this. Hell, you've got your job to worry about. Besides, when I bust outta here, somebody's liable to get hurt. I don't want it to be you."

Zeb grinned. "Is that so? Well, lemme ask you this. How the hell are you gonna bust outta here without help? Somebody's gotta get your horse and your belongings. How are you gonna get past that sentry standin' outside the door? What are you gonna do—just say, 'Sorry, boys, but I'm leavin' now'?"

"I guess it does sound a little foolish," Matt admitted, "but I'm damn sure not going back to Virginia to stand trial for somethin' I didn't even do." He glanced at Molly, who wore an expression of complete dismay. "You shouldn't even be hearing this talk. I don't want you to get in trouble." He jerked his head back to stare at Zeb again. "Why in hell are you so all-fired determined to stick your neck out for me, anyway?"

Zeb's face broke out in a wide grin. "Because I'm sick of the settlements, and I'm tired of scoutin' for damn fools like Lieutenant O'Connor. I hear you talkin' about goin' up to the Wind River country and the Bitterroots. Dammit, I wanna go with you. I know you think you're pretty much a loner, but a man needs a partner to make it in that country. Besides, I know that country. It's been a while, but I still know which way the wind blows up that way." He walked over to the bed and stuck out his hand. "Whaddaya say? Partners?"

Matt shook his head, hardly able to believe what he had just heard. One thing he was forced to admit—it was highly unlikely that he could pull off his escape without help. "Why, hell," he said. "Why not? If you're that anxious to get shot, then why not?" He took Zeb's hand, and they shook on it.

The one person in the room without a grin on her face was Molly. Once again, her shining knight in buckskin was about to say good-bye—this time for good, in all likelihood. She was not sure she could stand the prospect of never seeing Matt again. But she understood his need to try to escape. If he allowed himself to be taken back to Virginia, he would probably be hanged. She could not bear the thought. It would be better for him to risk his life on the chance that he might success-fully escape. As for her, sorrow seemed to be her lot. She would learn to accept it, knowing that she could never love another after Matt Slaughter.

Plans were quickly laid for an escape attempt the fol-lowing night. Zeb took it as his responsibility to get rid of the guard outside Matt's door—his proposed means a bottle of whiskey. From that point on, the plan was simple enough. The two of them would walk across the parade ground to the post trader's building. Zeb would have the horses tied behind the building. From there, they would simply ride away. It would have been easier for Matt if he had more time to heal, but they both felt the timing was right at the moment, when all troops on the post were on alert because of all the Indians pulling out from the talks.

Matt glanced at Molly, who was listening to every word. He wondered what she might be thinking about it. He knew she wanted to go with him, but he didn't see that it was possible, and certainly it was no life to thrust upon her. Bringing his mind back to the planned escape, he said, "I'm not of much use without my rifle."

"Already taken care of," Zeb answered immediately. "Friend of mine, Darren Murphy, was on stable duty the night you got shot. He told me that as of this mornin' your saddle with the rifle still in the sling and all your possibles were still in the tack room. Shouldn't be too hard to get at."

Matt nodded. Murphy—the name rang a bell. Then he remembered. Zeb had told him Murphy was the trooper who prevented O'Connor from putting another bullet in his back. He looked Zeb in the eye then. "You've already been plannin' this thing, haven't you? Before you even talked to me about it."

Zeb grinned and winked. "Your job is to get a helluva lot better overnight," he said. He glanced over at Molly. The young girl was obviously worried. "Don't you worry, missy. It'll be easier than teachin' a fish to swim. I'll be gettin' along now, so's you two can visit." With that he prepared to leave. "See ya tomorrow night, partner," he said to Matt as he went out the door, almost bumping into Dr. Riddler on his way in.

The doctor nodded briefly to Zeb, then turned his attention to his patient and the young lady. "Well, Molly," he said, "I thought I might find you here. How's the patient?" He directed the question to Matt.

"I expect I'll live," Matt responded. "But I'm too weak to stand up," he added, thinking it might be best if Riddler thought he was still too weak to warrant any concerns about escape.

"Well, I just wanted to check your bandage before I

go home to supper." After a brief examination, he nodded his satisfaction, then turned to Molly. "Are you about ready to go home? I expect Martha will be looking for you to help with supper." She nodded, but remained seated. "Well, I'll see you back at the house then," he said and departed, pulling the door closed behind him.

She got up from the chair and went to Matt's bedside. There was no need for speech. Her eyes told him of the pain in her heart as she gazed longingly into his. A tear slowly formed in the corner of her eye, and his heart was captured in that moment. He reached out to take her hand. As soon as his hand touched hers, she came to him, resting her cheek against his shoulder. He held her there for a long moment before speaking. "Molly, I'm sorry things turned out this way. I ain't got much choice in the matter. I've got to get away from here."

She rose and placed a finger on his lips to silence him. Smiling bravely, she took his face in her hands and kissed him. Her lips were soft and gentle at first touch, but then the tide of her passion could be held back no longer, and she kissed him hard and feverishly, releasing the longing that filled her soul. In that brief moment of time, she was at last able to realize complete contentment. He responded to her kiss with passion equal to hers, lost in that special moment. But then the realization that he must say good-bye told him that this was not to be. He gently pushed her away, and whispered softly, "You'd better go now. I'll see you tomorrow." Reluctantly, she pulled away, stood gazing at him as if to fill her eyes before leaving, then turned and left him.

* * *

Molly came to sit by Matt's bed for most of the following day, until the evening guard was posted, and Zeb stopped in briefly before putting his plan into operation. Matt was prepared to climb into his buckskins, which Molly had procured for him that afternoon. Ready to leave as soon as he got a signal from Zeb, he could do nothing but wait.

The plan, however, was not at first successful. Zeb managed to persuade the sentry to have a drink or two, but the soldier politely declined to drink himself drunk. In an effort to tempt the sentry to take one more drink, Zeb consumed most of the bottle himself, and ended up asleep outside Matt's room. At the changing of the guard, the sergeant on duty had Zeb carried out and unceremoniously dumped on the ground behind the hospital. Stiff and sick the next morning, a truly mortified Zeb limped into Matt's room to apologize and promise that he would not make the same mistake again.

Actually, the extra day gave Matt some much needed time to further recuperate. He agreed to let Zeb try his plan one more time before abandoning the idea. Their luck was considerably better on the next night, for Private Dewey Starks drew the ten-to-midnight tour of duty outside the prisoner's hospital room. Starks was a notorious drunk. Previously a corporal, he had already been busted back to private for drinking on duty. Zeb was almost prompted to laugh when he entered the hallway a few minutes after ten and discovered Starks seated in the chair outside Matt's door.

"Well, I'll be damned," Zeb called out cheerfully, "if

it ain't Private Starks. How you doin', Dewey?" He held the full whiskey bottle casually so that Starks could see it.

"Howdy, Zeb," Starks replied, his eyes fixed upon the bottle. "Whatcha got there?"

"Oh, this?" He gave the sentry a little wink. "I just come by to give my friend a little shooter to help him sleep. You won't let on to nobody, will you?"

"Maybe not," Starks replied, grinning, "if you was to give me a little shooter, too."

Zeb paused, his hand on the doorknob. "I wouldn't wanna do anything to get you in trouble — you bein' on guard duty and all."

"Hell, ain't nobody gonna know but you and me."

Zeb still hesitated as if trying to decide. "Well, maybe just one. Lemme give Slaughter a little snort first, and then we'll both have us a shot. All right?" Dewey nodded, his grin reaching from ear to ear. Zeb entered the room to find Matt sitting on the side of the bed, waiting. "Get your clothes on, partner. We'll be walkin' out of here before midnight when they change the guard."

Sergeant of the guard Billy Harmon halted his guard detail in front of the hospital and ordered the first man at the head of the squad to fall out. After ordering the rest of the detail to stand at ease, he told the replacement sentry to follow him. As soon as he entered the hallway, he knew something was wrong. The chair by the door to Slaughter's room was vacant.

"Damn that Starks," he muttered, and hurried to the

door of the room, mumbling obscenities as he ran. He thrust the door open and stuck his head inside. The patient was in bed, apparently asleep. Relieved to find the prisoner had not escaped, he turned to Starks' replacement. "Go find that son of a bitch—look out back, he might be taking a piss. I'll look down the other hallway." They split up to search for the missing guard. "I'll have his hide for this," Harmon promised as he stalked toward the end of the corridor.

Starks was nowhere to be found. Sergeant Harmon gave up the search after a few minutes. There was no time to comb the area for the missing sentry. The other guards had to be posted. "You see that you stay alert, dammit," he ordered as he left to attend his duties.

Private Goodman stood at parade rest until Harmon disappeared. Then he settled himself in the chair. After a few moments, he had second thoughts, and decided he'd better have a look at the prisoner to make sure everything was all right. He eased the door open and nodded to himself, satisfied that the patient was still asleep. He started to close the door when something peculiar caught his eye. The patient had kicked the sheet out on one corner of the bed. It struck Goodman as mighty strange that the man had gone to bed with his boots on. Curious, he pushed on through the door and approached the bed. Pulling the sheet back, he was startled to find Dewey Starks peacefully sleeping off a drunk.

Sergeant Harmon was fit to be tied. "There's gonna be hell to pay for this. Starks can kiss his ass good-bye." He stormed out of the room to confront Goodman and a sleepy hospital orderly who had just been roused from his cot. "Go find Lieutenant O'Connor," he ordered Goodman.

Harmon waited. After more than a quarter of an hour, Goodman returned alone, and reported that he could not find O'Connor. This did nothing to calm the sergeant's rapidly growing irritation. The officer of the day was supposed to be available any hour of the night. "Did you look in the guardhouse?" Harmon asked, knowing that it was probably the first place Goodman had looked. When the private answered that he had, Harmon threw up his hands in defeat. "Well, dammit, I don't know what to do. We've got an escaped prisoner loose somewhere, and the damn officer of the day ain't nowhere to be found." He fumed for a minute while he decided what to do. "I reckon we'll go wake the damn major up. He ain't gonna be too happy with O'Connor." The thought caused a malicious grin to appear. Like most of the enlisted men on post, he had no love for the lieutenant.

"I'm sorry you have to walk a piece, but I was afraid if I brought the horses to the hospital, somebody mighta noticed," Zeb said as the two men made their way across the deserted parade ground.

"It's all right. I'm makin' it just fine." Still unsteady, and experiencing a dull pain from the chunk of lead lodged in his back, Matt was making every effort to simulate a casual stroll. A growing dampening of his shirt, however, told him that the wound was bleeding. *No matter,* he thought. He'd rather bleed out and die right there on the parade ground than go to the gallows in Virginia. "Where the hell did you leave the horses, anyway?"

"Behind the sutler's store—we only got one little problem. I ain't been able to get in the tack room to get your saddle and stuff. It weren't no problem gettin' your horse. I just got in behind 'em when they drove 'em all out to graze down by the river. Hell, I coulda cut out two or three more. But the damn stables was busy as hell all day. I reckon there was a big to-do about the Injuns pullin' out. There ought'n to be nobody there this time of night 'cept one guard, though."

As Zeb had figured, there was one man standing guard at the stables. He walked a post around the three buildings and the corral. It seemed a long circuit for one man to make, but when Matt questioned it, Zeb said that he had seen only one man walking the post, although it had seemed odd to him as well. It was ridiculously easy to simply wait until the guard was at the far corner of his post, beyond the next two barns, and then slip in the back of the first barn.

Walking hurriedly between the line of stalls, they headed to the tack room to recover Matt's belongings. About to enter the room, Zeb held Matt back with a quick grasp of his arm. "Well, lookee here," he whispered, and pointed to the floor just in front of his feet. "I damn near stepped on him." It was a man sleeping, obviously another guard who should have been walking the post with his partner. They stepped around him very carefully. While Matt searched through assorted gear for his saddle, Zeb looked for some rope. Finding several coils looped over a post, he selected one and returned to secure the sleeping soldier. Before the guard was fully awake, he was tied and gagged. And by the time he was alert to what was taking place, he was helpless to do anything about it.

Unfortunately, it was too dark in the room to distinguish Matt's outfit from several others lining the walls. "I'm gonna have to light that lantern there by the door," Matt said. "I can't see what I'm doin'."

"Wait till I run back to the door, and I'll tell you when the guard is walking around the far building," Zeb said. "I don't think there's much chance he can see the light. He'll be on the other side of the building."

Zeb was right. The third barn completely blocked the guard's line of sight for several minutes. In half that time, Matt collected his saddle and rifle, and the two fugitives were hustling toward a little clump of trees where their horses waited—the guard none the wiser.

The midnight raid on the stables did not go completely undetected, however. Lieutenant James O'Connor, officer of the day, stopped in his tracks when he saw a light suddenly appear in the tack room of the first barn. Smiling smugly to himself, he hurried toward the barn, certain that he had caught one of his sentries away from his post, possibly even sleeping while the other guard acted as lookout. He had been determined that there would be no slacking on his tour as OD, and he had been showing up unexpectedly at other guard posts throughout the night. This was the first sign of dereliction of duty, and he was eager to spring his trap on the unsuspecting slacker.

Before he reached the corner of the corral, the light went out. He stopped to look and listen. About to move again, he paused when he saw two figures slinking away in the darkness, carrying something toward a small stand of trees several yards past the stables. *Ha!* he thought. *Looks like I've stumbled upon a little larceny.* Feeling pleased with the opportunity to come down hard on a couple of enlisted men, he made his way quickly toward the stand of trees.

"Want me to do that for you?" Zeb asked, watching Matt strain to throw his saddle on the paint.

"No," Matt replied. "I'm a mite weak yet, but I can manage to saddle my own horse." He was reaching under the horse's belly to tighten the girth strap when suddenly both men froze simultaneously at the distinct sound of a hammer cocking.

"That's right," O'Connor said. "You'd best not move a muscle." He stepped into the small clearing where the horses had waited, realizing only then whom he had happened upon. "Well, as I live and breathe," he blurted, hardly believing his eyes. "If it isn't Mr. Slaughter, and Mr. Benson—I believe I've discovered a jailbreak in progress." He kept his revolver pointed at them while he moved to position himself better. "You were damn lucky the first time, Slaughter, but this time you're going to be shot dead while trying to escape." His hatred for the tall scout came boiling to the surface. "Damn you," he spat, "you should have died when I shot you before." He glanced briefly at Zeb. "Sorry, Benson, I've really got nothing against you, but you're here with the prisoner on your own accord, and I don't want any witnesses." He fairly quivered with excitement, anticipating the sweet taste of revenge, knowing that he had both men helpless before him. Though he was trembling, it was far from the fearful nervousness he had felt the first time, when he'd shot Slaughter in the back. This time Slaughter was weak and vulnerable.

"Why, you yellow piece of shit," Zeb snarled. "You think you can kill both of us before one of us gets to you?"

O'Connor smirked, enjoying his moment of power. "I think I can empty this gun before either one of you takes a step toward me."

"Would it be easier for you if I turned my back?" Matt asked. "That's how you work best, ain't it?" He was pressing for time, hoping to keep O'Connor talking. His rifle was secured in the saddle sling out of his reach, and he wasn't sure how fast he could move to get it. It didn't look good. The odds were not in his favor. His greatest regret at the moment was that Zeb had been pulled into it.

Realizing that he had better finish the job before one or both of them decided to jump him, O'Connor raised the pistol and aimed it at Matt's chest. Seconds before his finger tightened upon the trigger, he suddenly felt the cold, hard steel of a double gun barrel pressed against the back of his neck, and the metallic clicks of both hammers cocking. He froze, unable to move, consumed by the mental image of what both barrels of a shotgun would do to his head. Though the distraction was for only for a second, Matt was instantly upon him,

his hand locked on the man's wrist. Zeb was right behind, neither one of them knowing what had happened
to cause the lieutenant to freeze, but both reacting automatically.

With O'Connor disarmed and pinned to the ground
under both men, there was time to discover the slight figure in the shadow of the oaks. Clearly as frightened as the
lieutenant, but with deadly resolve, Molly stepped into
the clearing. Visibly shaken, she carefully released the
two cocked hammers on Dr. Riddler's double-barreled
shotgun while silently giving thanks that she had not had
to pull the triggers.

"Molly," was all Matt could say at the moment, still
amazed by her sudden appearance. He would have gone
to her at once, but he was occupied at the moment with
the unfortunate lieutenant.

Zeb, seated now on the lieutenant's legs, grinned up
at the young lady, enjoying the irony of O'Connor's fortune. "Always a pleasure to see you, ma'am," he called
out with a chuckle. Looking back at Matt then, he asked,
"What are we gonna do with this pup?"

"I don't know," Matt replied at first, then said, "We
need some rope."

"There's plenty back in that barn," Zeb said. "Wait
till that sentry walks up to the other end, and I'll run
back and get some." He hesitated a moment. " 'Course
it'd be a whole lot easier to just cut his throat, and then
we wouldn't have to tie him up."

"That's true," Matt replied, stroking his chin as if
considering the suggestion, fully aware that Zeb was

merely japing the lieutenant. "That would be the smart thing to do."

Lying pinned to the ground with one man sitting on his legs, the other on his shoulders, and his own revolver pressed against the back of his head, O'Connor was terrified. He was certain they meant to kill him. At first, he attempted to threaten certain retribution by the army. "If you kill me," he stuttered between quivering lips, "the army will hunt you down. You're both good as dead."

"The army might thank us for doin' them a favor if we kill you," Zeb replied. "Hell, we might even get a medal. Whaddaya say, Slaughter, you wanna cut his throat, or you want me to do it?"

Knowing time was running out before the guard would be discovered in his hospital bed, Matt quit the game. "The sentry's headin' up toward the far end. You'd best get that rope. I'll take care of the lieutenant here."

Without another word, Zeb got up and disappeared in the shadows of the oaks. Feeling the weight removed from his legs, O'Connor started to struggle. "You just hold still," Matt warned. Fearful moments before to the point of soiling himself, the lieutenant now realized that they did not intend to kill him. Feeling less frightened, and more authoritative, he demanded, "Get off of me!" When there was no response from Matt, he tried to yell out. "Help!" was as much as he got out before Matt brought the pistol barrel down hard upon his skull.

In a matter of minutes, Zeb returned with a coil of rope. They used it all, trussing O'Connor up like a mummy. With the end of the coil, they looped a turn around his belly, threw the free end over a limb, and hoisted him up off the ground. Satisfied with the job, Zeb gave the suspended body a little push, and they left him swinging gently under the oaks.

The lieutenant taken care of, Matt focused his concern upon Molly, who had stood patiently by, watching the activity. What to do about her was the next question. She had saved their lives, but in doing so she was now involved in his escape. He should have realized that the decision was not his, and in fact had already been made. She turned and disappeared back into the darkness of the trees to return moments later, leading her horse with all her things secured in a saddle pack. Matt didn't know what to say. She had made up her mind to go with him before the incident with O'Connor.

Zeb said it for him. "Well, Molly, darlin', we're mighty pleased you could join us. Ain't we, Matt?"

Matt stood there, struck speechless as he gazed at the slender young girl, her eyes searching his for an answer. Then she slowly brought her hand up before her. Placing it over her heart, she then pointed to him.

"I reckon," he said softly.

Zeb did not miss the subtle exchange between the two young people. He nodded his head in approval, a pleased smile spreading across his rough features. "Yes, ma'am," he allowed. "It's a good thing to have a woman along, especially if she don't tend to chatter a lot."

With a few hours of darkness remaining, the three rode away from Fort Laramie, leaving a confused sergeant of the guard searching for an escaped patient as well as a missing officer of the day. Matt, Molly and Zeb were all fugitives now, and didn't give a damn. They turned their horses north and west, toward the Wind River Mountains and beyond. A smile of contentment firmly in place, Molly knew she was finally where she was meant to be. She could not tell in the darkness, but somehow she knew that Matt was smiling, too.

There were many things that were not yet settled. Matt thought about Ike. There was still a void in his life that would always be there. He had thought a lot of the huge man. Iron Claw was still out there somewhere west of the Powder, but Matt decided to let fate dictate the next meeting between the two. It would come. He had a strong feeling about that. Foremost in his mind at the present was to find a safe place for Molly. After that, there would be time for Iron Claw and the promise he had made over Ike's grave. There was bound to be a war, since Red Cloud and the other Sioux chiefs had pulled out of the peace talks. The Powder River country was going to be bloody. He thought about Cooter Martin and wondered where a war between the Sioux and the U.S. Army would leave the old man.

Then he glanced up ahead at Zeb. The rough-hewn old scout was most probably close to the same age Ike had been. It was hard to tell. Matt still marveled that Zeb would sacrifice his job as an army scout and cast his lot with an outlaw, all because he missed the high mountains and yearned to see them again. There was more to it than that, Matt figured. Zeb was already act-ing the part of an uncle. *Uncle Zeb,* Matt thought, grinning at the notion.

Riding up ahead of the two young people, Zeb had a grin on his face, too. It was brought on by the image he had in his mind of the arrogant Lieutenant O'Connor swinging from the limb of an oak tree like an ornament on a Christmas tree.

SIGNET

Charles G. West

**"RARELY HAS AN AUTHOR PAINTED THE
GREAT AMERICAN WEST IN STROKES SO
BOLD, VIVID AND TRUE."
—RALPH COMPTON**

DEVIL'S KIN

0-451-21445-5

Jordan Gray is hunting down his family's killers.
But when he crosses paths with a ruthless posse,
Jordan learns that he doesn't have to take the law
into his own hands to wind up an outlaw.

Available wherever books are sold or at
penguin.com

No other series has this much historical action!

THE TRAILSMAN